W9-ANM-632

THE RECKONING

OTHER FIVE STAR WESTERN NOVELS BY ETHAN J. WOLFE

The Last Ride
The Range War of '82
The Devil's Waltz
The Cattle Drive
The Regulator
Murphy's Law
All the Queen's Men
One If by Land

A YOUNGBLOOD BROTHERS WESTERN,
BOOK 2

THE RECKONING

ETHAN J. WOLFE

FIVE STAR
A part of Gale, a Cengage Company

Farmington Hills, Mich • San Francisco • New York • Waterville, Maine
Meriden, Conn • Mason, Ohio • Chicago

LIBRARY OF CONGRESS CATALOGING-IN-PUBLICATION DATA

Names: Wolfe, Ethan J., author.
Title: The reckoning / Ethan J. Wolfe.
Description: First Edition. | Waterville, Maine : Five Star, a part of Gale, Cengage Learning, [2019] | Series: A Youngblood Brothers Western ; book 2 Identifiers: LCCN 2018032041 (print) | LCCN 2018035090 (ebook) | ISBN 9781432850012 (ebook) | ISBN 9781432850005 (ebook) | ISBN 9781432849993 (hardcover)
Subjects: | GSAFD: Western stories.
Classification: LCC PS3612.A5433 (ebook) | LCC PS3612.A5433 R42 2019 (print) | DDC 813/.6—dc23
LC record available at https://lccn.loc.gov/2018032041

First Edition. First Printing: April 2019
Find us on Facebook—https://www.facebook.com/FiveStarCengage
Visit our website—http://www.gale.cengage.com/fivestar/
Contact Five Star Publishing at FiveStar@cengage.com

Printed in Mexico
1 2 3 4 5 6 7 23 22 21 20 19

For Michael P, a Truly Gifted Friend

PROLOGUE

During his fourteen-year tenure as Indian Affairs Agent for the reservation located in the Ozark Mountains near Fort Smith, Arkansas, Henry Teasel was responsible for many positive changes.

The population had tripled. Tipis were replaced by log cabins and homes with porches and flowerpots in the windows. Many of the cabins had indoor water pumps. A school and church centered the establishment that was quickly becoming a town. The education level was as high as many towns in most states. Most inhabitants farmed the land. Some raised horses that were sold to the army. Medical care was available to all in the small, but well-supplied doctor's office.

It always struck Teasel funny that he, a college graduate, was considered a highly educated man and he spoke just one language. English. Yet most folks on the reservation were still considered savages by many, and they spoke English, French, Spanish, and at least three different languages inside their Native culture.

However, slow as it came, the progress of acceptance was being made, and by both whites and Natives.

It took Teasel more than six months to broker the deal that finally came to fruition with the tribes on the reservation, the government in Washington, and the niece of John Chisum: One thousand head of cattle, two bulls, and a dozen milking cows at the below-prime rate of eighteen dollars a head. Everybody on the reservation pitched in, and the government matched the total, hoping that if ranching succeeded in Fort Smith, it could succeed on reservations elsewhere.

Many of the men on the reservation were fine cowboys, having learned the trade working for the army. Supplying drovers would be no problem.

The train ride from Fort Smith to Roswell in New Mexico took nearly twelve hours by railroad. Even ten years ago, the trip would have taken weeks by horse and longer by wagon.

For much of the trip the train traveled at speeds of fifty-five and even sixty miles per hour.

It arrived in Roswell just after midnight. The streets were dimly lit by lanterns mounted on posts. Just a few saloons were open. The train usually stopped in Roswell just once per week, unless it was cattle drive season. Then a train loaded with boxcars stopped nearly every hour for a week or more.

John Chisum had the largest cattle ranch in the country, and it was situated just a few hours' ride south of Roswell. To feed the general population and the army, Chisum needed a way to move his vast herd quickly and in an orderly fashion, and the railroad agreed to build a station in Roswell.

As he exited the train and carried his suitcase along the platform, Sheriff Dan Pietrie met Teasel at the end.

"Mr. Teasel, Miss Sally Chisum asked me to escort you safely to the hotel," Pietrie said.

"Thank you, Sheriff, but it's just a few blocks' walk to the hotel," Teasel said.

"Maybe so, but you're carrying a bank draft for twenty thousand dollars," Pietrie said. "It's hard to keep something like that under your hat."

"I suppose you're right," Teasel agreed.

They walked the four blocks to the Hotel Roswell, a four-story structure on Main Street.

"I rented a buggy for the morning," Pietrie said at the steps of the hotel. "Miss Sally asked me to ride you over right after breakfast."

"Fine. Will you join me for breakfast?" Teasel said. "Say eight-thirty?"

"See you then," Pietrie said.

Teasel's room was on the third floor facing the street. The room had a balcony, and he sat out for a bit as he wasn't yet tired and the night air was hot.

He had a small flask of bourbon whiskey. He mixed some with a glass of water and sipped as he enjoyed a cool westerly breeze.

There were ranches much closer to Fort Smith that could have sold him the thousand head of cattle. But the Chisum Ranch was the largest of its kind, and John Chisum was an old friend of Judge Isaac Parker, the federal judge who ruled over the entire western district of Arkansas, including the reservation.

A year ago, when John Chisum died in Arkansas, Parker spoke at the funeral. Even though Teasel didn't know Chisum, Parker had him attend the funeral.

At the funeral was where Teasel met Sally Chisum.

Six months later, Teasel wrote her about the idea he had for purchasing cattle for the reservation, and she replied that she would be more than willing to supply his needs.

The first step was to hold a town hall meeting on the reservation and pitch the idea of raising cattle to the Natives. A thousand head could double very quickly with two prime bulls in the mix. Most Natives agreed to help finance the operation only if the government agreed to keep its nose out of it and allow the Natives to succeed or fail on their own accord.

After several trips to Washington, the Bureau of Indian Affairs decided to match the funds raised on the reservation and to keep entirely out of the business except for Teasel's involvement as overseer.

Then it was just a matter of details and arrangements.

Close to two in the morning, Teasel felt the need for sleep and turned in for some much-needed rest.

The buggy ride to the Chisum Ranch took about an hour. The ride from the front arch of the ranch to the ranch house took just as long.

Chisum's spread was enormous, to say the least.

The house was large enough for a family of twelve, but Sally Chisum lived alone except for her cook and maid. The ranch hands, of which there were many, all resided in a large bunk house a quarter mile away.

Sally met the buggy herself when it arrived at the corral in front of her house.

"Good morning, Sheriff, Mr. Teasel," Sally said.

John Chisum never married, but his brother's daughter, Sally, was his heir apparent. She lived with him for many years and learned the cattle business from the bottom up. After Chisum's death, Sally assumed the role of the country's largest cattle baron.

During the late Lincoln County War, John Chisum befriended Billy the Kid at one time, and Billy and Sally became close friends.

"Miss Sally, I need to return to town," Pietrie said. "The train will return to pick up Mr. Teasel at ten tonight."

"I shall see that Mr. Teasel doesn't miss his train," Sally said.

The rest of the morning and well into the afternoon was spent shopping for cattle. Teasel was far from an expert on cattle, but Sally, as young as she was, rivaled her uncle when it came to knowledge on livestock.

They took her private buggy and, with Sally at the reins, they traveled many miles of open range. By late afternoon, the one thousand cattle had been selected, along with the dozen milking cows and two bulls.

When they returned to the house, Sally's cook had a full supper ready and waiting in the dining room.

Sally and Teasel dined alone in the large dining room.

Conversation was divided between business and Sally's exploits with her uncle.

"I noticed that your hands are divided between Natives, Mexicans, blacks, and whites," Teasel said.

"My uncle held no prejudices when it came to hands," Sally said. "A man was worth the work he could do regardless of his race or color. I was raised to believe the same, and I do."

"I'm curious about something," Teasel said.

Sally smiled and said, "Are the stories in the newspapers about Billy the Kid and our friendship true?"

"I'm just curious," Teasel said. "You don't have to answer, Miss Chisum."

"My uncle did friend him, and so did I during the Lincoln County War," Sally said. "William knew a thousand jokes, was a wonderful dancer, and loved to play croquet."

"Croquet?" Teasel said.

"Yes, and he was quite good at the game," Sally said. "And I'll tell you something else. He wasn't left-handed, as many stories reported."

"It was sad the way it ended," Teasel said.

"Indeed," Sally said.

"Thank you for humoring me," Teasel said.

"Now, let's talk about your cattle," Sally said. "Have you asked the Santa Fe to make a special stop to transport the cattle?"

"I spoke with them. They said they couldn't afford to make a special run for so small a herd," Teasel said. "I'm afraid we're going to have to do this the old-fashioned way and drive the herd east to Fort Smith."

"Even for my experienced hands, that's a three week or more journey," Sally said. "But if you travel on good grazing ground, it's an opportunity to fatten them up along the way. I shall ask my ramrod to draw up a map of the best open-range grazing lands for you to give to your men."

"That is much appreciated. My drovers will arrive in one week," Teasel said. "Eight good men from the reservation and all experienced. Can I trouble you to purchase a chuck wagon for us? I will pay for it and supplies, and we will provide the horses."

"I have several chuck wagons that don't get much use these days," Sally said. "I will donate one to your cause, and you can supply it in Roswell."

"I appreciate that very much, Miss Chisum," Teasel said.

"You are welcome, and please call me Sally."

The maid entered the dining room and said, "The buggy for Mr. Teasel is ready, Miss Sally."

"Please tell Judge Parker I asked about him," Sally said. "And that I could use a letter from him."

"I will," Henry said. "And thank you for everything."

Judge Isaac Parker was known in many circles as the "Hanging Judge" because many an outlaw was hanged under his jurisdiction. His snow-white hair and beard made him appear much older than his forty-nine years and also added a darker shade to his character.

In the years Teasel knew and reported to Parker, he had never known the judge to be anything other than fair-minded and even-tempered.

After reporting to Parker upon his return to Fort Smith, the judge broke out a bottle of whiskey and filled two small glasses.

"It is quite an accomplishment, Henry," Parker said. "I have to hand it to you. This contract will mean a great deal to the reservation and its people."

"Thank you, Judge," Teasel said. "But the job has just started. I have to get the men to the Chisum Ranch, and then it's at least a month to Fort Smith."

"Pick the best men available, Henry," Parker said. "Pay Emmet Youngblood a visit. He knows the best drovers on the reservation."

"I'll do that, Judge. Thanks," Henry said.

"How is Sally?" Parker said. "I haven't seen her since John's funeral."

"She's fine, Judge. She said to give you her regards and she could use a letter," Teasel said.

"Well, I'm due in court," Parker said. "I'll talk to you more about this later."

Emmet Youngblood was the Chief of Reservation Police for the reservation. Teasel found him in his office, located in the center of the settlement.

"Good morning, Emmet," Teasel said as he entered the office.

"Morning, Henry. Fresh coffee on the stove," Emmet said.

Teasel filled a tin cup from the pot on the woodstove and then sat in the chair opposite the desk.

"How did your trip to Roswell go?" Emmet asked.

"That's why I'm here, Emmet," Teasel said. "I need eight good drovers and a man to drive the chuck wagon."

"Let's talk to the elders," Emmet said. "We'll find you the men."

"How is your mother these days?" Teasel asked.

"Fine. She's at the school at the moment," Emmet said. "And she put two hundred dollars of her own money into your project, so if you value your health, you best not lose it."

Three days later, Emmet, Teasel, and nine men from the reservation took the train from Fort Smith to Roswell. At Judge Parker's insistence, Emmet accompanied Teasel and the men to ensure a smooth start to the operation.

Sally Chisum recognized Emmet from her uncle's funeral.

"Mr. Youngblood, you are the head of the reservation police as I recall," Sally said. "I remember you from my uncle's funeral."

"Nice to see you again, Miss Chisum," Emmet said.

They were on the porch of the Chisum home.

Sally looked at the nine Natives standing just off the porch.

"They look very capable," she said.

"They can cowboy, if that's what you mean," Emmet said.

"Come into the house," Sally said. "I sent for my ramrod. He has a detailed map of the route back to Fort Smith."

Three weeks later, the ramrod of the reservation cowboys decided to let the herd rest along green grazing lands near the Red River in Texas. The ramrod, a full Apache who served as a scout and then as a drover for the army, knew that fattening up a herd made them more likely to travel a greater distance on a given day.

The eight drovers and driver of the chuck wagon were murdered during the second night they camped along the Red River.

The drover standing watch had his throat cut. The remaining eight were shot as they slept in their bedrolls. The chuck wagon was stripped of all supplies and left behind when the herd was stolen.

The dead lay as they were for three days, until some passing cowboys spotted circling buzzards in the distance and went to investigate.

What they saw made them sick to their stomach.

CHAPTER ONE

Captain John Armstrong of the Texas Rangers had seen many things in his tenure as a member of the chief law enforcement agency in Texas. As the man responsible for capturing the infamous John Wesley Hardin in eighteen seventy-seven, Armstrong was no stranger to violence.

He thought he'd seen the worst man had to offer. What he witnessed along the Red River just made him plain sick right down to his soul.

Armstrong could have telegraphed the news, but he decided to take the railroad to Fort Smith and see Judge Parker in person.

He had been in Dallas testifying in a case when the local sheriff informed him of the slaughter on the Red River. After riding to the site, Armstrong decided the news was too terrible for a telegram.

The trip from Dallas to Fort Smith took just half a day, and he arrived at three in the afternoon, a few minutes ahead of schedule. He used the six hours on the train to gather his thoughts and search for the right words to say to Judge Parker.

He had never been to Fort Smith before and didn't know what to expect from a town with so wild a reputation. As he walked the streets from the station to the courthouse, Armstrong observed that Fort Smith wasn't so different from Dallas or Houston.

A deputy marshal was on duty in the lobby of the courthouse.

"Captain Armstrong of the Texas Rangers, and I'm here to see Judge Parker," Armstrong said.

"Check your gun," the deputy said. "And I'll walk you up."

Armstrong was also curious about the famous hanging judge. And like Fort Smith itself, Parker wasn't at all what Armstrong expected.

Shorter in person, his white hair and beard making him look older than he was, Judge Parker was actually soft spoken and polite.

"What is so famous a Texas Ranger doing in Fort Smith?" Parker asked as he shook Armstrong's hand.

"Bringing bad news, I'm afraid," Armstrong said.

Armstrong removed a folded paper from a pocket and set it on the desk. "Have you seen this paper before?" he said.

Parker picked up the paper, unfolded it, and scanned it quickly.

It was the bill of sale for the cattle purchased from Sally Chisum.

"Where did you get this?" Parker asked.

"Who is Henry Teasel?" Armstrong asked. "The man who signed this document."

"The Indian Affairs Agent for this territory," Parker said.

"Would it be possible for him to be present so I don't have to tell this twice?" Armstrong asked.

Henry Teasel's face drained of all color as Armstrong told him the news.

"They . . . they can't be dead," Teasel said.

"I assure you, Mr. Teasel, they are very dead and very buried," Armstrong said.

"Buried? Buried where?" Teasel said. "Those men have families. They . . ."

"Mr. Teasel, those men had been lying in the sun four days with buzzards eating the flesh off their bones by the time I reached them," Armstrong said. "They needed to be put into the ground, and that's what we did."

"The herd?" Teasel said.

Armstrong shook his head. "My trackers followed the tracks across the Red River and lost them after the crossing."

"How do you lose an entire goddamn herd?" Teasel said.

"Henry, no call for that kind of talk," Parker said.

"It's all right, Judge," Armstrong said. "Mr. Teasel is justifiably upset. To answer your question, Mr. Teasel, by the time my trackers arrived, a week had passed. A bigger herd would leave a larger trace, but a thousand head does minimal damage to the grass. It starts to grow back inside of two days, and after five there is hardly a trace. The murderers could have moved the herd east or west in the shallow part of the river and surfaced miles away from where they crossed. I'm sorry, but that's just the way it is, sir."

Teasel broke out in a cold sweat.

"What do I tell their families, all the people who invested in this?" Teasel said. "They trusted and put their faith in me."

"And you did nothing to violate that trust, Henry," Parker said.

"Judge, I—" Teasel said.

"Now listen to me carefully, Henry," Parker said. "I'm giving you a direct order. I want you to go home to your wife and children and speak of this to no one. If you feel you must, you can tell your wife, but no one else. Report to me first thing in the morning. Do you understand me?"

"Yes, Judge," Teasel said.

"Captain Armstrong, it's close to suppertime," Parker said. "Would you be my guest?"

"I have to catch the eight o'clock train back to Dallas," Armstrong said. "I'm due to testify in court in the morning."

★ ★ ★ ★ ★

The steak house a block from the courthouse served the most expensive cut in town at five dollars a plate.

"I'm used to those dollar steaks in Austin," Armstrong said. "Tough as the leather in my boots."

"It's in the marbling," Parker said. "The more marble in the cut, the tenderer the steak."

"Judge, as good a steak as this is, what's really on your mind?" Armstrong said.

Parker sighed. "Captain Armstrong, I'm going to have to do something about this mess," he said. "I don't have the jurisdiction in Texas to ask the Rangers for help, but I would appreciate any assistance you could lend me."

"I'll do what I can, Judge," Armstrong said. "The crime was committed on the Texas side of the Red River."

"I appreciate that, Captain," Parker said.

Teasel parked his buggy next to the corral and took his horse to the small barn behind his home.

He patted the horse's neck as he closed the door to the stall.

"I'll see to you as soon as I see my family," Teasel said.

Teasel's wife of fifteen years, Harriet, was in the kitchen preparing supper. She greeted him with a kiss and asked about his day.

"Fine, dear," Teasel said. "Where are the girls?"

"In their room, doing their schoolwork," Harriet said.

"I'll say hello and then see to the horse before supper," Teasel said.

"Hi, Poppa," his daughters said when he entered their bedroom.

"How are your studies doing?" Teasel asked.

"Fine, Poppa," the oldest girl said.

"We're doing mathematics," the younger girl said.

"I won't keep you, but how about a kiss for your old pa?" Teasel said.

Warm from hugs and kisses from his girls, Teasel returned to the barn where he fed the horse grain while he brushed and groomed him.

He spoke to the horse as he ran the soft bristle brush along his powerful chest.

"I love those people," Teasel said. "The Comanche, the Sioux, the Apache, I love them all. How am I going to tell them I lost their money, and the cattle, to boot? How?"

Finished with the grooming, Teasel placed a warm blanket over the horse's back.

He went to the workbench in the corner of the barn, removed a .32 caliber revolver from a drawer, and took it to the rocking chair beside the small Franklin stove.

Teasel sat in the chair, put the barrel of the revolver in his mouth, cocked it, and pulled the trigger.

Harriet was taking an apple pie from the oven when she heard the gunshot.

Chapter Two

Maria Youngblood, Emmet's wife of three months, handled an ax as well as any man. As she chopped wood for the outdoor barbecue pit, she wiped her brow and glanced down the road at the approaching buggy.

She paused to look up at the roof of the home she and Emmet were building. He was laying roofing shingles. Shirtless in the heat of the day, Emmet's muscular torso was covered in a fine sheen of sweat.

Maria didn't see Emmet look down the road, but she knew he spotted the approaching buggy. When it was just one hundred yards away, Emmet stopped working, climbed down the ladder, picked up his shirt, and walked to Maria.

"Judge Parker," Emmet said.

Maria added some kindling to the barbecue pit and said, "Ask him if he'll stay for lunch."

Emmet removed his pipe from the shirt pocket, stuffed and lit it, and then reached for the coffee pot on the grill. He filled a cup and puffed on the pipe until Judge Parker arrived.

Emmet met the buggy when Parker brought it to a stop beside Emmet's wagon.

"Afternoon, Judge," Emmet said. "Stay for lunch?"

"I'm afraid I don't have much of an appetite," Parker said. "I could use a cup of that coffee though."

Maria filled a cup and gave it to Parker.

"Thank you, Maria," Parker said. "Emmet, a word in private."

"I'm just going to tell her later, Judge," Emmet said.

"All right," Parker said. "Let's find some shade. This will take a while."

"Aw, Henry," Emmet said.

Maria started to cry at the news. She knew the Teasel family only in passing from church and around town, but in her twenty-seven years, she had seen more horrible deaths and enough destruction to last a dozen lifetimes, and her emotions ran over.

"This is a sad day, Emmet," Parker said. "But justice needs to be and will be done. Your brother is due back tomorrow. I'd like to see you both in my office after he arrives."

Emmet nodded.

"I best get back to town," Parker said.

After Parker left, Maria said, "I don't feel like working anymore. I'm going back to the house."

Emmet nodded, kissed Maria, and said, "I'll be along in time for supper."

Maria took the wagon. Emmet had ridden from his office to the construction site on his pinto and would ride him home later.

The ride was just a quarter of a mile, and when she arrived the house was quiet. Amy, Emmet's mother, was teaching school in the settlement. His daughters, Mary and Sarah, were with her as students.

Maria parked the wagon and then led the horse into the corral. She would see to him a bit later. She went into the house and made a fire in the woodstove in the kitchen. There was fresh meat in the icebox, and she gathered the makings for a stew.

Then she put on a pot of coffee and took a cup to Amy's rocking chair and sat to drink it.

After a few sips, Maria set the cup on the floor and started crying again. She knew her emotions were getting the better of her, but the scars from last year were still fresh in her mind.

Just eight months ago, renegade Comanche warrior Two Hawks left the reservation after his wife died and started a war that lasted months and resulted in many deaths. She had been working for the mission that had raised her at the time, and Two Hawks led a war party on the mission and killed everyone except for her and Father Ramon, the priest in charge.

She was taken hostage, along with Father Ramon, and brought to a secret camp in the Ozark Mountains.

Emmet led a daring rescue party to the secret camp, only to find it abandoned except for her and Father Ramon.

Two Hawks fooled them all and attacked the army outpost near Fort Smith, killed the soldiers, and then disappeared without a trace.

Before the raid on the mission, a chance meeting with Emmet and his brother, Jack, took place at the mission. For Maria and Emmet, it was love at first sight. After the attack on the army outpost, Emmet brought her home to meet Amy and his children from his first wife, who died in childbirth.

They started construction on the house in the fall before the snow came and resumed in the spring. In between, they were married at the church in Fort Smith.

Maria didn't have to wait for Emmet to return from the meeting with Judge Parker tomorrow to know that he and Jack would be sent to hunt down the men who murdered the Natives who'd been bringing the cattle to the reservation.

She was hoping to tell him the news that she was pregnant this Sunday before church, but now she would have to keep it from him a while longer. A lawman hunting criminals can't be distracted with thoughts of home. It made him careless, and carelessness often resulted in a shortened life span.

Maria was so lost in thought that she didn't hear Amy's buggy arrive and was startled when Emmet's daughters burst into the room with all of the energy of an eight- and ten-year-old.

Immediately their mood changed when they saw Maria crying in the rocking chair.

"Maria, what's wrong?" Sarah said.

Amy was right behind them.

"Yes, Maria, what is wrong?" Amy said.

Maria stood up from the rocking chair.

"Girls, can you watch the stew while I speak with your grandmother?" Maria said.

"Henry Teasel, my good God," Amy said. "A kinder, gentler man I've never known."

Maria wiped tears from her eyes and looked at Amy. They were on the porch and each had a cup of coffee, but Maria's was untouched.

"Judge Parker will send Emmet and Jack to hunt the men responsible," she said.

"Of course, he will," Amy said. "Jack is a US marshal and Emmet is the chief of reservation police. It's to be expected."

"Emmet is to take the bar exam in four months," Maria said.

"That's in four months," Amy said. "Right now my son has his responsibility to see to. Both of them."

"Don't you worry that when they ride out they might never return?" Maria said.

Amy sipped her coffee and looked at Maria.

Maria remembered that Amy's husband, a US marshal, was killed in the line of duty when Emmet and Jack were just young boys, and she felt foolish for making so stupid a remark.

"I'm sorry, Amy. Forgive me," Maria said.

"There is nothing to forgive, Maria," Amy said. "Men have a sense of duty they must fulfill, even if most of them are nothing but big children at heart. We can patch their wounds and fill their bellies and darn their socks, but we can't change their nature."

"I would never want to change Emmet's nature," Maria said. "But there is something else."

Amy sipped coffee and waited.

Maria seemed lost for words.

A sudden, sweeping noise sounded from behind the screen door.

"Mary," Amy said.

"Yes, Grandmother," Mary said.

"Come out here," Amy said.

The screen door opened and Mary came out to the porch, holding a broom.

"What are you doing?" Amy asked.

"Sweeping the floor," Mary said.

"What did I tell you about snooping on people?" Amy said.

"I wasn't . . ." Mary said.

"There is another use for that broom," Amy said. "Would you like me to demonstrate it for you?"

"No, Grandmother," Mary said.

"I suggest you find your sister and see to supper," Amy said.

Mary nodded and went inside.

Amy looked at Maria. "How far along are you?" Amy asked.

Maria took a deep breath, and then exhaled slowly. "Close to three months. How did you know?"

"I bore two sons, one of them a damned giant, and helped deliver a dozen more, including my nosy little granddaughter in there," Amy said. "I know the look of fresh bread in the oven."

"Emmet will . . ." Maria said.

"You don't tell my son," Amy said. "You don't say one word. You won't show until after he's left, so keep your lips closed. The surest way to get him killed is to give him something besides his job at hand to think about. Do you understand?"

Maria nodded. "I do, and I won't say a word."

"If you do, I'll show you that other use for a broom," Amy said. "We best see to the girls before they burn the house down."

Late in the afternoon, Emmet came down off the roof, satisfied that most of it was done. He tossed on his shirt and saddled his pinto.

Between building the house, his duties on the reservation, and studying for the bar exam, time was short these days.

And it was about to get a great deal shorter.

As he rode back to Amy's house, Emmet wondered what could drive a man like Henry Teasel to suicide.

It wasn't pride. Henry Teasel wasn't a prideful man in any way. It had to be shame.

He took the blame for what happened and made the shame all his own.

There was no other explanation for his action.

Judge Parker would send him and Jack and maybe a few others to hunt down the men responsible. Instead of late spring as a completion date for the house, it would probably be early fall before the work was done.

As he neared the house, Emmet could see his mother on the porch.

Amy had recently turned sixty, but she showed no signs of slowing down. She stood when he reached the corral and dismounted.

"Hello, Mother," Emmet said when he reached the porch.

"Before you tend your horse, sit for a minute," Amy said.

Emmet took the chair next to Amy.

"Maria told me about Henry Teasel," Amy said. "I expect Judge Parker will send you and your brother on a manhunt again."

"He's so much as said so," Emmet said.

Amy nodded.

"You keep your mind on the job and not your pretty new wife," Amy said. "And you will make it back to her."

"Don't worry, Mother," Emmet said. "Besides, I'll be riding with that big oaf you call my brother, and who better to watch my back."

"Go see to your horse," Amy said. "Supper is almost ready."

Chao-xing Fong was a striking beauty, for sure. As she stepped out of the dry-goods store wearing a blue skirt, white blouse, two-inch-high, button-hook shoes, and carrying two bundles of fabric, she turned the head of every man on the streets of Fort Smith.

And every man in Fort Smith kept their distance, as it was well known to all that she was Jack Youngblood's woman, and there would be certain hell to pay if she was accosted in any way.

She crossed the ocean from China in sixty-one when she was just a child. Her father was an engineer, and he went to work for the Southern Pacific Railroad and helped build the transcontinental railroad.

After its completion, her father stayed on and helped build many of the connecting tributaries that still existed.

Ten years ago, her father, after accumulating a goodly amount of wealth, decided to return to China where the family would live in prosperity. Before they could depart, Chao-xing's parents were murdered for their wealth, and Chao-xing found herself stranded in Arkansas virtually penniless.

Working with her mother, Chao-xing had learned the laundry and seamstress trade, and she went to work in a Chinese laundry to make ends meet. A chance encounter brought her to Jack when, late one night, two drifters attempted to rape her in the laundry.

Jack was a deputy marshal then and didn't waste time or words when he happened by that night. He simply shot the two men dead and asked questions later.

Now she wore his engagement ring and lived in the house he grew up in on a tree-lined street in Fort Smith. The two-story home was a disaster when she moved in, as Jack was not much of a housekeeper and his duties kept him too busy for housework. During the past six months, Chao-xing had given the house an overhaul, even painting the exterior. The parlor was the only room that reflected her Chinese culture. She decorated the room with her doll collection and vases.

A skilled seamstress, Chao-xing ordered a Singer sewing machine from a catalogue at the dry-goods store and began making Jack his shirts. He was so large a man that he had difficulty finding shirts that fit properly. Once his fellow marshals noticed his shirts, she began custom-making shirts for them, and, soon after, for those in town who could afford her fifteen-dollar-per-shirt price tag.

The two bundles of material she carried home were for orders placed by several marshals and some local businessmen.

When she reached the edge of town and turned down the tree-lined street where the house was located, Chao-xing paused for a moment when she saw Judge Parker's buggy parked outside the gate of the picket fence.

She knew the news would be bad.

Parker stepped down from the buggy as she approached the house.

"Is he dead?" Chao-xing asked.

"If you mean Marshal Youngblood, he's due back tomorrow midmorning," Parker said.

"Well, you're not here to order a shirt," Chao-xing said.

Parker sighed. "We need to talk, Chao-xing," he said.

"I'll make some tea," Chao-xing said.

"Jack's been gone three weeks, and you want to send him out again for who knows how long. Why?" Chao-xing said. "You have a dozen other marshals who can . . ."

"When Jack is hunting a man, he's the meanest son of a bitch ever born, and that's what this job calls for, Chao-xing," Parker said. "I'm sorry, but I have to do this. I wanted to let you know before Jack returned. I figure I owe you that much."

Chao-xing took a sip of her tea. "I understand," she said. "How long do you think he'll be gone this time?"

"I'd say count on a month," Parker said.

"Well, why not let me fit you for a new shirt?" Chao-xing said.

"I suppose I could use a few new shirts," Parker said.

CHAPTER THREE

The citizens of Fort Smith always lined both sides of Main Street whenever the prisoner wagon returned to town. It had to take that route to reach the courthouse and holding jail.

The atmosphere was as electric as if the circus had just arrived with elephants leading a parade.

Shortly before noon, Jack, atop his tall horse, led the wagon into town. Behind the wagon, two deputies followed, and a third deputy held the reins on the four-horse team. The wagon itself was a covered wagon with a steel cage added to it.

Nine men were inside the cage.

Citizens wondered who they were, what they had done, and if they would hang or not. Most cheered as the wagon rolled past them.

As was his custom, Parker waited at the steps of the courtyard for the wagon to arrive. Six armed marshals waited with him.

Chao-xing was allowed to wait for Jack on the courthouse steps. She held a parasol to keep the sun off her neck.

The wagon rolled to a stop at the steps and Jack dismounted. Three weeks' worth of beard covered his face. His shirt was ripped in several places, but it didn't matter to Chao-xing. Seeing Jack always made her heart flutter.

The other two marshals dismounted and Jack said, "Open her up. We ain't got all day here."

A marshal opened the cage and the prisoners filed out, except one.

31

Jack went to the cage.

"Well, come on," Jack said.

"You go to hell, you son of a bitch," the prisoner said.

Jack reached in, grabbed the prisoner by his shirt, yanked him out of the cage, and tossed him like a doll to the muddy street. As the prisoner stood up, Jack kicked him in the rear end and the prisoner landed face-first into the mud.

The crowd laughed.

Chao-xing hid her grin at the sight.

"Marshal Youngblood," Parker said.

Jack turned. "Judge," he said.

"A moment, please," Parker said.

Jack walked to the steps.

"Ten warrants and nine prisoners," Parker said.

"One resisted arrest," Jack said. "I had to show him the error of his ways."

"And where is he?" Parker asked.

"Resting comfortably," Jack said. "In boot hill."

Parker turned and looked up the steps at Chao-xing.

"Chao-xing, take your man home, clean him up, and have him back here at five o'clock," Parker said.

As Jack soaked in a hot tub full of Chao-xing's bubble bath and oils, she sat on the rim of the tub and carefully shaved him.

"You smell like a wet goat," Chao-xing said.

"Three weeks in the saddle, what do you expect?" Jack said. "Roll me a smoke, would you, honey?"

"Hold still, you stupid oaf, before I cut your throat," Chao-xing said. "I'm almost finished."

Chao-xing scraped the last bit of stubble from Jack's face and stood up.

"Dunk under," she said.

Jack submerged under the water for a few seconds, and when

he surfaced, Chao-xing had a cigarette ready and placed it between his lips.

"Thanks, hon," he said.

Chao-xing struck a match and lit the cigarette.

"Jack, I've been wearing your ring for six months now," Chao-xing said. "When are you going to marry me?"

Jack dropped the cigarette into the tub.

"What's the rush, hon?" he said.

"I want to have babies," Chao-xing said.

Jack swallowed hard. "Well, jeeze, hon, and here I was thinking about . . ."

"I know what you were thinking about," Chao-xing said. "When are you going to marry me, Jack? I want babies."

"Do we have to talk about this now?" Jack said.

"Yes."

"Damn," Jack said. "Can't it wait until after I see the judge?"

"No."

"I swear, you are the most stubborn woman I ever met," Jack said.

"Did you meet many women while you were away, Jack?"

"That's not what I meant," Jack said.

"When?" Chao-xing said.

Jack sighed.

"When?" Chao-xing said.

"Let me see what the judge wants, then you can plan a wedding," Jack said.

"I'm going to put on some tea," Chao-xing said. "Think of something amusing we can do while the water boils."

Chao-xing turned and left the bathroom.

Jack thought for a moment and then stood up.

"Well, hell," he said and climbed out of the tub.

Emmet was already in Judge Parker's chambers when Jack arrived wearing a brand-new shirt Chao-xing made for him while he was away.

"Hey, little brother," Jack said and shook Emmet's hand.

"Well, gentlemen, here it is," Parker said.

While Jack was meeting with Parker, Chao-xing packed his saddlebags with clean shirts, socks, underclothes, and soaps for his razor. She would add fresh provisions in the morning in the way of canned goods.

Jack owned a silver flask, and she filled it with bourbon whiskey and tucked it into the saddlebags.

Then she made some tea, took it to the parlor, sat, and started to cry.

Amy and the girls were at school. Emmet rode to his office before riding to town to see the judge.

That's when the morning sickness struck and Maria vomited into the sink. When her stomach settled, she cranked the pump to wash the sink clean.

Then she sat with a cup of coffee at the table.

The thought that Emmet might never return to see his child born washed over her like darkness, and she started to cry.

"Henry Teasel, Jesus Christ," Jack said.

"I know," Parker said. "And I'm sorry to do this to you boys, but I have to send you as soon as possible. Emmet, I'm going to deputize you as a deputy marshal so you have full federal jurisdiction. Pick one of your reservation police deputies to fill in for you while you're away."

"We could use a few more men, Judge," Jack said.

"So could I, but Reeves and Tillman are up north, and I need six to run the jail and courthouse," Parker said.

"We'll need expense money," Jack said.

"I drew three thousand," Parker said. "And not one drop goes to liquor, you hear me, Jack."

"Judge, I'd never—" Jack said.

"Be quiet," Parker said. "Now tell me what you need and what your plans are to get started."

"We'll need a tracker," Jack said. "Someone really good. We'll need to pay him well, too."

"It occurs to me that it would be fairly easy to spot a thousand head with the Chisum brand on them, so they would have to change the brands. That's not hard to do, but a thousand plus will take some time. They may be closer than we thought."

"What's the prime rate on Chisum beef these days?" Jack said.

"Twenty a head," Parker said.

"In Mexico and Canada?" Jack asked.

"Twenty, maybe twenty-two in Mexico, even higher in Canada," Parker said. "What's on your mind, Jack?"

"What Jack is trying to say is they might have rustled more than one herd to make the risk worthwhile," Emmet said. "Maybe you could send out a few telegrams asking if other herds were recently stolen."

"I should have thought of that myself," Parker said.

"Let's take a look at a map," Emmet said.

They moved over to Parker's conference table where he had a large book of maps. "I circled the area along the Texas side of the Red River where the herd was stolen," he said.

"There's a lawman you should see in Dallas," Parker said. "Captain Armstrong of the Texas Rangers. I asked him for some help across the border."

"I've met Armstrong," Jack said. "He's a good man. Wire him we're coming."

"When do you want us to leave?" Emmet asked.

"There's a service for Henry tomorrow at ten," Parker said.

"I expect you to be ready to leave as soon as you finalize your plans and secure a tracker."

"We'll be ready," Emmet said.

"Emmet, raise your right hand so I can swear you in," Parker said.

Jack and Emmet sat on the courtroom steps after they left Parker's office.

Jack rolled a cigarette. Emmet lit his pipe.

"Damn bad luck," Jack said. "I just got home."

"I'm building a house and studying for the bar exam," Emmet said. "This could set me back months."

Jack mused while he sat on the steps.

"Chao-xing wants us to get married," he said.

Emmet grinned. "And you're upset this trip might delay those plans, huh?"

"Dammit, Emmet, I don't know if I'm cut out to be married like you," Jack said.

"That's how I felt the first time when I married Sarah," Emmet said.

"Who you stole from me, by the way," Jack said.

"Don't start that nonsense again, Jack," Emmet said. "We both know it's nothing of the sort."

"Well, what am I supposed to do?" Jack said.

"Do what your heart tells you is the right thing to do," Emmet said.

"Excuse me, gents, but are you the Youngblood boys?" a man of about sixty said as he approached the steps.

"We are," Emmet said. "And you are?"

"My name is Stanly Duff. I purchased the newspaper in town."

"The *Gazette*?" Emmet said.

"Yes. I own the paper in Little Rock and . . ."

"What is it you want, Mr. Duff?" Jack said.

"Yes, well, it's like this, boys," Duff said. "I'd like to see your mother and would like your—"

"What do you mean 'see'?" Jack said.

Emmet grinned. "He means he wants to court Ma, Jack."

Slowly, Jack stood up and towered over Duff.

"I've seen her around town, and she's a lovely woman and I . . ." Duff said.

"Come within a hundred feet of my mother, and I will pull your arms out and beat you to death with them," Jack said.

"Jack, shut up," Emmet said.

"I meant no disrespect, Marshal," Duff said.

"Mr. Duff, have you spoken to our mother?" Emmet said.

"No, I haven't," Duff said. "I was hoping you boys might give me your blessing to do so."

"Tread lightly in that regard, Mr. Duff," Emmet said. "Our mother is the only soul on this earth my brother is afraid of."

Duff looked at Jack.

"He's . . . I see," Duff said. "Well, I assure you my intentions are purely honorable."

"Mr. . . . Duff, is it? I don't care what your intentions are," Jack said. "If I see you inside a hundred feet of my mother, I'll shoot you dead on the spot."

Jack turned and walked toward the courthouse corral to fetch his horse.

Duff looked at Emmet.

"Is he . . . was he serious?" Duff said.

"Mr. Duff, I wouldn't try my brother," Emmet said. "Those who do tend to have a shortened life span. Now, excuse me, sir."

Emmet walked to the corral and caught up with Jack just as Jack was mounting his tall horse.

"Jack, hold on a second," Emmet said.

"That popinjay is asking for trouble," Jack said.

"Jack, Ma doesn't exactly need our permission to have a man caller," Emmet said. "Now forget it and bring Chao-xing to the house for supper tonight. We may not be together again for a while."

Jack nodded.

"Don't be late," Emmet said.

CHAPTER FOUR

Jack tossed a baseball with Mary and Sarah near the corral where there was lots of room. The game of baseball became popular during the war when bored soldiers took to playing it to pass the time.

During his travels, Jack had seen a few games played by professional teams. Not long ago in Little Rock, he saw a game played between the team from Boston and the team from Cincinnati. After the game, the balls that were too scuffed to reuse were tossed to the fans. Jack caught such a ball and saved it for just such an occasion as this.

While Jack tossed the ball with the girls, Emmet chopped wood at the side of the house. There was a full cord of chopped wood, but he wanted to make sure there was enough to last while he was away. The wood wasn't needed for heat during summer months, but it was a necessity for cooking and bathing.

In the house, Amy, Maria, and Chao-xing set the table.

"Emmet doesn't know you are pregnant?" Chao-xing said to Maria.

Maria shook her head. "I thought it best not to tell him until after he returns from assignment," she said. "I don't want him distracted when he's after dangerous men."

"I understand," Chao-xing said.

"What about you and Jack?" Maria said.

"He wants to get married, but he's afraid," Chao-xing said.

"My son is as dumb as he is big," Amy said. "You girls finish setting the table."

Amy went outside to the porch and watched Jack toss the baseball with the girls. His Colt was slung over the porch railing and his shirt was untucked and, with a smile on his face, Jack appeared the friendliest of souls.

But Amy knew Jack could and often would be the most deadly of men at the slightest provocation.

"Jack, a moment please," Amy called to him.

Jack tossed the baseball to Mary. "Be right back," he said.

He went up to the porch.

"Ma," he said.

"You either marry that girl or let her go," Amy said.

"Chao-xing?" Jack said.

"No, Queen Victoria," Amy said. "Of course Chao-xing."

"Ma, I . . ."

"Be quiet," Amy said. "The cow will give away the milk for free for only so long, John. There will come a time when the buyer has to pay up or the cow leaves the barn."

"Jesus, Ma," Jack said.

"He would agree with me, you fool," Amy said. "Now, what's the problem?"

Jack looked at the porch floor. He stood six-foot, four inches, and towered over Amy by a foot or more, yet in her presence he always felt like a child.

"Well, what is it?" Amy asked.

"I don't know, Ma," Jack said. "It's just the thought of being tied down scares me some."

"Then let her go," Amy said.

"I can't, Ma. I love her," Jack said.

"Then she will let you go, and you will spend the rest of your days wondering about her in the arms of another man," Amy said. "You'll grow old haunted by memories. Is that what you want?"

Jack sighed.

"I'll talk to her after dinner," Jack said.

Amy looked down the road, and Jack turned to see what she was looking at.

"Girls," Jack said loudly.

Mary and Sarah looked at Jack.

"Come up here right now," Jack said.

They raced up to the porch.

"Go inside," Jack said.

They didn't question Jack and entered the house.

Jack tucked in his shirt, reached for his holster, and strapped on his Colt, and, just like that, the little boy was gone and the US marshal appeared.

"Ma, inside," Jack said.

Amy turned and entered the house.

Jack stepped down from the porch and walked to the corral. There was no need to call Emmet; he was suddenly behind Jack, shirtless and dripping sweat.

"Do you know him?" Jack said.

Emmet peered at the approaching rider.

"Red Moon," Emmet said.

"Comanche?" Jack said.

"Sioux," Emmet said. "He scouted for Sherman, Grant, and Custer. He visits his people on the reservation from time to time and always checks in with the police. I wonder what he wants."

"We'll find out soon enough," Jack said.

A few minutes later, Red Moon arrived, riding a large mustang stallion. He stopped in front of Jack and Emmet and made the Sioux hand greeting for hello.

Emmet returned the greeting.

"I am seeking the one called Emmet Youngblood," Red Moon said.

"I am Emmet Youngblood," Emmet said.

"My services as scout are yours," Red Moon said.

"Do you drink coffee?" Emmet asked.

"Have you sugar?" Red Moon said.

"Yes."

"Then I drink coffee."

Amy filled four cups with coffee and then sat next to Jack on the porch.

Red Moon looked at her.

"You have the look of Sioux," he said.

"Partly," Amy said. "And some Mexican Apache."

Red Moon sipped coffee and nodded.

"Very good," he said.

"So, Red Moon, why are you here?" Emmet said.

"The news of the attack on your people on the Red River has traveled south to the Llano and as far north to Nebraska," Red Moon said. "The news reached me at the fort in Ogallala, where I am chief scout. The fort commander gave me permission to scout for you when you go after these men. That is why I am here."

"Mind me asking how old you are?" Jack said.

"In white man years I am sixty-one," Red Moon said.

"What are you in Sioux years?" Jack asked.

"Many moons old," Red Moon said with a sly grin.

"Well, we need a seasoned scout," Emmet said. "Will you join us for supper, and we'll talk."

Behind the screen door, Chao-xing, Maria, Mary, and Sarah turned away and went to set another place at the table.

Red Moon proved to be an entertaining dinner companion. He told stories of his days as a scout with Grant, Sherman, and Custer. Mary and Sarah barely touched their supper, they were so engrossed in his tales.

After supper, Jack, Emmet, Red Moon, and Amy took coffee on the porch.

Jack rolled a cigarette while Emmet and Red Moon smoked pipes.

"We leave tomorrow on the two o'clock train to Dallas," Emmet said. "If you still want to scout for us, we'll be on that train."

"I was told in town that there is a ten o'clock service at the church for the man called Teasel," Red Moon said. "I would like to attend."

"Then you can stay here and sleep in our one extra bed, and we'll ride into town together," Amy said.

"I don't wish to put you out, ma'am," Red Moon said.

"You won't," Amy said. "You can tell some more tales of your adventures at breakfast to the girls."

"Then I accept," Red Moon said.

"Well, I best get Chao-xing and head home," Jack said. "I'll see you at the church."

"Remember what I told you," Amy said.

"I remember," Jack said.

As Jack and Chao-xing rode away in their buggy, Amy and Emmet stood on the porch and watched them.

"What did you tell Jack?" Emmet said.

Amy turned to her son.

"Do you remember when you were eight and I caught you snooping at the door?" Amy said.

"I do remember that," Emmet said.

"Do you recall what I told you?"

"Before or after the spanking?"

"After."

"Let's see," Emmet said. "Something like, a man who minds

his own business has a longer life expectancy than a man who doesn't."

Amy looked at Emmet and then she went into the house.

"Well, at least she didn't spank me," Emmet said.

"The night is young," Amy said from the open window.

Jack smoked a cigarette as he waited in bed for Chao-xing. A lantern on the dresser cast the bedroom in a yellowish glow.

He could hear her washing her face in the basin in the bathroom. After a few minutes, the splashing stopped and Chao-xing appeared in the dark doorway.

"Jack," she whispered.

"In bed."

Chao-xing walked in front of the lantern, and her entire body was exposed through the sheer, silk robe she wore. Her skin seemed to glow in the pale light.

Immediately, Jack felt the excitement in his stomach start to build.

Chao-xing went to the bed, sat and removed the covers from Jack, then took the cigarette from his lips and placed it into the ashtray on the table.

Jack stared at her.

"My God, you're a thoroughbred," he said.

Chao-xing burst into tears.

Jack sat up. "I was hoping for a more romantic response," he said.

"Idiot," Chao-xing said in Chinese. "Stupid buffoon always in a hurry to get himself killed," she continued in Chinese.

"I can't . . . I don't know what you're . . ." Jack said.

"Be quiet when I'm talking," Chao-xing said in English. Then she said in Chinese, "You're the size of a bear with the courage of a lion, but you're nothing but a mama's boy at heart. I don't know why I waste my time on a stupid fool like you."

"I don't . . ." Jack said.

"You're afraid to marry me," Chao-xing said in English. "That's the truth, isn't it?"

Jack sighed heavily.

"The truth is, I'm afraid to lose you," he said.

"And I'll tell you something else, you . . . what did you say?" Chao-xing said.

"I said I'm afraid to lose you," Jack said.

"Do you really mean that?"

"I mean it enough to ask my mother to make you a wedding dress," Jack said.

"When did you do that?"

"Before we left tonight."

"Why didn't you tell me?" Chao-xing said.

"You was too busy yelling at me in your gibberish," Jack said.

"That gibberish is thousands of years older than your English," Chao-xing said.

"Well, do you want to keep yelling at me or do you want to make up?" Jack said.

"Making up is the best part of having a fight," Chao-xing said as she stood and removed the robe. Then she positioned herself on top of Jack, kissed him softly, and said in Chinese, "Even if you are a dumb ox."

CHAPTER FIVE

The church in the center of Fort Smith held three hundred people. By nine-thirty every seat was taken, the reverend opened the doors, and people lined the walls. Five hundred from the reservation arrived in town and they gathered in front of the church to hear the service.

Tables were set up behind the church with refreshments and food for those who wished to mingle afterward.

Amy, the girls, and Maria assisted the reverend at the refreshments tables after the service for Henry Teasel concluded.

Jack and Emmet broke away from Chao-xing and Maria to speak privately with Judge Parker.

"Henry had it all wrong," Parker said. "They don't hold against him what happened. If he could have seen the Natives turn out for him today, he would never have done what he did."

"We have a train to catch, Judge," Emmet said. "I'll need that expense money before we board. And some extra for our scout, Red Moon."

"Walk over to the courthouse with me and I'll see to it," Parker said.

"You go ahead, Emmet," Jack said. "I'm going to pick us up some extra ammunition. I'll meet you at the station in one hour."

Jack held the Colt Peacemaker in his hand and compared it to his own. The bluing was perfect. The black ivory handle had the same gold crucifix inscribed on the right side.

"Emmet's no gunman, so I set the trigger pull to seven pounds," the gunsmith said.

Jack nodded and picked up the perfectly made brown holster. Eighteen slots lined the rear of the belt for extra ammunition.

"Let me have four boxes of ammunition for the Colts and two for our Winchesters," Jack said.

"What about your derringer?" the gunsmith said.

Jack's right boot had a special sleeve on the inside that held a derringer chambered in .38 long.

"Toss in a box for that," Jack said.

"This be cash, Marshal?" the gunsmith asked. "I ask because if you get killed, I'll never collect from the judge."

"I'll pay cash," Jack said.

"That's sixty for the custom Colt, fifteen for the holster, and fifteen for the ammunition," the gunsmith said.

Judge Parker stood on the railroad platform and shook hands with Jack, Emmet, and Red Moon. Jack held a sack from the gunsmith.

"I'll expect a telegram as soon as possible," Parker said.

"You'll get it," Emmet said.

Parker looked at Jack. "And Marshal, do try to keep the body count low."

"I'll do my best, Judge, to cooperate with those who don't want to," Jack said.

Parker nodded to Red Moon, then turned and left the platform.

Jack turned to Emmet.

"This is for you, little brother," Jack said and handed Emmet the sack.

Emmet opened the sack and removed the new Colt and holster.

"Jack, I like the iron I wear," Emmet said.

"That Dragoon you carry weighs near nine pounds loaded," Jack said. "It's useless unless you can find a fence post to lean it on."

Amy, Chao-xing, Maria, and Mary and Sarah approached Jack and Emmet on the platform.

"Emmet, listen to your brother," Amy said. "He knows more about such things than you."

Emmet removed his holster and replaced it with the new Colt. He gave the Dragoon to Amy.

"You take care of it for me, Ma," he said.

Amy placed the holster over her shoulder.

"Girls, say goodbye to your father," she said.

Emmet got down on one knee and hugged Mary and Sarah.

"You girls mind your grandmother and Maria," he said.

"We will, Pa," Mary said.

"Girls, we'll wait for Maria and Chao-xing at the end of the platform," Amy said. "Jack, a word in private after you say goodbye to Chao-xing."

"I'll be on the train," Red Moon said.

Emmet stood and hugged Maria.

"Don't do anything stupid like get yourself killed," she said.

Chao-xing held Jack tightly around his waist.

"Don't make me a widow before I'm a wife," she said.

"Worry about the bad guys, hon," Jack said. "They're the ones that need it."

Chao-xing took Jack's hand and walked with him to Amy.

Amy led Jack twenty feet away.

"I expect you to watch out for your brother," she said. "He is not the gunman you are, and he is too newly married to leave behind a widow."

"Emmet can take care of himself, Ma," Jack said.

"You're not so big I can't still slap you into next week," Amy said. "Now promise me."

"Do you even need to ask?" Jack said.

Amy looked up at her son.

"No, I guess not," she said.

"I best get moving before the train leaves without me," Jack said.

"Jack?" Amy said.

"I know, Ma," Jack said. "I love you, too."

Shortly after the train left the station, Jack, Emmet, and Red Moon went to the dining car and ordered coffee.

Emmet held a leather briefcase. Once they were seated, he dug out a stack of papers and set them on the table.

"What's all this?" Jack asked.

"Reports on stolen herds from the past six months," Emmet said. "North and south of the Red River and as far west as Arizona."

"Do you think the same bunch as those that stole the herd bound for the reservation stole those, too?" Red Moon asked.

"Hard to say," Emmet said. "These herds range in size from fifty to two hundred and fifty. Ours was a thousand. If it is the same bunch, they've grown more daring."

"Or stupid," Jack said. "A larger herd is easier to track."

"Well, no one has seen a hair of them yet," Emmet said. "These other papers are reports from local cattlemen's associations. Judge Parker wired them to be on the lookout for altered brands at auctions. Anything that looks like an altered Chisum brand is to be set aside."

"Excuse me, gentlemen," the waiter said.

"Yes?" Emmet said.

"I've been asked to ask your friend to kindly leave the dining car," the waiter said.

"Why?" Emmet asked.

"Yeah, why?" Jack said.

"I don't know, sir. I didn't ask," the waiter said.

Jack looked around the dining car. Except for a plump man of about fifty seated with a woman of about the same age, the car was empty.

Jack stood up.

"No trouble, Jack," Emmet said.

Jack walked to the man's table. "Are you the one who asked our friend to leave?" he said.

"I am," the man said.

"Why?"

"My dear sir, the man is . . ."

"Don't call me sir," Jack said. "This badge on my chest comes with a title."

The man looked at the badge.

"Marshal, the man is a savage," the man said. "I have my wife's honor to think about."

"That man seated over there is wearing the uniform of the United States Cavalry," Jack said. "His rank is Sergeant Major. He scouted for Grant, Sherman, and Custer. Now we can end this conversation two ways. One is that you apologize to my friend and offer to buy the three of us dinner tonight. Two is I open that window behind you and toss your useless ass out onto the tracks, and I'm sure your wife wouldn't mind all that much. Which will it be?"

"Marshal, you can't be serious?" the man said.

Jack reached over and slid open the window.

"Try me, you carpetbagger," Jack said.

The man stood up. He took his wife's arm as she stood.

"Pay the waiter for dinner and throw in a bottle of bourbon whiskey," Jack said.

The man and his wife approached the waiter.

"I would like to buy the marshal and his friends dinner

tonight," the man said and produced his wallet.

Jack returned to the table after the man left and took his chair.

"Was all that really necessary, Jack?" Emmet asked.

"Our ma is part Sioux," Jack said. "That makes us part Sioux. The hell with that man and his wife."

"He'll complain," Emmet said.

"Let him."

"Would you really have thrown him out the window?" Red Moon said.

"Naw, his fat ass wouldn't have fit," Jack said.

"Jesus, Jack," Emmet said. "Can we get back to business now?"

Jack looked at the waiter. "What time you serve dinner?"

"Six o'clock, Marshal," the waiter said.

"We'll have three steaks with all the fixings and a bottle of bourbon," Jack said.

Red Moon looked across his seat at Jack, who was sound asleep in his chair with his hat over his eyes. Emmet sat next to Red Moon, and Red Moon nudged him.

"We just sat down ten minutes ago. How is it he's asleep?" Red Moon said.

"Jack has always had the ability to fall asleep whenever he wants to," Emmet said. "I think it's because he's as dumb as an ox and his mind is always free of worry."

Without moving a muscle, Jack said, "I heard that."

Emmet grinned.

"Let's take a look at these maps again," he said.

Unable to sleep, Maria tossed on a robe and went outside to the porch and sat in a chair. The night air was cool, and the soft breeze felt good on her face. The moon was up and large in the sky, and her night vision was good.

Wearing a shawl over her shoulders, Amy opened the screen door and joined Maria, taking the chair to her left.

"I was the same way whenever my husband left after some outlaw," Amy said. "Unable to sleep or eat, worried every minute of every day until he returned."

"Did you ever get used to it?" Maria asked.

"No," Amy said. "And you won't either if you really love your husband."

"I feel guilty for not telling him about the baby," Maria said.

"Don't," Amy said. "I know my Emmet. At heart, he is a kind and caring man. Kind and caring is not the way to hunt outlaws. Give him something to dream about and he won't make it home. Now, how about I warm us some milk so we can go back to bed?"

Chao-xing tossed and turned until she finally gave up trying to sleep and got out of bed. She lit the lantern on the bedside table and walked to the kitchen. The floorboards creaked under her bare feet.

It was odd how, whenever Jack was home, she never heard all the noises the house made. The creaking floorboards, the drafty windows, the little drip from the water pump in the kitchen sink.

Jack was always so loud in whatever he was doing, he drowned out all other noises.

Chao-xing opened the icebox. The pan was full of water. She carried it to the sink, dumped it, and then replaced it. She checked the ice. It would last at least another week or more.

She removed a bottle of milk, filled a glass, and sat at the table. She sipped and thought about Jack. As long as he was a US marshal, there would always be the threat that one day he would not return home.

And Jack would always be a marshal. Chao-xing knew in her heart that Jack was born to be a lawman. He knew nothing else and didn't want to do anything else.

What kind of life together would they have?

The last hour or so, Red Moon dozed in his chair. When he awoke, Emmet was engrossed in a thick, leather-bound book.

"Is that a bible?" Red Moon asked.

"To some," Emmet said. "It's a law book. I'm studying for the bar exam."

"Bar exam? Like a saloon?"

"I went to law school, but in order for me to practice law, I need to pass a test they call the bar exam," Emmet said.

"So you're going to quit as police chief and become a lawyer?" Red Moon said.

"For Judge Parker's court as a public defender," Emmet said. "And as official defender for the reservation."

Red Moon nodded to the sleeping Jack. "And him?"

"Jack will always be the lazy slob you see before you," Emmet said.

Without moving a muscle, Jack said, "I heard that."

A conductor entered the car. "Ten minutes to Dallas," he said.

CHAPTER SIX

Dallas was a cowboy town, a stop for local ranchers taking their beef to markets by railroad. Built near the Trinity River before Texas became a state, it boasted a population of fifteen thousand residents and many tall buildings of six stories or more.

After retrieving their horses from the boxcar, Jack, Emmet, and Red Moon walked them to the center of town.

"I wired the Hotel Fort Worth and reserved rooms for two days," Emmet said.

"Ten o'clock at night and it's ninety degrees in this town," Jack said.

As they reached the street where the hotel was located, they passed several open saloons.

"A cold beer might sit well about now," Jack said.

"We're not here for the beer, Jack," Emmet said.

Emmet looked at Jack.

"Or the saloon dancing girls," Emmet said.

They passed a saloon that had a second-floor balcony. On the balcony a few saloon girls looked down at them.

"Hey cowboys, how about a cold beer and a warm girl?" one of them called out.

Jack looked up and winked at the girls.

"Remember what's waiting for you at home," Emmet said.

"If you mean a leash around my neck, I remember," Jack said.

"There's the hotel," Emmet said.

The Hotel Fort Worth stood six stories high, and the rooms facing the street had balconies. Its private livery stable was next door, separated by an alleyway.

"Let's stable the horses before we check in," Emmet said.

A man was on duty in the livery. Jack, Emmet, and Red Moon took their rifles and saddlebags with them when they entered the hotel lobby.

"I'm Marshal Emmet Youngblood," Emmet said. "I wired this morning to reserve three rooms."

The desk clerk looked at Red Moon.

Jack looked at the desk clerk. "If you give me any shit about him not being welcome, I'll . . ."

"He is most welcome," the clerk said in Sioux.

"We appreciate that," Emmet said in Sioux.

"You have the blood?" the clerk said in Sioux.

"And some Comanche," Emmet said in Sioux.

"And the large one?" the clerk said in Sioux.

Emmet looked at Jack. "He hardly speaks English, he's so dumb," Emmet said in Sioux.

"Enough with this gibberish," Jack said. "Send up some cold beers to our rooms. In the bottle in a bucket of ice."

"I see what you mean," the clerk said to Emmet in Sioux.

Stripped down to their underwear, Jack and Emmet sipped cold bottled beer on the balcony of their room.

As he rolled a cigarette, Jack said, "Why does he get his own room?"

"He's our elder, Jack," Emmet said. "It's a sign of respect. Besides, this way I'll know where you are all night."

Jack lit the cigarette with a wood match and tossed the match over the balcony.

"This Ranger, Captain Armstrong, is supposed to meet us here in the morning," Jack said.

"He wired the judge he'd be on the ten o'clock train from Austin," Emmet said. "We'll pick up what supplies we need for a week and head out as soon as he's ready."

"Red Moon may be a first-class tracker, but I have little hope we'll find the men who did this," Jack said.

"I can't say I disagree with you, but it's our job to try," Emmet said. "Before Armstrong arrives, we'll check in with the local cattlemen's association and see if there's been any more rustling around here."

Jack blew a smoke ring, sipped beer, and said, "What's it like being married, Emmet? Really like."

"It's like your soul is out there floating around searching for something to complete it," Emmet said. "And when you find the right woman, that's just what happens. You feel whole inside, like a complete man."

"But you get told what to do a lot," Jack said.

"Absolutely," Emmet said.

"And nagged a lot."

"Count on it."

"And you don't get to do the things you want to do," Jack said.

"Never," Emmet said.

"Well, who needs a life like that?" Jack said.

"You do, Jack," Emmet said. "More than any man I know. You think on that. I'm going to bed."

After an early breakfast in the hotel café, Jack, Emmet, and Red Moon took coffee on the porch. Not yet seven-thirty, the streets of Dallas were alive and bustling.

"We have plenty of time before the train arrives," Emmet said. "I'll walk over to the telegraph office and send a wire to Ma and the women. When I get back, we'll visit the cattlemen's association."

Jack rolled a cigarette and said, "Don't hurry."

"Mind if I tag along?" Red Moon asked.

"Come on," Emmet said.

After Emmet and Red Moon left, Jack smoked his cigarette and sipped his coffee and watched the streets.

A man of about fifty, wearing the badge of sheriff, approached the hotel and stepped up to the porch.

"I'm Sheriff Lang. I heard a couple of marshals and a tracker were in town," Lang said.

"Jack Youngblood," Jack said.

"I've heard of you," Lang said. "You're out of Fort Smith under Judge Parker."

"That's right," Jack said.

A waitress from the café appeared on the porch. "Want a refill, Marshal?" she said.

"I do, and bring a cup for the sheriff," Jack said.

The waitress filled Jack's cup and returned to the café.

Lang sat in a chair next to Jack.

"You're waiting on Armstrong," Lang said. "He wired me yesterday from Austin that he'll be on the ten o'clock train."

"We got the same wire," Jack said.

The waitress returned with a cup of coffee for Lang.

"Thank you," Lang said.

After the waitress returned to the café, Lang said, "I know why you're here, Marshal. What happened to those Indians should never have happened. I'd like to ride along with you to the Red if you wouldn't mind."

"I don't mind, Sheriff, but if you ask me, we're wasting our time," Jack said. "Too many weeks have passed and those that done it are long past gone."

"I can't say as I disagree, but it's necessary to try," Lang said.

"My brother said that very thing," Jack said.

Emmet and Red Moon returned to the hotel and climbed the

steps to the porch.

"Emmet, this here is Sheriff Lang," Jack said. "He wants to go with us to the Red."

"It's several days in the saddle from here," Emmet said. "And back."

"I've done it before," Lang said.

"What time does the cattlemen's association open for business?" Emmet said.

"Eight," Lang said.

"We'll talk about it over lunch after Armstrong arrives," Emmet said.

The Dallas chapter of the Cattlemen's Association was located three blocks from the hotel.

The president of the chapter was a man named Larkin, and he saw Emmet and Jack in his office.

"The one thing we can't abide is theft of cattle," Larkin said. "From white man or Indian, either one. Small numbers of cattle are always rustled, but nothing like what happened to those Indians has happened in Texas in a decade."

"Mr. Larkin, you have a registry of every cattle brand in the country," Emmet said. "Those who stole that cattle and murdered those nine men need an outlet to sell the cattle to or they're worthless."

"I understand what you're saying, Marshal, but we can't monitor every auction house from New York to California," Larkin said.

"No, but what you can do is request reports on any new brands that recently sold at auction," Emmet said. "Even if they split up the herd into groups and sold them at different locations, the brands would still need to be recorded at the auction houses and copies sent to the association."

"I can do that," Larkin said.

"Good," Emmet said. "Now, can we see your registry for new brands registered during the last six months?"

After an hour of flipping pages in the registry, Emmet noted nine new cattle brands registered at auctions from several different states and territories.

"May I give you my opinion?" Larkin said. "Those cattle were driven south into Mexico where brands don't matter to the buyers, unlike Canada, where our association does close business with theirs."

"I can't say as I disagree with you, Mr. Larkin," Emmet said.

The ten o'clock train was ten minutes late. Emmet, Jack, and Red Moon waited at the station house for its arrival.

When it finally arrived, about forty passengers got off, one of whom was Armstrong.

He carried a satchel and his saddlebags and Winchester rifle, and immediately walked to Emmet, Jack, and Red Moon.

"I'm Captain Armstrong of the Texas Rangers," Armstrong said.

"I'm Marshal Emmet Youngblood, and this is my brother, Jack," Emmet said. "This is our scout, Red Moon."

"Let me get my horse," Armstrong said. "We can talk at the hotel."

Emmet, Jack, Armstrong, and Red Moon sat at a table on the hotel porch. Each had a cup of coffee and a slice of apple pie.

Armstrong had a detailed map, and he traced a path with his fingers.

"It's a hundred and fifty hard miles to the Red River where we buried the bodies," Armstrong said. "We'll need a mule and supplies for the trip. If we leave right after lunch, we can make twenty miles before dark."

"May I ask what tracks or signs you found?" Red Moon said.

"I wish I could say we found something, but we didn't," Armstrong said. "It was as if the entire herd vanished into thin air."

"Well, herds don't vanish into thin air, and I don't fancy a sore ass before we even get started," Jack said.

Jack stood up and walked down the steps.

"Jack, where are you going?" Emmet said.

"To hitch a ride," Jack said and walked away.

"What's he talking about?" Armstrong said.

"I don't know," Emmet said. "But I'm going to find out."

Emmet, Armstrong, and Red Moon followed Jack as he walked back to the railroad station.

At the station, Jack opened the door and approached the ticket counter.

"Are you the station manager?" Jack asked the man behind the counter.

The station manager looked at Jack's badge. "I am," he said.

Emmet, Armstrong, and Red Moon entered the station and stood behind Jack.

"When is the next train to Tulsa?" Jack asked.

"Nine tomorrow morning," the station manager said.

"Does it make any stops?"

"Runs express the entire way."

"Not tomorrow it doesn't," Jack said. "Tomorrow it will stop on the Texas side of the Red River."

"Why would it do that?" the station manager asked.

"Because I need it to," Jack said.

"That's out of the question."

"I'm United States Marshal Jack Youngblood, and my position is federally appointed," Jack said. "The railroad is also a federal enterprise, and that makes it at my disposal in times of emergency, which this is. Now I'm after men desperate enough to kill nine men and rustle a herd, so that train will stop where I say it will stop."

"You haven't the jurisdiction to make such a demand," the station manager said.

"My jurisdiction is wherever the hell I happen to be standing," Jack said. "And I'm sure Washington would not like to hear that your railroad refused to aid a US marshal in his duties, any more than I would like to tell them that."

The station manager sighed and looked at Jack.

"I'll wire the railroad and make the special request," the station manager said.

"Good," Jack said. "And I'll see you at nine tomorrow morning."

"I can hardly wait," the station manager said.

Walking back to the hotel, Emmet said, "That was good thinking, Jack. That saves us four days' ride."

"I just didn't see the need for days in the saddle when a few hours on the train will do," Jack said.

When they reached the hotel, Jack kept walking to the livery.

"Where are you going?" Emmet asked.

"Take my horse for a ride," Jack said. "I'll see you for supper."

Jack rode his tall horse about five miles west of Dallas. He stopped in a field of wildflowers and let his horse munch grass while he sat and smoked a cigarette.

"It's not that I don't love her. I do," he said to his horse. "I just don't know if I'm the right sort to settle down."

The horse looked up and turned his head to Jack.

"Women expect you to be faithful to them, you see," Jack said to his horse. "Especially when you're married to one of them."

The horse ignored Jack and continued eating grass.

"At home, I don't see a problem," Jack said. "But when I'm

away, there's girls in every saloon just waiting to tempt a man, and I'm easily tempted, as you well know."

Jack finished the cigarette, sprawled on his back, and looked up at the clear blue sky overhead.

"Hell," he said and closed his eyes.

When he opened his eyes, it was because Emmet was standing over him after nudging him on the shoulder.

"What are you doing?" Emmet said.

"Taking a nap," Jack said.

"You've been gone for hours," Emmet said.

Jack sat up and rolled a cigarette.

Emmet sat next to Jack.

"What's eating you, Jack?" Emmet asked.

Jack struck a match and lit the cigarette. "I don't think I can do it, Emmet."

"Do what?"

"Chao-xing."

"If you feel that strongly about it, then don't marry her," Emmet said.

"Oh, I can marry her," Jack said. "The problem is, I don't know if I can be faithful to her. I don't think it's in my nature."

"Jack, if you can't be faithful to Chao-xing, you shouldn't marry her," Emmet said.

"Then I'll lose her," Jack said.

"You will," Emmet said.

"You are no help," Jack said.

Emmet grinned. "Jack, if you feel the need to take up with some saloon girl when you're away from home, think about how you would feel if you found out Chao-xing was holed up with some saddle bum while you were gone."

"She would never do that," Jack said.

"But if she did."

"I suppose I'd feel sick to my stomach."

"That's how she would feel if she discovered you betrayed her," Emmet said. "Now let's get back to town. Supper's waiting on us."

"Sheriff Lang, I don't see the need for you to make this trip," Armstrong said. "Chances are we'll find nothing, and Dallas will be without a sheriff for a week or more."

"I have six highly qualified deputies," Lang said. "And I figure you'd be making the trip back alone. Two is a safer way to ride than one, wouldn't you agree?"

Armstrong looked at Emmet and Jack.

"What do you boys say?" Armstrong said. "This is your party."

They were in the hotel restaurant eating steaks. Emmet sliced off a piece and before placing it into his mouth he said, "The sheriff has a point. Two can ride safer than one on a long journey."

Armstrong looked at Jack. "What do you say?"

"I believe I'll have me a slice of apple pie for dessert," Jack said.

Chapter Seven

"You girls mind Maria while I'm gone," Amy said. "I know it's Saturday, but you still have homework to do, and I expect it done by the time I get back."

Maria, Mary, and Sarah stood on the porch and watched Amy climb into her buggy.

"What time will you be back?" Maria asked.

"Around sundown, I suppose," Amy said.

Amy tugged on the reins and the horse moved the buggy forward.

"Maria, you take it easy today," Amy said.

"I will," Maria said.

Once Amy was on the road, Maria said, "Come on, girls. Let's wash the breakfast dishes."

Jack rolled a cigarette and watched with amusement as Emmet and Red Moon tried to move the mule into the boxcar. Emmet held the reins as Red Moon pushed the mule from the rear.

"How much did you pay for that bag of glue?" Jack said.

"Wisecracks don't help, Jack," Emmet said. "This mule is carrying a hundred pounds of supplies, so why don't you give us a hand."

Jack struck a wood match and lit the cigarette, then stepped onto the loading ramp and held the match to the mule's rear end.

Singed, the mule lunged forward, up the ramp, and into the

boxcar, knocking Emmet to the floor of the car in the process.

"Happy to oblige, little brother," Jack said.

Standing barefoot and in just her underwear, Chao-xing was motionless while Amy took her measurements.

At five-foot-one inches tall, Chao-xing was nearly fourteen inches shorter than Jack.

"I'm measuring the dress long to accommodate your high-heeled shoes," Amy said. "Of course, you might need a stepladder to kiss Jack at the altar."

Amy wrote down the measurements on a pad and said, "Okay, let's look at material."

Chao-xing put on a robe, and she and Amy sat at the table where dozens of samples of materials were laid out.

After sampling the materials, Chao-xing chose a soft, off-white pattern.

"I'm an American citizen sworn in by Judge Parker himself. I'd like an American dress for my wedding," Chao-xing said.

"I'll walk over to Greenly's and pick up the material, but you'll need to try on shoes later to make sure they fit properly," Amy said. "I won't be long."

"I'll fix lunch while you're gone," Chao-xing said.

Stanly Duff watched the streets of Fort Smith through the large window of his newspaper office.

Directly across the street was Greenly's General Store, and by chance he happened to see Amy Youngblood enter the store.

He grabbed his hat, crossed the street, and stood outside Greenly's to wait. When she came out twenty minutes later, Amy was carrying a large wrapped bundle.

"Excuse me, Mrs. Youngblood," Duff said. "My name is Stanly Duff. I run the *Gazette* newspaper."

"How can I help you, Mr. Duff?" Amy asked.

"I would like to speak with you for a moment if I may."

"I'm walking six blocks from here," Amy said. "Can you walk and talk at the same time?"

"Yes, of course," Duff said.

"Most men can't," Amy said and started walking, leaving Duff behind.

Duff scurried to catch up to her.

"Mrs. Youngblood, last week I asked your sons for permission to call on you," Duff said.

"Call on me?" Amy said. "And what did they say?"

"The big one, he said something along the lines that if I came within a hundred feet of you he'd beat me to death."

Amy grinned. "That would be Jack."

"Yes, well, Mrs. Youngblood, I would like to call on you sometime if I may," Duff said.

"Then you have a death wish, Mr. Duff," Amy said.

"I can take care of myself," Duff said. "I was on the boxing team at Yale."

Amy laughed. "Mr. Duff, my son Jack would pull you apart at the seams like a rag doll. However, I give you high marks for your courage."

"So may I?" Duff asked.

"May you what?" Amy said.

"Call on you."

Amy paused in front of Chao-xing's house. She looked at Duff carefully. He was a handsome man in his way, well dressed and educated. It might do her some good to have a conversation with someone of her generation for a change.

"Come to Sunday supper tomorrow night," she said. "Take the road onto the reservation and take the first fork in the road southwest three miles. Dinner is at six. Don't be late."

Amy turned and entered the house, leaving Duff open-mouthed on the street.

Jack, Armstrong, and Lang stood beside their horses and watched as Emmet and Red Moon struggled to get the mule out of the boxcar.

A conductor approached the boxcar.

"Come on, boys, move that mule out," he said. "This unscheduled stop has put us behind schedule as it is."

Frustrated, Emmet looked at Jack. "Would you do the honors?" he said.

Jack walked up the loading ramp, past the mule, and stood beside Emmet. Jack lit a wood match, touched the mule's backside, and it all but flew down the ramp.

"All right, boys, let's get mounted," Armstrong said. "I'll ride you west to where we buried those souls."

After lunch, Amy finished measuring the material for Chao-xing's wedding dress.

"Why not stay at the house with me while Jack is away," Amy said. "That way I don't have to worry about you, and we can work on the dress."

"I have clients waiting for shirts," Chao-xing said.

"You can make them at the house just as easily and ride them into town when you're finished," Amy said. "Pack some bags. I'll wait."

Chao-xing had seven shirts ready for delivery, and she placed a sign on the door to pick them up at Greenly's store. She loaded her sewing supplies and materials into Amy's buggy, and as they rode out of town, Amy stopped at the meat market on Main Street.

Horace, the butcher, was behind the counter.

"Mrs. Youngblood," he said.

"I'd like to pick up a fresh turkey after church tomorrow," Amy said. "At least eighteen pounds."

"Special occasion?" Horace said.

"As you are the town gossip, if it was a special occasion you would be the last person I would tell," Amy said. "I'll pick up the turkey around eleven. Good day."

They stood at the site of the nine graves with hats in hand. Each grave had a cross fashioned with sticks and strips of leather.

"We fashioned crosses because some of them wore a cross and chain," Armstrong said.

"Most on the reservation have converted to Christians," Emmet said.

Red Moon studied the surrounding grass.

"Two weeks is enough time for the grass to grow back, but not the divots," he said. "I can see them headed northeast to the river."

"That's what my trackers said. We lost the trail at the water," Armstrong said.

Red Moon walked his horse to the edge of the river. Jack, Emmet, and Armstrong followed with their horses and the mule in tow.

Red Moon left his horse and waded down a bank into the shallow shore of the Red River.

"They entered here," he said. "I can tell by the damage the herd made on the shoreline when they entered the river."

Red Moon returned to his horse. "Let's ride the river for a bit and see if we can find where they came out."

"The mule might cross the river, but he's not going to walk around in it," Emmet said.

"Follow us along the banks," Red Moon said. "Jack, you and the captain work each side of the river east. I'll go west with

Sheriff Lang. Fire a shot if you find the crossing. I'll do the same."

"I'll follow Red Moon," Emmet said.

Jack took the Oklahoma side of the river while Armstrong took the Texas side. They rode in shallow water, searching for any signs of a disturbance.

After an hour, Jack crossed over to Armstrong.

"They wouldn't have come this far to hide their tracks," he said.

"I agree," Armstrong said.

"Let's turn around and catch up to Red Moon," Jack said.

Jack and Armstrong turned their horses and headed west. After about thirty minutes, they heard a shot fired.

"That's Red Moon," Jack said.

After hugging Chao-xing, Mary and Sarah helped her carry her sewing supplies into the house.

The rest of the day was spent measuring, cutting, and sewing material for Chao-xing's wedding dress.

Chao-xing borrowed a pair of high-heeled shoes from Maria so Amy could measure the wedding dress properly.

"When is the wedding?" Mary asked.

"When he returns, we will pick a day," Chao-xing said.

"Will Uncle Jack have to wear a suit and tie?" Mary asked.

"Of course," Amy said.

Sarah giggled. "Uncle Jack won't wear a tie," she said.

"A man will do a lot of things he wouldn't normally do for the woman he loves," Amy said. "And that's enough talk. We'd best see to dinner."

Jack studied the riverbank on the Oklahoma side of the Red River.

"They took the herd north," he said. "That doesn't make

sense. Mexico is the place to sell stolen beef."

"I'll scout ahead and see if I can find a trail," Red Moon said. "Might as well make camp for the night. I'll be back in two hours."

After tending to the horses and mule, Jack built a fire and Emmet starting cooking the evening meal.

Red Moon returned shortly before sunset.

"They moved the herd northwest," he said as he dismounted.

Emmet handed him a cup of hot coffee.

"I lost them in the foothills, but I can pick up the trail in the morning," Red Moon said.

"That doesn't make sense," Armstrong said.

"Unless they have a buyer already arranged," Emmet said.

"Where? Who?" Armstrong said.

Emmet dug out his maps. "Red Moon, show me where you lost the trail."

Red Moon used his finger to trace a path on the map. "We are here," he said. "And I lost them here."

Emmet studied the map.

"There is nowhere in Oklahoma or Arkansas they can sell those cattle at auction," he said. "Every lawman, including Joe Lefors, will be watching the auction houses."

Armstrong looked at the map. "Dodge City is a good place to dump a thousand head with no questions asked," he said.

"Can you cross Oklahoma unnoticed with a thousand head?" Emmet asked.

"If you know the country, you can cross ten thousand without attracting a soul," Red Moon said. "You cross the Canadian River, the Cimarron and Arkansas Rivers, and that'll take you right into Dodge. As long as you stay in open-range country, you can travel for weeks without seeing so much as a mule deer."

"How long will that trip take?" Emmet asked.

"From this spot, about three weeks at a steady pace," Red Moon said.

"They could be in Dodge already," Emmet said. "As we have no other evidence to go on, I suggest we ride straight to Dodge."

"I'm afraid we can't go with you that far out of our jurisdiction," Armstrong said.

"No, but you can ride with us to Tulsa and catch the train back to Dallas," Jack said. "Me, Emmet, and Red Moon can take the train to Dodge and save us weeks in the saddle."

Emmet nodded. "That is what we will do," he said.

"Good" Jack said. "Let's eat."

With his back against his saddle, Red Moon smoked his old pipe and looked up at the stars.

"When I was a small boy, Texas was still part of Mexico," he said. "My people roamed free on lands in Colorado, New Mexico, and Nebraska. We didn't speak English, French, or Spanish and knew very little of the white man's ways. We lived above the Canadian River, and the Mexicans had little interest that far north."

Emmet smoked his pipe, sipped coffee, and looked at Red Moon.

"I was ten or eleven before I saw my first white man," Red Moon said. "Some of my friends and I went to kill a buffalo on the Nebraska plains and wandered too far from our village settlement. We had our little bows and arrows and tomahawks so dull, they couldn't open a turtle shell, but we were determined to kill a two-thousand-pound buffalo. We were hiding in some tall grass and watching the buffalos when we saw some white men in the distance. Mountain men they were. One of them had a .50 caliber Hawken Rifle—a plains rifle they called it back then. The buffalo hunter killed a buffalo from four hundred yards away with one shot. Even though I was just a boy, I knew the country would become a white man's country. That was the year of the Alamo. That is the way of things, and we accept it or we die."

"Did you know Ten Bears?" Emmet asked.

"I did know Ten Bears," Red Moon said. "He was a great leader of my people. He wanted only peace with the government in Washington. In the end, that was his undoing."

"Maybe so, but when old Ten Bears was a young buck, he whipped a lot of white ass north of the Canadian," Jack said.

"Those were the good old days," Red Moon said.

Jack had his flask and took a sip and passed it to Red Moon.

"To the good old days of long ago," Jack said.

Red Moon took a sip from the flask and passed it to Emmet.

"Personally, I prefer a soft bed beside the fireplace than a cold floor in a tipi in my old age," Red Moon said.

Emmet took a sip from the flask and handed it to Armstrong.

"At any age," Armstrong said.

"If we catch these men, they won't allow us to take them in," Red Moon said. "We will in all likelihood have to kill them."

There was a moment of silence and then Jack said, "I'm counting on that."

Emmet looked at Jack and nodded.

"For what they did, for once I agree with you, brother," Emmet said.

Chapter Eight

Amy left the butcher shop carrying an eighteen-pound turkey wrapped in brown paper.

"Is that a turkey, Grandmother?" Mary asked.

"It is," Amy said.

"We haven't had a turkey since Christmas," Mary said. "It today a special occasion?"

Chao-xing took the turkey and placed it in the rear of the buggy.

Amy climbed into the buggy and took the reins from Maria. "We have a guest for supper tonight," she said.

"Who, Grandma?" Sarah said with excitement.

"Yes, who?" Mary asked.

Amy cracked the reins. "Let's play a game on the way home," she said.

"Let's do, Grandmother," Mary said.

"All right," Amy said. "Let's see which one of you girls can ask the most nosy questions on the way home."

"What do we win, Grandma?" Sarah asked.

"The winner gets to cook the turkey all by herself," Amy said.

Maria and Chao-xing grinned, and the ride home was very silent.

"I'm afraid I underestimated my fifty-year-old back," Lang said as he stretched after dismounting.

"You're not alone," Armstrong said. "This country is hard on a man's bones."

Emmet started a fire to cook lunch and make a pot of coffee.

"We'll give the horses two hours' rest," he said. "We should be able to make another twenty miles before dark."

"The Canadian is just ahead," Red Moon said. "After that we cross the Arkansas, and then we'll be in Tulsa in twenty-four hours."

"I didn't ask, but Red Moon, have you seen signs the herd came this way?" Emmet said.

"Many," Red Moon said. "I believe our guess is correct that they were driven to Dodge City. The more important question is, why is someone following us?"

"Who? Who is following us?" Emmet asked.

"That is for us to find out," Red Moon said. "Tonight, when we allow them to catch up with us."

"Why would we allow them to catch up with us?" Emmet asked.

Rolling a cigarette, Jack said, "So that Red Moon can kill them."

Mary and Sarah stared at Amy as she emerged from her bedroom. Wearing her blue dress and black shoes, her hair in a French braid, Amy appeared a decade younger.

"How grand you look, Grandmother," Mary said.

"Thank you, but you and your sister need to change," Amy said.

"Into what?" Mary asked.

"Those yellow dresses you wore at Maria's wedding," Amy said.

"Why, Grandma?" Mary asked.

"We have company for supper."

"Who?" Sarah asked.

"A gentleman caller," Amy said.

"What's a gentleman caller?" Sarah said.

"It's about the size of my backhand if you don't go put on those dresses right now," Amy said.

Mary and Sarah scurried to their bedroom.

Amy walked out to the porch. Maria and Chao-xing followed her.

"A gentleman caller?" Maria said.

"Just Mr. Duff, who runs the newspaper," Amy said. "I guess last week he approached Jack and Emmet and asked permission to call on me."

"And Jack didn't kill him?" Chao-xing said.

"I suspect he would have if Emmet hadn't been there," Amy said.

"We better change," Maria said.

Grinning, Maria and Chao-xing went inside to change.

"Here is a good place to make camp," Red Moon said. "I can backtrack before the moon is up and kill whoever is following us."

"Maybe you could just capture whoever it is so we can find out why he's dogging us," Emmet said.

"I have to agree with the marshal," Armstrong said. "We just can't kill a man without knowing the reason."

"Which marshal do you mean?" Jack said.

"Red Moon, don't listen to my brother," Emmet said. "We'll capture him and find out why he's trailing us. I'll go with you."

"You'll only slow me down," Red Moon said. "However, I will take him alive if you wish."

"You look old," Sarah said to Duff as they gathered at the dinner table.

"Those are not proper table manners," Amy said to Sarah.

"It's quite all right," Duff said. "The child is correct, I am old. However, not so old I can't tell a good dinner story."

"Tell us a story," Mary said.

"I will if you will allow me to carve the turkey," Duff said.

All eyes fell upon Amy, and she gently nodded.

Duff stood and began to carve the turkey. "Let's see now," he said. "I believe I was reporting for the *Kansas Star Ledger* back in seventy-one and Wild Bill Hickok was the town marshal. It was a wild place full of adventure."

Amy sighed and rolled her eyes.

"Make the fire a little bigger so he doesn't lose sight of us," Red Moon said as he sat and removed his boots.

"Any bigger, and they'll see it in Fort Smith," Jack said as he tossed a log into the fire.

Red Moon put on moccasins and stood up. About to pick up his rifle, he paused and looked west into the darkness.

"I won't have to go out after all," he said.

"Why not?" Emmet asked.

"Because he's coming in," Red Moon said. "About a hundred yards to the west. One rider."

Except for Jack, who sat against his saddle with a cup of coffee and a cigarette, all eyes turned west.

"Give him a moment," Red Moon said.

About a minute passed, and then a voice in the dark called out.

"Hello to camp," the voice said.

"We hear you," Emmet said. "What do you want?"

"A cup of that hot coffee and some grub. I been on the trail for weeks, the last two days without food."

"Come in, but know we have five rifles on you," Emmet said.

Slowly, the rider approached camp and dismounted by the fire. He looked at Jack, who hadn't moved from his saddle and grinned. "I make it four rifles," Tom Horn said.

Emmet walked to the rider and said, "Why you're young Tom Horn, the army scout. What are you doing out here, Tom?"

"Working for the Cattlemen's Association as stock detective," Horn said. "They hired me on account of all the recent rustling. I was trailing some horse thieves who stole sixteen horses off the Ladder Six Ranch out of Colorado. This is a bad bunch. They killed a foreman and his crew and a few others along the way."

Red Moon filled a plate with stew from the pot on the fire, filled a cup with coffee, and handed them to Horn.

"Thanks," Horn said. "I ran out of grub forty miles back. I was hoping to pass a town and resupply before I lost the trail."

"Tom, this is Captain Armstrong of the Texas Rangers and Sheriff Lang from Dallas," Emmet said.

"Howdy," Horn said as he spooned in some stew.

"This bunch you're after, how many men?" Armstrong asked.

"Five," Horn said.

"And if you catch them, what do you plan to do against five men who will kill for ponies?" Armstrong asked.

"Ride for the nearest army outpost," Horn said.

"Tom helped scout for us last year when we were chasing Two Hawks and his bunch," Emmet said.

"Sorry about the way that turned out," Horn said.

"How far ahead are these men?" Armstrong asked.

"A full day to the east," Horn said.

Emmet walked to Jack and sat beside him. "What do you think?"

Jack stood up and walked to Horn. Emmet stood and followed.

"We can't lose sight of the cattle thieves we're after," Jack said. "I'll ride with young Tom. You and Red Moon continue on to Tulsa. I'll catch up with you in Dodge."

Emmet sighed. "All right, but you catch the train straight to Dodge. No sidetracks, Jack."

Jack looked at Horn.

"Okay, Tom?" Jack said.

Horn nodded.

"Good," Jack said and he returned to his saddle, sat, and placed his hat over his eyes.

Amy and Duff took coffee after supper on the porch.

"Would you object to my smoking a cigar?" Duff asked.

"I would not," Amy said.

"Thank you," Duff said as he removed a cigar holder from his jacket pocket. "I'm afraid a good cigar is a weakness of mine."

"Mr. Duff, what is it you want?" Amy asked.

"I thought I made my intentions clear," Duff said. "I want to enjoy the company of a woman of my own age. I didn't set out to do so, but I have amassed quite a bit of wealth. My wife is gone fifteen years now, and money doesn't provide good company and good conversation for a man."

"That's what you're looking for? Company and conversation?" Amy said.

"Don't sell good company and conversation short, Mrs. Youngblood," Duff said.

As he struck a match and lit the cigar, Amy said, "Most men aren't satisfied with just conversation from a woman of any age, Mr. Duff."

Duff paused and looked at Amy.

"Mrs. Youngblood, I would never dare to assume to . . ." he said.

Amy stood and walked to the screen door and turned her back to it. She kicked backward with her right shoe, struck Mary in the head, and knocked the girl backward, then quietly returned to her chair.

Still holding the lit match, Duff dropped it when it burned his fingers.

"Please continue, Mr. Duff," Amy said.

"I . . . I'm at a loss for words," Duff said.

"That's a bold confession for a newspaper man," Amy said.

"I suppose it is."

"Do you like picnics, Mr. Duff?" Amy said.

"I . . . I suppose so."

"Maybe you would like to go on one next Saturday?" Amy said. "Around eleven o'clock would be fine if you're so inclined."

"I would," Duff said.

"It's getting late, and you'd best be on your way while the moon is up," Amy said.

Armstrong led Emmet away from the fire after Armstrong was sure Jack was asleep.

"You can't let your brother ride after five dangerous men like that," Armstrong said. "Even with Horn, it's five against two."

"With my brother on their tail, I'd be more worried about the five," Emmet said.

Armstrong nodded. "It was just a thought."

"Don't let it worry you none," Emmet said. "We'll make Tulsa by tomorrow night, and I'll buy you and Lang the best steak they have."

Emmet went to where Jack was asleep and spread out his bedroll. As he lay down and looked up at the stars, Emmet looked at Jack.

"You best not get yourself killed," Emmet said. "I'd hate to have to face Ma with that kind of news."

CHAPTER NINE

"You watch yourself, Jack," Emmet said after they broke camp.

"See you in Dodge, little brother," Jack said.

As Jack and Horn rode east, Emmet, Red Moon, Armstrong, and Lang rode north to Tulsa.

Jack and Horn rode until noon and then stopped to rest their horses for one hour. Jack made a fire and boiled a pot of coffee, and he and Horn ate hard biscuits with sticks of jerked beef.

"Any notion who these five men are?" Jack asked.

"A few of the men on the Ladder Six said it might be this horse thief called Moon and his bunch," Horn said. "They operate out of Utah and Idaho as far as I know, but they could have moved around to avoid the law."

"It don't add up to my way of thinking to take a ride as hard as this for less than twenty horses," Jack said. "Never mind risking a noose. Something bigger is afoot here, Tom."

"I'm suspecting that myself, Marshal," Horn said. "What do you propose?"

"We'll see when we get closer to these bushwhackers," Jack said.

While Emmet, Armstrong, and Lang made noon camp, Red Moon scouted ahead. He returned after an hour, dismounted, and took a plate of beans and bacon from Emmet.

"They traveled west to the Arkansas River," Red Moon said.

"The trail went cold from there, but I suspect they took the herd to Dodge, as we believe."

"When do you figure we'll reach Tulsa?" Emmet asked.

"Around midnight tomorrow," Red Moon said.

"There should be a train to Dallas sometime the following day," Emmet said.

"I've been studying on something," Armstrong said. "Suppose this bunch is part of a bigger outfit, what then?"

"If we discover that as a fact, I'll get the army involved in hunting them down," Emmet said.

"Mind a personal question?" Armstrong said. "I sense you have higher aspirations than that badge on your chest."

"It's no secret," Emmet said. "I plan to take the bar exam this fall, practice law in Judge Parker's court, and also represent the Natives on the reservation under Parker's jurisdiction."

"In that case, I better make sure you don't get killed," Red Moon said.

At sundown, Jack and Horn dismounted and made camp.

"Tend the horses while I make us some supper," Jack said.

Jack built a fire and put on a pan of beans and bacon and coffee and cut thick slices of cornbread.

"How far you figure they're ahead of us?" Jack asked as he filled a plate for Horn.

"Those were fresh tracks we were following," Horn said. "Four hours at most."

"Finish your supper, Tom," Jack said. "As soon as the moon is up, we're going for a ride."

"Where?"

"Into the Ozarks," Jack said.

Jack led Horn through a narrow notch in the Ozark Mountains

that went on for several miles and ended at the base of a box canyon.

They dismounted. Jack stood very still for several seconds and smelled the air.

"Smell that, Tom?" he said.

Horn nodded. "Campfire."

"Let's go," Jack said.

"Where?"

"Up."

After securing the horses, Jack and Horn climbed a canyon wall that stood about a thousand feet high.

Once on the plateau, they walked to a ledge and looked down.

Forty or more horses were penned inside a corral made of posts and rope. In a separate corral made in the same fashion, Jack counted seventeen horses. Fifteen men slept beside a large campfire, while two men with rifles stood watch.

"It's a bigger operation, as I feared," Jack said. "Let's go."

Jack lifted the coffee pot from the still smoldering ashes of the fire, filled two cups, and handed one to Horn.

"Seventeen men is too much for just the two of us, Marshal," Horn said. "We'll need to go for help. The army is . . ."

"Three days' ride from here," Jack said. "I expect these boys are waiting on more ponies before they ride the bunch to Mexico where they can get three hundred dollars American a head for a good horse. We'll get help, but not from the army."

"From who?" Horn asked.

"Don't trouble yourself over that, young Tom," Jack said. "We best get some sleep. Those ponies aren't going anywhere tonight."

"What's that book you got your nose buried in, Marshal?" Armstrong asked.

By the fire, Emmet smoked his pipe as he studied his law book.

"That's his bar exam study book," Red Moon said.

"That's right," Armstrong said. "You'll be a lawyer soon, won't you, Marshal?"

"That remains to be seen, Captain," Emmet said. "Most fail the test three times before finally passing. With my limited time to study, I expect it might take me a while."

"That's the thing about lawmen," Armstrong said. "Most of us know so little about the actual laws we're paid to enforce."

"Times are changing, for sure," Lang said. "It won't be long before we'll have to do more than raise our right hand and say 'I do' to wear a badge."

Emmet closed the book and set it aside. "We have a forty-mile ride tomorrow," he said. "Best get some sleep."

"Where are we going?" Horn asked as he and Jack rode deep into the Ozark Mountains.

"To see a friend and ask for help," Jack said.

CHAPTER TEN

Jack dismounted at a narrow pass in the mountains and looked up at the canyon walls.

"Dismount, young Tom," he said. "We're afoot the rest of the way."

Jack led the way through the pass that was so narrow they had to walk single file.

"This doesn't suit me, Marshal," Horn said. "I'd like to know who we're going to see at the end of this journey."

"Best learn the fine art of patience, young Tom," Jack said. "The impatient man oftentimes ends up on the wrong end of a rope."

"I will try to remember that," Horn said.

They reached the end of the pass and Horn said, "Now what?"

"Now we ride a ways and hope we don't get ourselves shot," Jack said.

"By the people you're asking for help?" Horn said.

"Life sometimes is a mystery," Jack said.

They rode several miles until Jack dismounted at another narrow pass.

"We walk again. On the other side, whatever you do, keep your guns holstered," Jack said.

The narrow pass was about a mile long and opened up to a wide valley between two mountains.

Horn went to mount his horse and Jack said, "Stay afoot,

Tom. We're walking."

"To where?"

"Those rocky hills you see there in the distance."

"That's a quarter mile," Horn said.

"You're a good judge of distance," Jack said. "How are you at common sense?"

"I don't follow," Horn said.

"Do what I tell you when I tell you, and you might not get shot," Jack said.

"*Might* not?"

They walked the quarter mile, and Jack stopped them at the base of a steep hill. He looked up.

"Maybelle Shirley, it's Marshal Jack Youngblood come a calling," Jack shouted.

"Who is . . . ?"

"Belle Starr, and don't say another word unless I tell you to," Jack said.

"*The* Belle Starr?" Horn said.

From the top of the hill, hidden from view, Belle Starr shouted, "Who's that with you, Marshal Jack?"

"Army scout and stock detective Tom Horn," Jack shouted.

"Why should I not shoot you and your stock detective dead where you stand, Jack Youngblood?" Belle shouted.

"Hear what I have to say first, Belle," Jack said. "I didn't come empty-handed, you know."

"What have you for whiskey?" Belle asked.

"An unopened bottle of Kentucky whiskey," Jack said.

"Tie your mounts and bring up the whiskey," Belle said.

Jack and Horn tied their horses to nearby trees and climbed the steeply slanted hill to the top where Belle Starr and fourteen men waited. Each man held a rifle in his arms. Belle Starr wore a two-gun holster.

Jack handed Belle the bottle of whiskey.

"Thank you kindly," she said and looked at Horn. "What about your runt? Is he empty-handed?"

"Who are you calling runt?" Horn said.

Holding the heavy whiskey bottle by the neck, Belle swung it like a club and struck Horn in the jaw. Horn tumbled backward and rolled down the hill.

"He's young, Belle, but he's a good man," Jack said.

"Come up to the porch, Marshal Jack," Belle said. "We'll have a drink and discuss why I shouldn't let my men shoot you."

Not far from the edge of the hill stood a large cabin, barn, corral, outhouse, and bunkhouse. Several patches of land had vegetables growing.

Belle and Jack walked to the porch with her men following close behind. The men were a mixture of Mexican Apache, white, mixed Sioux, and Comanche.

After opening the bottle, Belle filled two shot glasses with whiskey and gave one to Jack.

"Sit," Belle said. "We'll talk some before I kill you."

Jack took a sip of whiskey, set the glass on the porch, and started to roll a cigarette.

"Do one for me, Jack," Belle said.

Jack gave her the cigarette and rolled another. He lit both off a wood match.

"I need your help, Belle," Jack said. "Young Tom was tracking some horse thieves and murderers when I come across him. They killed innocent people and are holed up with forty ponies. There's too many of them for just Tom and me, but if you lend your men we can take the lot of them."

"Why should I help you?" Belle said.

"I'll let you keep half the ponies," Jack said.

"I could just keep them all," Belle said.

"Young Tom needs something to bring back for his trouble," Jack said.

"Too thin, Marshal Jack," Belle said. "You'll have to do better than that to suit my taste."

"Where's your husband, Belle?" Jack asked.

"He's in Judge Parker's jail waiting trial on a phony horse-theft charge, as you well know," Belle said.

"Have you visited him?" Jack asked.

"You know damn well Parker has a warrant on me," Belle said. "I show my face in Fort Smith, and he'll hang me for sure."

"In exchange for your help, I'll have Judge Parker issue you and Sam full pardons," Jack said.

"You'll put that in writing," Belle said.

"I have some official writing paper in my saddlebags," Jack said.

"You put in writing that both Sam and me get full pardons and I keep twenty ponies, and you got my help," Belle said.

"Deal," Jack said.

Belle spat in her right hand.

"Spit," she said.

Jack spat in his right hand, and they shook.

"Let's have us another drink while you give me details," Belle said.

"Maybe I should see to young Tom first," Jack said.

Belle, Jack, and Horn sat at the table in the kitchen of the cabin. On a piece of paper, Jack drew a map with a pencil.

"It's a box canyon, Belle," Jack said. "A narrow pass from the east, another from the west, with cliffs on both sides. We go in with five men from each pass and six on the cliffs with rifles; we can take them while they sleep without too much of a problem.

Tomorrow will be a good moon, and they will have a fire going."

"What do you say, young Horn?" Belle asked.

"I think my jaw is broken is what I think," Horn said.

"It's just a bruise," Belle said. "My men wanted to kill you just out of boredom, so be grateful I didn't let them. Go stir the cook pot."

Horn stood and crossed the room to the large fireplace, where a black pot of stew hung from a tripod. He used a long wood spoon to stir the stew.

Belle filled three glasses with whiskey as Horn returned to the table.

"Drink that, runt," Belle said. "It will numb your jaw."

Horn drank half the glass of whiskey in two long swallows.

"How long a ride is it to this canyon?" Belle asked.

"Maybe four hours. No more than that," Jack said.

"We'll move out at sunset tomorrow," Belle said. "Marshal Jack, you and the runt can sleep in the cabin tonight."

Alone on the porch, Jack sipped whiskey from a glass and smoked a cigarette. There was a nice moon, and his night vision was good. Horn was asleep in the spare bedroom.

The screen door opened with a creak and Belle emerged wearing a robe. She took the chair beside Jack.

"Roll me a cigarette," she said.

Jack rolled a cigarette, lit it, and handed it to Belle. "What do you hear of Blue Duck these days, Belle?" he said.

"Blue Duck?" Belle said. "Ain't seen him since before the Comanche attack on Fort Smith last year. Why?"

"Just asking."

"I come to ask you to share my bed tonight," Belle said as she inhaled on the cigarette.

Jack looked at her. Belle, despite her rough exterior, was a beautiful woman with many exciting attributes.

"What would Sam say if he heard you make such an offer?" Jack said.

"Sam's been in jail for months and you've given me the itch and it needs to be scratched," Belle said.

"Belle . . . I have a woman waiting on me," Jack said. "We're to be married when I get home."

"She's at home and Sam's in jail and I'm here, and I can be very womanly when I'm so inclined, Marshal Jack," Belle said.

"Dammit, Belle, don't be tempting a man so," Jack said.

Belle stood up and walked to the screen door. "I'll go wake the runt," she said. "Maybe his jaw ain't aching him so badly he can't please a woman."

"That's a good idea," Jack said.

"That girl you got waiting at home, she must be some woman," Belle said.

A mile from Tulsa, Emmet, Armstrong, Red Moon, and Lang dismounted and walked their horses into town.

"Our horses will need two days' rest and grain before we can ride them any distances again," Red Moon said. "We pushed them hard."

"And then some," Emmet said. "But we won't need to ride them for a while at least. Red Moon and I will wait in Tulsa for Jack and the captain, and Sheriff Lang can head back to Dallas tomorrow."

"I hope there's a place we can get a good steak this time of night," Armstrong said. "I've had enough beans to last me forever."

"I care more about a soft bed at the moment than food," Lang said.

"Let's face it, Sheriff, we're becoming old men," Armstrong said.

"I can hear piano music from a saloon," Red Moon said.

"And smell a steak cooking," Armstrong said.

As they neared the town limits, Tulsa was alive with activity. Dozens of cowboys off the trail were drunk in public, and saloon girls tempted them from the balconies above the saloons.

Deputies patrolled the streets, keeping the peace.

"They have a saloon here with dancing girls that put on a show every hour and electric lights that come on above the bar to announce their entrance," Emmet said.

"I thought you was a happily married man, Marshal," Red Moon said.

"I am," Emmet said. "My brother isn't."

Chapter Eleven

Emmet, Red Moon, Armstrong, and Lang met for breakfast in the restaurant located in the lobby of the Hotel Tulsa.

"There's a train back to Dallas at ten," Armstrong said. "I reckon me and Sheriff Lang will be on it."

"Maybe we can ride together again someday," Lang said.

"I checked the train schedule," Red Moon said. "We can catch the one o'clock to Dodge this afternoon."

Emmet stood up from the table. He shook hands with Armstrong and Lang. "It was a pleasure riding with you boys," he said. "Red Moon, I'm going to check in with the sheriff and see if there is any word from my brother."

Jack was killing time with some of Belle's men by tossing knives into a circle for a quarter a point when Horn emerged from the cabin with a cup of coffee.

Horn arched his back and walked a bit stiff-legged down the porch steps to Jack.

"What's the matter, young Tom? Sleep poorly?" Jack said.

"Damn," Horn said.

Belle came out to the porch holding a cup of coffee and said, "Marshal Jack, come up here and talk with me a spell."

Jack handed Horn his knife. "I'm up six bits, don't lose it," he said.

"Roll me a smoke," Belle said when Jack reached the porch.

Jack rolled two cigarettes, lit them both, and gave one to Belle.

"Blue Duck is down on the Llano last I heard," Belle said. "South of the Canadian, but I also heard he's moving around a lot these days."

Jack nodded.

"Now tell what your interest in Blue Duck is?" Belle asked.

"Before I got sidetracked with young Horn there, me and my brother were tracking some men who murdered nine off the reservation that were droving a thousand head of cattle from the Chisum Ranch to Fort Smith," Jack said. "It's something Blue Duck is capable of doing."

"Blue Duck will hang one day for many things, but that isn't one of them," Belle said. "That old bastard knows better than to steal a herd he can't unload outside of Mexico, and he has too many who would shoot him on sight to risk a trip south of the Rio."

"I expect you're right, Belle," Jack said.

"So what have you planned for tonight?" Belle said.

Emmet checked the telegraph office, but there was no word from Jack. He sent a telegraph to Judge Parker with his plans and then sent a second to Maria and Amy.

From the telegraph office, Emmet went to see the sheriff. He was in his office and his name was Peal.

"Weren't you in town six months ago with your brother?" Peal asked.

"You've a good memory, Sheriff," Emmet said. "You heard about the cattle rustled and nine dead from the reservation at Fort Smith?"

"Who hasn't in these parts?" Peal said.

"My tracker has them moving northwest," Emmet said. "Maybe to Dodge City where it would be easy to sell a thousand head without too many questions."

"Dodge would be the place for that," Peal said.

"Do me a favor," Emmet said. "I sent a few telegrams. If I get replies when I'm in route, would you forward them to Dodge?"

"Sure thing, Marshal," Peal said.

As Belle saddled her horse, she turned to her men. "I expect to find Tom Horn alive when me and the marshal return from our scouting."

Jack led Belle to the hidden pass where they hobbled their horses and then climbed the cliff that overlooked the outlaw camp.

"I count seventeen men and forty-three horses," Belle said. "And no lookouts posted."

"They're too overconfident in their hideout to post watch," Jack said.

"How do you want to do this?" Belle asked.

"Five of your men take the west pass in," Jack said. "I'll take the east. The . . ."

"Alone?"

"I work best alone, Belle," Jack said. "The rest of your men and Horn take the cliffs. When I go in and take out the lookouts, your men come in and you start shooting from the cliffs. Whoever is left alive, Horn takes to Fort Smith along with twenty ponies. You keep the rest as payment."

"Don't forget the letter to Judge Parker."

"I'll write it as soon as we get back to your cabin."

"Obliged, Jack," Belle said as she reached out and gently took hold of Jack's rear end and gave it a squeeze.

"What are you doing, Belle?" Jack asked.

"Feeling me a man," Belle said. "What's it look like?"

"Let go, Belle. You had your pleasures last night with Horn," Jack said.

"He was too tuckered out for a romp this morning," Belle said.

"I done told you, Belle. I got a woman waiting on me back in Fort Smith," Jack said. "She's wearing my ring. It wouldn't be right."

"Let's get back then," Belle said. "Maybe Horn has regained enough strength for a poke by now."

"The train is late," Red Moon said.

Emmet was smoking his pipe while seated on a bench with his law book in his lap. He glanced at the station clock mounted on the wall of the ticket office. The train was fifteen minutes overdue.

Their horses were tied to the hitching post on the platform. Emmet looked at them. "They seem well rested," he said.

Red Moon sat next to Emmet.

"It will take about eight hours to reach Dodge. Maybe there will be word from the marshal when we get there," he said.

"If you're worried about my brother, don't," Emmet said. "Jack plays dumb as an ox, but he's not and he's as tough as iron."

"I see the train coming," Red Moon said.

Emmet stood up.

"Let's get the horses," he said.

On the porch of Belle's cabin, Jack stripped his Colt revolver, cleaned and oiled it, and then loaded it with fresh ammunition. He always kept an extra revolver in his saddlebags, and he cleaned and loaded it as well.

The sun was low in the sky by the time his guns were cleaned and loaded, and Jack smoked a cigarette, drank a cup of coffee, and watched the sky glow various colors.

Chao-xing weighed heavily on his mind. It was odd how he felt a twinge of guilt even though he rejected Belle's advances. Belle was a desirable woman, for sure, and Chao-xing would have never known he'd strayed, but that thing Emmet would call his conscience nagged at him in the back of his mind and kept him on the right path.

Maybe he really was ready for marriage and commitment as a husband?

The screen door suddenly burst open and Belle emerged with loud fanfare. Dressed in black pants with a matching shirt and boots, she wore her two-gun rig around her waist.

"I best wake my men from their napping, Jack," she said. "We got some riding to do tonight."

Belle stepped off the porch and walked to the bunkhouse.

The screen door opened again and Horn limped out.

"Hell, I can barely walk," he said.

"That will teach you to give into temptation, Tom," Jack said.

"Temptation, hell," Horn said. "I call it assault."

"I don't see him, Belle," Horn whispered as he lay on his belly and looked down upon the outlaw camp.

"You won't see Jack until he wants to be seen," Belle whispered. "Now be quiet before you spook them lookouts."

Horn watched the outlaw camp below. Fifteen were in their bedrolls around a campfire. Two sat awake with rifles, on lookout. Between the moon and fire, the camp was well illuminated.

The night air was hot, and Horn felt his shirt stick to his back. He strained his night vision as he looked at the pass from the east where he knew Jack was waiting, but couldn't see anything.

Five of Belle's men waited in the shadows of the pass from

the west. Nine of her men were prone on the cliff alongside Belle. Each had a Winchester rifle.

The two lookouts seemed bored and after a time their heads grew heavy and slumped as they dozed.

"Ready yourself, boys," Belle whispered.

Horn had seen Jack in action once before when he watched him ride down on some outlaws and shoot them from atop his horse, but this time was completely different. He would be walking into a camp holding seventeen armed men, and all of them killers.

Suddenly, Jack emerged from the shadows of the east pass and walked directly into the outlaw camp. His Colt was held loosely by his right side. The spare Colt was tucked into his pants. The two lookouts heard his approach and glanced up, but the campfire dimmed their night vision.

"Who's there?" one of the lookouts shouted.

Jack cocked his Colt and shot the man dead. Then, before the second lookout could cock his rifle, Jack shot him dead, too.

"Marshal Jack has balls of iron," Belle said as she stood up. "That's it, boys. Let them have it until they surrender or they're all dead."

Belle's five men emerged from the west pass with their revolvers and rifles blazing. Jack shot and killed four more of the outlaws as Belle, Horn, and her men opened fire.

The battle was over in seconds. Nine of the outlaws lay dead before the others tossed their weapons and surrendered.

"Marshal, wake up," Red Moon said. "We're in Dodge."

Slumped in his seat, Emmet opened his eyes.

"What time is it?" he asked.

"One-thirty in the morning," Red Moon said. "We were delayed a bit because of a brush fire on the track."

"I wired ahead and reserved two rooms at the Hotel Dodge,"

Emmet said. "We'll check in with the local marshal and telegraph office in the morning."

After retrieving their horses from the boxcar, Emmet and Red Moon walked past a half dozen cattle auction houses and pens filled with cattle. Guards armed with shotguns were posted along the pens.

As they walked their horses past a pen, a guard said, "Stop and state your business."

"Marshal Emmet Youngblood and army scout Sergeant Major Red Moon," Emmet said.

A lantern rested on a fence post. The guard lifted it and said, "Come into the light so I can see you."

Emmet and Red Moon walked closer to the lantern. The guard looked at Emmet's badge and Red Moon's uniform.

"Sorry, Marshal, we're mite testy right now," he said.

"Why?" Emmet asked.

"A small herd of six hundred from the Dillon Ranch was rustled a few nights ago," the guard said. "They ambushed the six drovers during the night and made off with the entire herd."

"Killed the men?" Emmet asked.

"One is still alive," the guard said. "He's over at the doc's office."

"The sheriff's office?" Emmet asked.

"Three doors down from the Long Branch, but he's out with a posse," the guard said. "The town marshal is in though. His office is across the street from the sheriff."

"Thanks," Emmet said.

"Sure, and sorry about the mix-up."

Emmet and Red Moon entered town and located the marshal's office. The saloons were closed for the night and the streets were dark and quiet, but a lantern glowed inside the marshal's office.

Two men inside the office were at a desk drinking coffee.

One standing, the other seated.

Emmet opened the door and entered the office, followed by Red Moon. Immediately the man standing drew a massive Smith & Wesson .44 revolver and aimed it at Emmet.

"Easy with that cannon," Emmet said. "I'm Marshal Emmet Youngblood. This is army scout Red Moon."

The man holstered the large revolver.

The man at the desk said, "I'm Town Marshal Bat Masterson. My friend with the jumpy gun is Wyatt Earp."

Red Moon glanced at Emmet.

"Youngblood?" Masterson said. "You wouldn't happen to be relations to Jack Youngblood?"

"He's my brother," Emmet said.

"What brings you to Dodge?" Earp said.

Jack sipped coffee as the sun rose over Belle's cabin. On the ground, the remaining eight outlaws were roped in a circle as Belle's men stood watch over them.

Belle and Horn emerged from the cabin with cups of coffee and took chairs next to Jack.

"Any of your men unwanted by the law?" Jack asked Belle.

"Five," Belle said. "The rest would hang if brought to town."

Jack removed a folded paper from his shirt pocket and gave it to Horn.

"You take Belle's five men and ride these *hombres* to Fort Smith along with twenty ponies," Jack said. "You give this document to Judge Parker. He'll honor it in my name."

"I will," Horn said.

"I'm obliged to you, Marshal Jack," Belle said.

"Stay clear of the wrong side, Belle," Jack said. "If I hear you crossed over, I'll be back for you."

"Don't you worry none," Belle said. "As soon as Sam gets back, we'll start a new righteous path."

"Glad to hear it," Jack said, then he stood and walked down to his horse.

CHAPTER TWELVE

"How did you sleep?" Emmet asked Red Moon as they ate breakfast in the restaurant inside the Hotel Dodge.

"Like a baby," Red Moon said.

Bat Masterson and Wyatt Earp entered the restaurant and joined them at the table.

A waitress came to the table.

"We'll have what they're having," Masterson said.

"What time does the telegraph office open?" Emmet asked.

"Ten," Masterson said.

"We'll have time to check the auction houses before the telegraph office opens," Emmet said. "If it's the same bunch, I doubt they brought a stolen herd to town, but I need to check anyway. Then I want to talk to that cowboy who survived and see if he knows anything."

"The sheriff should be back sometime today with his posse, but I doubt he has anything to report," Earp said.

"Mind a question, Mr. Earp?" Red Moon said. "I heard you went west to California with your brother."

"I did," Earp said. "Bat and I are friends from the old days of the Dodge City War. He fancies himself a journalist these days and invited me to Dodge to write my biography. Next thing I know, he roped me into being his temporary deputy while he writes the story."

"Journalist?" Red Moon said.

"My lawman days will soon be behind me," Masterson said.

"I plan to become a newspaper man and write for the New York City newspapers."

"In the meantime, I'm roped into helping Bat control this Godforsaken town when hundreds of cowboys off the trail get liquored up on a Saturday night," Earp said.

"And you love every minute of it," Masterson said to Earp.

A man entered the restaurant and approached the table.

"Excuse me, but the sheriff is back early," the man said.

"We lost them in the Arkansas River headed west," Sheriff Brady said from behind his desk. "Even the scouts from the Fort Dodge Reservation couldn't pick up the trail, and we followed well out of my jurisdiction."

Brady paused to sip coffee from a cup.

"Six hundred head vanished like a ghost," he said.

"It's got to be the same bunch that ambushed the nine off the Fort Smith Reservation and made off with a thousand head a few weeks ago," Emmet said.

"The Arkansas goes deep into Colorado," Red Moon said. "It's shallow this time of year, but in Colorado anybody in it would drown."

"My guess is they used the river to lose us and then headed north," Brady said. "But why north? A stolen herd is much easier to sell in Mexico."

"Good question," Emmet said. "I'll check in with you later, Sheriff."

A tour of the auction houses proved fruitless. All cattle purchased during the past month came from registered brands and had been shipped out to the slaughterhouses in Kansas City and Chicago.

Emmet checked in with the telegraph office, but there was no word from Jack as yet. He sent a telegram to Maria and Amy and one to Judge Parker.

Masterson and Earp went with Emmet to visit the surviving drover from the ambush. He was just eighteen years old and, although he would live, he had a concussion.

"You have ten minutes, and don't go bouncing him around," the doctor said.

The kid was awake and sitting up in bed. He was boyishly handsome with hair the color of straw. A white bandage was wrapped around his forehead.

"Emmet, this here is Harry Longabaugh," Masterson said. "Harry, this is Marshal Youngblood."

Longabaugh nodded. "I expect you want to hear about what happened?" he said.

"Where are you from?" Emmet said. "You have an accent I can't place."

"A little town in Pennsylvania," Longabaugh said. "I came west with my family three years ago. I been working on the Dillon Ranch the last year or so."

"So tell me what happened," Emmet said.

"It's like I told the sheriff," Longabaugh said. "It's just a sixty-mile drive from Mr. Dillon's ranch to Dodge, and he had six hundred head he wanted to sell to the army. Me and five of the boys headed out and figured on a three-day drive. I guess we was twenty miles outside of Dodge when they hit us during the night."

"How many?" Emmet asked.

"Can't say for sure," Longabaugh said. "It was dark, and I was asleep. We had one man at a time on watch. A shot woke me up. When I got out of my bedroll, all I had was a few seconds before somebody shot me. The bullet creased my skull, and the doc said I was lucky to be alive. They must have figured I was

102

dead. Hell, I don't even own a gun. There was maybe eight or nine of them, and they all wore spook hats."

"Spook hats?" Emmet said.

"White sacks over their faces with holes cut out for their eyes," Longabaugh said.

"Spook hats," Emmet said.

"Yes, sir, spook hats," Longabaugh said.

"How did you get to Dodge?" Emmet asked.

"I don't know," Longabaugh said.

"Mr. Dillon sent a few of his hands to check on things when the drovers didn't show in Dodge," Masterson said. "They found young Harry here wandering around in a daze and brought him to town."

"Thanks for the information, son," Emmet said. "Get better soon."

"Thanks, Marshal," Longabaugh said.

Masterson and Earp caught up with Emmet and Red Moon at the livery where Emmet and Red Moon were saddling their horses.

"Headed out?" Masterson asked.

"I'm waiting on my brother," Emmet said. "While I wait, I'd like to check that site where the cattle were stolen. I should be back sometime tomorrow afternoon. If any telegrams arrive for me, I'd appreciate it if you'd hold them."

Judge Parker heard a commotion outside his office window, and he stood up from his desk to see what caused it.

The last thing he expected to see was nine men roped together in a loop on their horses with one man in the lead, five in the rear, and a string of horses all tethered together.

"What in blazes?" Parker said.

He went down to the courthouse steps and waited. The streets were lined with people, buzzing with excitement.

The lead rider rode to the steps and looked at Parker.

"Are you Judge Parker?" he said.

"I am. Who are you?"

"Horn. Tom Horn. I have a letter from Marshal Jack Youngblood."

Parker read Jack's letter of request at his desk. Horn sat in a chair opposite him and politely waited for Parker to finish.

Finally, Parker set the document aside.

"Jack Armstrong is the best marshal I've ever run across, but sometimes he has the sense of a goat," Parker said. "He could have been killed in a shootout like that."

"I don't think that ever occurred to him, Judge," Horn said.

Parker sighed. "Probably not, the idiot," he said. "He headed to Dodge to meet up with his brother?"

"That's what he said," Horn said.

"I'll arrange to have your prisoners transported to Denver for trial," Parker said.

"Thank you, Judge," Horn said.

"Do me a favor," Parker said. "On your way out, would you ask a deputy to bring Sam Starr to my office?"

Sam Starr, escorted by two deputies, stood before Judge Parker.

"Against my better judgment, Sam Starr, I am issuing you and Belle Starr a full pardon effective immediately. Do you understand the word *pardon*?"

Sam Starr grinned and nodded. "I do," he said.

"Get cleaned up, get your horse, and ride out of Fort Smith," Parker said. "And remember, this pardon doesn't protect you against punishment for future crimes."

When Jack opened his eyes, he was alone in a bed at Madam

Orr's brothel in Tulsa. His head pounded as the hangover kicked in immediately upon waking up.

The room was frilly, with red lace drapes and a red-domed lantern on the table.

Jack moaned as he sat up.

The door opened and Madam Orr entered, carrying a tray that held a coffee pot, cup, pitcher of water, and glass.

"Good morning," Madam Orr said.

"No need to shout," Jack said.

Madam Orr set the tray on the table and opened the drapes and bright sunlight entered the room.

Jack shielded his eyes.

"Jesus," he said as he stood up.

Madam Orr opened a small envelope and poured a white powder into a glass and filled it with water. She stirred it with a spoon and handed the glass to Jack.

"What's in it?" Jack asked.

"Crushed willow root for your headache," Madam Orr said. "Drink it all down and then a second glass of plain water."

Jack gulped the water, then filled the glass and sat on the bed.

"After you finish that second glass of water, have a cup of coffee," Madam Orr said. "I'll have a bath ready for you in a few minutes."

"I could use a shave," Jack said.

"You could use a wet bar of soap," Madam Orr said. "Have you any clean clothes?"

"Some."

"I'll launder your dirty."

Jack sat in a hot tub of scented water and smoked a cigarette as Madam Orr sat in a chair and carefully shaved him.

"What's gnawing at you, Marshal?" Madam Orr asked as she

scraped his chin.

"Nothing. Why?"

"You show up at ten o'clock last night," Madam Orr said. "You don't want a woman; just a bottle, and you lock yourself in a room and get drunk alone. I'd say something's eating at you pretty good."

Jack tossed the cigarette into the water and looked at Madam Orr.

"I . . . I'm supposed to get married when I get home," he said.

"And you don't want to?"

"No, I do," Jack said. "I love her."

"And the problem is?"

"Women expect their husbands to be faithful to them," Jack said.

Madam Orr grinned. "And you don't think you can be?"

"Hell, I don't know," Jack said. "Temptation is a mighty strong force when it tugs at a man, especially if he's away from home a lot like I am."

"You seemed to resist last night," Madam Orr said. "Little Jewel was asking for you, and you practically slammed the door in her face."

The door to the bathroom opened and Jewel walked in with a basket of Jack's clean clothes. She set the basket on a counter and smiled at Jack.

"Anything else I can do for you, Marshal?" Jewel said, faking wide-eyed breathlessness.

"Yes, you can get the hell out of here," Madam Orr snapped.

Jewel winked at Jack as she left the bathroom.

Jack started to stand up. Madam Orr said, "Sit your dumb ass down, you big oaf. You go chasing after Jewel and you'll regret it the rest of your days."

Jack sat, sighed, and rested his head against the rim of the tub.

"Love is a difficult thing to find, Jack," Madam Orr said. "If you're one of the lucky ones to find it, don't never do anything to crush it. You treat it like it was all the gold in the world, you hear me? Because if you don't, it will slip right through your fingers."

Jack sighed again.

"And if I catch you in my place again, I'll shoot you myself," Madam Orr said.

Jack sent a telegram to Emmet in Dodge and then walked his horse to the railroad station to wait for the train.

CHAPTER THIRTEEN

The train arrived in Dodge City at four forty-five in the afternoon. Still a bit hungover and with a mild headache, Jack slept most of the nine hours it took to make the trip from Tulsa.

He walked his horse into town to the hotel where Emmet had reserved rooms. The streets were full of cowboys off the drive looking to spend their wages in the saloons and brothels that lined the downtown streets. They were unarmed, though. Dodge, like many other cattle towns, had an ordinance forbidding firearms to be worn on the streets from Friday to Monday to reduce the number of drunken shootings.

The Hotel Dodge had its own livery and, after checking his horse in, Jack took his saddlebags and rifle into the lobby to register.

"Are you Marshal Jack Youngblood?" the desk clerk asked.

"I am," Jack said. "My brother registered here and reserved me a room."

"Yes, sir, but there's a telegram waiting for you at the marshal's office," the clerk said.

"Let me settle my things and I'll walk over," Jack said.

Emmet rested his horse along the banks of the Arkansas River while Red Moon scouted ahead. It was late in the day, and he built a fire and put on some coffee. When it boiled, he filled a cup and smoked his pipe.

When Red Moon returned, he dismounted near the fire,

grabbed a cup, and filled it with coffee.

"I picked up their trail a few miles from here," he said. "It wasn't difficult. They left the drags behind."

"Any notion where they're headed?" Emmet asked.

Red Moon turned and pointed to the large mountain in the distance. "Mount Sunflower, the tallest mountain in Kansas."

"I thought Kansas was flat," Emmet said.

"Everybody thinks that who hasn't been to Kansas," Red Moon said.

"The other side of that mountain is Colorado," Emmet said. "At least another day's ride from here. We'll have to turn back to Dodge for my brother."

"I could go on without you and wait on the other side in Colorado," Red Moon said.

"Neither Jack nor I is that good of a tracker," Emmet said. "We best stick together."

"We'll lose time," Red Moon said.

"Better we lose time than each other," Emmet said.

"In that case, what's for supper?"

Jack was drinking coffee with Bat Masterson and Wyatt Earp at a corner table in the Long Branch Saloon. The tables were full of hard-drinking cowboys and card players, and a piano player plunked out tunes on an upright piano in the corner.

"You know, it occurs to me that I never did thank you for helping with the Dodge City War a few years back," Masterson said to Jack.

"I was passing through anyway," Jack said. "Wyatt, how is Jose?"

"Fine, just fine," Earp said. "She's in San Francisco with her family until I'm done here. We're thinking of trying our hand at a gold mine in Alaska."

"Alaska?" Jack said.

"Jose's the kind of woman craves excitement," Earp said.

"How long you been together now?" Jack asked.

"Four years," Earp said.

"And you're happy?" Jack asked.

"Only time I been happy in my life is after I met Jose," Earp said.

As he rolled a cigarette, Jack looked at Masterson. "What about you, Bat?"

"On the subject of marriage, I'm afraid Wyatt and I share different points of view," Masterson said. "I find there are too many women in the world who need pleasing to lock horns with just one."

"Even if you found you loved one of them?" Jack said.

"Especially then," Masterson said.

"Don't listen to him, Jack," Earp said. "Bat's a heathen."

Looking at Jack, Masterson said, "If I didn't know better, I'd say old Jack here might be thinking of settling down."

Before Jack could respond, a commotion broke out across the room.

A dusty cowboy jumped to his feet and shouted, "I ain't giving no damn money to no card cheat."

The man opposite him, a grizzled veteran dressed in a black shirt and pants, jumped to his feet, too. "No man alive accuses me of cheating," he said.

Neither man had a firearm, but the cowboy had a large Bowie knife; he pulled it and waved it at the other man.

"I do believe that cowboy is fixing to stab Texas Jack Vermillion," Masterson said.

Vermillion picked up a shot glass of whiskey and threw it in the cowboy's face and hair. As the cowboy blinked, Vermillion pulled a wood match from his shirt pocket, lit it, and held it at arm's length.

"Move that blade and you'll find out what the fires of hell

feels like," Vermillion said.

Earp stood up and walked across the bar to Vermillion.

"How you doing, Texas Jack?" Earp said.

"Fixing to roast me a cowboy," Vermillion said.

Earp looked at the cowboy. "Put that knife away, youngster, and I do mean now."

The cowboy slowly replaced the knife into its sheath.

"Come over to my table," Earp said to Vermillion. "Somebody I want you to meet."

Vermillion gathered up his money and followed Earp to the table.

"Bat, you remember Texas Jack?" Earp said.

"I do. Sit and have a drink," Masterson said. "I'm sick of this lousy coffee anyway."

Vermillion took a chair and started to roll a cigarette.

"Texas Jack Vermillion, this is Marshal Jack Youngblood," Earp said.

"Texas Jack, of the last ride of Wyatt Earp and his immortals?" Jack said.

"Don't believe everything you read, Marshal," Vermillion said. "The only thing I did was get my horse shot out from under me. Old Doc Holliday had to pull me out from under, or I'd a died for sure."

"How is old Doc, by the way?" Masterson asked.

"In a hospital in the mountains near Denver," Earp said. "I'm planning to stop and see him when I'm done here."

A waiter came to the table.

"Four shots of bourbon whiskey," Earp said.

The waiter went to the bar and returned with four filled shot glasses.

Vermillion picked up his glass and tossed back the bourbon, set the glass down, and looked at the stair that led to the second floor. "Well, my bean has an itch that needs to be scratched," he said.

Vermillion stood, walked to the stairs, and went up to the second floor.

"Well," Earp said.

Jack picked up his shot glass. "Let's go get a steak," he said.

Jack, Earp, and Masterson were having after-dinner coffee in the hotel restaurant when a deputy entered and approached the table.

"The doc wants to see you. That kid Longabaugh remembered something," the deputy said.

"Where's that other marshal?" Longabaugh asked.

"He went out of town," Earp said. "He'll be back tomorrow."

"What did you remember?" Masterson asked.

"I've been studying on things, like you said," Longabaugh said. "After that bullet creased my head and I was on the ground, I kept hearing things even though it was all fuzzy. I heard one of them say something like 'Good shot, Case or Casey.' Something like that."

"Case or Casey?" Masterson said. "Are you sure?"

"Like I said, I was all fuzzy, but I think so," Longabaugh said.

"All right, boy, you get some sleep now," Masterson said.

Jack, Earp, and Masterson checked the federal warrants book in Masterson's office.

"That's every federal warrant on record and not a Casey or Case in the lot," Masterson said.

"It's possible the boy got it wrong," Earp said. "He does have a concussion and was half unconscious at the time."

"I guess there's not much more we can do at this point,"

Earp said. "A few herds coming through tomorrow you're welcome to check, but it's doubtful stone-cold killers like this bunch would try to sell them legal."

"Thanks for the help, boys," Jack said. "I believe I'll turn in early."

Jack left the office and walked several blocks to the hotel, passing the Long Branch Saloon on the way. On the second floor balcony, three scantily clad women watched him as he passed.

"Hey, Marshal, you're a big one," one of the women said.

"For five dollars I'll make your dreams come true," another woman said.

Jack tipped his hat as he kept walking.

"I know this country well, although I've never crossed Mount Sunflower," Red Moon said.

Emmet and Red Moon were in their bedrolls, watching the night sky. It was bright and clear and millions of stars were visible.

"Denver is not a good place to sell stolen cattle, so there must be another destination," Red Moon said. "A place where they can gather the stolen cattle and have time to alter the brands."

"That requires a safe haven and lots of time," Emmet said. "And the special irons needed to change the brands. Would you know of such a place?"

"I do not," Red Moon said. "But the Colorado Rockies might be a good place to set up such an operation."

"We can't exactly search the whole mountain range," Emmet said.

"Cows and men leave tracks," Red Moon said. "Even on rock. If they are out there, I will find them."

"I believe you," Emmet said.

"I owe it to my people," Red Moon said. "And yours."

"Which of my people are you talking about?" Emmet asked. "The Sioux, Apache, or Irish side of the family?"

"You will make a fine lawyer someday," Red Moon said.

Emmet grinned and closed his eyes.

CHAPTER FOURTEEN

Around four in the afternoon, Jack was taking coffee on the porch of the hotel. Three or four herds had been driven in so far, and all the paperwork checked out as he knew it would be.

He was rolling a cigarette when he spotted Emmet and Red Moon riding into town along Main Street.

They stopped at the hitching post in front of the hotel, dismounted, and went up to the porch.

Emmet took the cup from Jack, sat in a chair, and said, "How did it go with Horn?"

"We got them," Jack said.

"How many did you kill?" Emmet asked.

"Six, but they had it coming," Jack said. "What about you, find anything new?"

"Red Moon found a trail leading to Mount Sunflower," Emmet said.

Jack looked at Red Moon.

"That's hard country," Red Moon said.

"And we're going after them?" Jack said.

Emmet sipped coffee and nodded.

"Still got the mule?" Jack asked.

"In the livery," Emmet said.

"We'll need him," Jack said. "And that kid, the one with the concussion, he remembered something. He said one of them called another Case or Casey. We checked every federal wanted poster, but there's nothing close to it."

"The kid probably doesn't know what he heard in the condition he was in," Emmet said.

"Probably true," Jack said.

Emmet set the cup aside.

"Right now I need a steak," Emmet said. "And then a bed. I figure we'll leave as soon as we resupply in the morning."

Masterson and Earp met Emmet, Jack, and Red Moon outside the general store.

"If Judge Parker sends a telegram for us, tell him we're headed into Colorado," Emmet said.

"The two of you, one tracker, and a mule, you got no chance of finding that bunch," Earp said. "You know that, right?"

"As much as I'd like to be home with my wife and girls right now, I owe it to the people on the reservation to try," Emmet said.

Jack mounted his massive horse. "Let's go if we're going," he said. "See you, Wyatt, Bat."

"Another hour and we'll be inside that pass through Mount Sunflower," Red Moon said as he ate beans, bacon, and cornbread from a tin plate.

"They must have a reason for taking the long way around the barn," Jack said. "They could be in Mexico by now. Hell, they could be halfway to South America by now."

"I've been giving that a lot of thought," Emmet said. "Suppose they have a place no one knows about to stash the cattle until the herd is big enough to sell. If they had enough time to change the brands, they could even sell them in Canada for top dollar. Twenty or more a head."

"And where is this place, because it sure as hell ain't in the Rocky Mountains?" Jack said. "Which is where we're headed, by the way."

"They may cut through the mountains to get where they're going, but wherever they are keeping the herd isn't in the Rockies," Red Moon said. "I've herded cattle for the army many times. They require open range, good water, and lots of room. The mountains don't offer much of that unless you're willing to climb, and cattle aren't."

"What about a valley in the mountains somewhere?" Jack asked.

"That's possible, but not likely if you're trying to hide a stolen herd from the law," Red Moon said.

"Can you track them?" Jack asked.

"I can track them," Red Moon said.

"You track them," Jack said. "And I'll kill them."

"All of them, Jack? We don't know how many of them there are," Emmet said.

"For making me sleep on the ground and miss my woman and for murdering those good men, I'll kill every last one of them sons a bitches," Jack said.

"What day is this?" Red Moon asked.

"Saturday," Emmet said.

Amy wore a light blue dress with a matching shawl and wore her hair in a complicated braid that took both Maria and Chao-xing an hour to complete.

She waited on the porch until she spotted the dust of a carriage, and then she went into the house because it wouldn't be proper for a gentleman caller to see her waiting on the porch.

Chao-xing and the girls were cutting a stale loaf of bread into small cubes.

"We're going fishing at the creek, Grandmother," Mary said. "Chao-xing said stale bread catches a lot of fish."

"Make sure you wear your old chores clothing," Amy said.

"We will," Mary said.

Maria entered the kitchen.

"Amy, Mr. Duff is here," she said.

"Thank you," Amy said and left the kitchen.

Maria, Chao-xing, Mary, and Sarah looked at each other and then quietly followed Amy to the living room and stood at the door.

Duff presented Amy with a fresh-cut bouquet of flowers.

"Thank you, Mr. Duff," Amy said. "They are lovely."

Amy turned, and Maria was right behind her with a vase.

"Would you . . . ?" Amy said as Maria took the flowers.

Duff had a box of chocolates under his left arm. "Would it be all right if I gave the young girls a box of chocolates?" he said.

Mary and Sarah dashed to Amy's side.

Amy sighed. "Girls, you may take Mr. Duff's gift, but only two pieces each. Maria and Chao-xing will keep count."

Mary took the box of chocolates. "Thank you, Mr. Duff," she said.

"Are you my grandmother's beau?" Sarah asked Duff.

"Let's play the counting game," Amy said.

"Let's not," Mary said, and she and Sarah dashed back to Chao-xing and Maria.

"Mr. Duff, the picnic basket is on the porch. Shall we go?" Amy said.

Duff held the door open, and they went out to the porch where Duff picked up the picnic basket.

As they walked down to his carriage, Duff said, "What's the counting game?"

"Get out of line, Mr. Duff, and you'll find out," Amy said.

As they rode through the pass of Mount Sunflower, Red Moon said, "When we exit this pass sometime tonight, we'll be in Colorado."

"That's exciting news there, Red Moon, but are we tracking

them or are we just out for a long scenic ride?" Jack said.

"We aren't tracking anybody," Emmet said. "Red Moon is doing the tracking. We're doing the following."

"Red Moon, are we following you because you're following their trail, or are we following you because we don't know any better?" Jack said.

Casually puffing on his pipe, Red Moon said, "Do you see all those disturbed rocks against the walls of the pass?"

Emmet and Jack looked at the walls.

"Those are made when a large herd passes quickly and they kick up rocks and debris," Red Moon said. "They passed this way, all right. We may have to ride for weeks to catch them, but we will catch them."

"That's assuring," Emmet said.

"Weeks more away from home. What's assuring about that?" Jack said.

"If you're thinking about Chao-xing, remember the saying, 'absence makes the heart grow fonder,' " Emmet said.

"I'll think about it if you tell me what the hell it means," Jack said.

Amy guided Duff to a shady spot under a large oak tree that overlooked a shallow creek. They spread out several blankets, and Amy unloaded the large picnic basket. The fried chicken she cooked earlier in the morning was still warm. So were the fresh rolls. The glass jars were full of cold lemonade. The pie tin held a freshly baked apple pie.

"Mrs. Youngblood, I . . ." Duff said.

"You may call me Amy."

"All right. Amy," Duff said. "And you may call me Stanly if you'd like."

Amy nodded. "What's on your mind, Stanly?"

"Mrs. Youngblood . . . I mean Amy, you are about the most

direct woman I have ever met," Duff said.

"Well, Stanly, I've lived through the Alamo, the rising of Texas, the Civil War, the Comanche Wars, given birth to two sons, I've been shot three times, and have taken four arrows in my sixty years. I don't have the time or the desire to be anything but direct," Amy said. "So what's on your mind?"

"I'm a lonely man," Duff said. "As I told you, I've been a widower for a long time. I have three newspapers and have acquired a fair amount of wealth, but I am lonely. I desire the company and conversation of a smart, strong-willed woman who can fill the void in me."

"And you think I'm that woman?" Amy said.

"I would like to find out," Duff said.

"Stanly, I won't change who I am for you or any man," Amy said.

"I wouldn't expect or want you to," Duff said.

"Good. Eat your chicken," Amy said.

About a mile ahead of them, Red Moon spotted a circle of buzzards in the sky.

"Emmet, Jack," he said.

"We see them," Emmet said.

They rode to the dead cow the buzzards were feasting on and dismounted. The buzzards had been picking on the cow for weeks, and it was close to bone without much meat left.

As they walked to the cow, the buzzards scattered and took to the air.

"Damn filthy creatures ate the brand right off her flesh," Jack said.

Red Moon inspected the carcass. "It would take weeks for them to eat this much flesh," he said.

"What do you suppose happened to her?" Jack asked.

"Could have been anything," Red Moon said.

"At least we know we're on the right trail," Jack said.

Jack mounted his horse and looked at the circling birds. "Come finish your lunch, you filthy bastards," he said.

Amy had packed a small coffee pot and cups and made a fire to boil a pot. She and Duff drank cups of coffee while they ate apple pie for dessert.

"Another slice?" Amy asked.

"I couldn't," Duff said. "My belt would bust."

Amy sipped her coffee. "What are your ambitions, Stanly?" she asked.

"I like Fort Smith," Duff said. "I figure to stay. Oh, I don't know if I can make the *Gazette* as big as my paper in Little Rock, but it can be a fine paper. I'm thinking of publishing it twice a week."

"I meant towards me," Amy said.

"Oh," Stanly said. "Can I be honest?"

"If you aren't, I'll know," Amy said.

"I was thinking of stealing a kiss from you," Duff said.

"It took you long enough to get around to that one," Amy said.

"May I?"

"You may."

They rested the horses for an hour, and Emmet took the time to study territorial maps.

"After we exit this pass, there's nothing for forty miles to the west," he said. "Then there's a town called Lamar."

"After the pass, they will turn north and avoid towns," Red Moon said.

"Why won't they turn south?" Jack asked.

"If they had ambitions of Mexico, they would have done so long before now," Red Moon said.

"I agree," Emmet said.

"Maybe we should head to this Lamar and see if they have a telegraph station?" Jack said. "Maybe there's some news?"

Emmet looked at Red Moon. "That's not a bad idea."

Red Moon looked at the map. "Two days' ride is not so far a detour, and we can resupply in Lamar," he said.

"Then let's get going," Jack said.

"Thank you for a lovely afternoon, Stanly," Amy said as he helped her down from the carriage.

"Allow me to carry the picnic basket to the door," Duff said.

"No need. It's much lighter empty," Amy said. "Besides, the little spies are probably behind the door. Will I see you in church tomorrow?"

"You will."

"Then sit with us."

An hour before sunset, Red Moon led Jack and Emmet out of the pass to wide open prairie.

"We could make Lamar in a day and a half," Red Moon said.

They rode about fifty yards, and the shot rang out so suddenly it spooked the horses. Emmet was nearly thrown.

Red Moon fell from the saddle with a gaping hole in his right lung.

Jack and Emmet jumped from the saddle and kept low as they raced to Red Moon.

A second shot missed Jack by a few feet.

"Get him to the cover of those rocks," Emmet said.

Jack lifted Red Moon and ran with him to cover behind several large rocks.

Emmet followed and said, "How bad?"

"Bad," Jack said.

"Damn bushwhacker," Red Moon said.

"Hello you three," a man called out. "All I want is one horse and your mule. You can keep the rest."

"Screw you, bushwhacker," Jack shouted. "You shot our tracker."

"Quit yelling and look for something," Emmet said.

"He's behind those rocks," Jack said and pointed to large rocks on top of a hill a hundred yards away.

"Give me your bandana," Emmet said.

Jack removed his bandana and gave it to Emmet.

"He's losing a lot of blood," Emmet said as he used the bandana to tie off Red Moon's wound.

"Listen to me, you three," the man yelled. "You can't go anywhere unless I allow it, so you might as well give me a horse and the mule. Then you can save your friend."

"Jack, Red Moon will die if we don't get him some help," Emmet said.

"All right," Jack shouted. "I'll ride one horse and the mule a hundred yards to the west. You come get them. Agreed?" he shouted.

"Toss your sidearm and rifle from the saddle first, and then come ahead," the man shouted. "I like that pinto."

"Figures," Jack said.

"Jack?" Emmet said.

"Tend to Red Moon," Jack said.

He stood and walked forward with his hands up.

"I'm removing my sidearm," Jack yelled.

"I see you," the man yelled.

Jack removed his gun belt and set it on a rock, then walked to the pinto and removed the rifle from the saddle sleeve and placed it beside his gun belt.

"Now ride that pinto and the mule a hundred yards and dismount," the man shouted. "Then you turn around and run back. I won't shoot no more. You got my word."

Jack grabbed the reins on the mule and then mounted the pinto. He rode at a slow pace about a hundred yards and then dismounted. As soon as his boots touched the ground, he turned and ran back to the rock.

Jack picked up the rifle, cocked the lever, and waited with the rifle by his side. The man came down from the left and slowly walked to the pinto. He looked back at Jack and then mounted the saddle.

The second he was atop Emmet's horse, Jack brought the rifle to his right eye, aimed carefully, and fired one shot. About one second later, the man fell from the saddle.

Jack set the rifle down, put on his holster, and then walked quickly toward the man. He reached him just as the man struggled to stand up. He was bleeding heavily from the bullet that had passed through his left lung.

"Ya done shot me," the man stammered.

"I'm United States Marshal John Youngblood, and of course I shot you, you bushwhacking jackass," Jack said.

"First ma horse threw me and ran off, and now I'm shot. Of all the rotten luck," the man said.

"Luck has little to do with it, you bushwhacker, and you're as dumb as you are dead," Jack said and drew his Colt, cocked it, and shot the man through the heart.

About a mile from Amy's house, Duff encountered a man walking on the road. He stopped the buggy beside the man and said, "Hello."

"Afternoon," the man said.

"Are you all right?" Duff asked.

"I was doing some odd jobs on the reservation," the man said. "My horse came up a bit lame, and I left him a few miles back. I could use a ride to town."

"Hop in," Duff said.

The man stepped up into the buggy. The moment he was in, he reached for the knife hidden in his right boot and shoved it to the handle into the right side of Duff's chest.

For a moment, Duff had no idea what just happened. Then, as blood gushed from the chest wound, he started to gasp for breath.

"Let's see what you got here," the man said and found Duff's wallet in his jacket pocket.

"Looks like a couple hundred dollars," the man said. He put his right foot against Duff's shoulder and shoved him out of the buggy.

Duff hit the ground on his back, bleeding and gasping.

The man took the reins. "I thank you for the hospitality and the use of your buggy," he said and rode away.

Duff struggled to breathe as he slowly rolled over and got to one knee. His lung was filling with blood, and he would die here on the road unless he did something about it.

Using all his strength, Duff managed to stand up, and then started walking back to Amy's house.

Maria and Mary were shucking corn on the front porch when Duff staggered off the road and collapsed thirty feet from the house.

"Get Amy. Quick," Maria said.

As Mary ran into the house, Maria ran to Duff. She knelt beside him and looked at the knife handle protruding from his chest.

A few moments later, Amy, Chao-xing, and Mary arrived.

Without hesitation, Amy said, "Chao-xing, take the buggy to Doctor Jefferson's house. Mary, you go with her to show her the way. Maria, help me get him to his feet."

"Did you kill him?" Emmet asked when Jack returned with the

pinto and mule.

"Course I killed him," Jack said. "He shot Red Moon; I should let him go for that?"

"We got to get him to a doctor, Jack," Emmet said.

His face covered in sweat, his shirt drenched in blood, Red Moon gasped, "I can ride."

"We need to get him to Lamar and a doctor," Emmet said.

"Pour some whiskey on that wound and tie it tight," Jack said. "I'll get some rope and we'll tie him to his horse."

"What about the bushwhacker?"

"Let the buzzards have him," Jack said. "I won't sweat digging a grave over that bastard."

Doctor Jefferson, the black reservation doctor, examined the knife protruding from Duff's chest.

Duff was in Amy's bed and unconscious.

"The knife has to come out before I do anything else," Jefferson said. "I'll need hot water and plenty of bandages."

"Chao-xing, you and Maria get the water and bandages," Amy said. "Mary, Sarah, please help them, and then stay out of here."

"Mrs. Youngblood, will you assist me?" Jefferson asked.

"Of course."

Around midnight, they rested the horses for two hours. Jack untied Red Moon and gently lowered him beside the fire Emmet built.

"Is he awake?" Emmet asked as he stirred bacon and beans in a pan over the fire.

"No, and I don't expect him to be," Jack said.

"Stir the food while I check his wound," Emmet said.

"That's all I can do for him tonight," Jefferson said. "He'll need rest and plenty of good food to build up his blood. Can I stay the night so I can keep an eye on him?"

"Of course," Amy said. "I'll have the girls make up the spare bed."

Maria entered the bedroom. "We made supper for you. Please come eat."

"Bring me a plate," Amy said. "I'll sit with Mr. Duff while the doctor gets some sleep."

Jack and Emmet sat around the fire as they ate.

"We'll ride to sunrise and rest the horses again," Jack said.

"This is damn near going to kill my pinto," Emmet said.

"The mule is slowing us down," Jack said. "Let's take what supplies we need and cut him loose."

"You take care of the mule," Emmet said. "I'm going to check Red Moon's wounds and change the bandage."

Amy sat in a rocking chair beside her bed. The house was still and quiet, as everyone but she was asleep. The lantern on the dresser was on low flame so the room had minimal light, just enough to see Duff by.

Duff's face was covered with sweat. He was probably running a fever. There was a basin on the floor, and she dipped a towel in the water and washed Duff's face to cool his skin.

Then she sat in the chair to wait for morning.

CHAPTER FIFTEEN

Jack and Emmet rode until sunrise and made camp for two hours. While they ate breakfast and drank coffee, Red Moon opened his eyes briefly, but quickly fell back into unconsciousness.

"He's in a bad way, Jack, and we still have a full day's ride ahead of us," Emmet said.

"I know, but we got no choice but to keep riding until we reach Lamar," Jack said.

"What if they don't have a doctor?" Emmet asked.

"Every town has somebody to do the healing, even if it's a barber," Jack said. "And the odds of him living are better if he's in a bed with someone tending him who knows what they're doing."

"We won't reach Lamar until after dark," Emmet said.

"Close to ten, I figure," Jack said. "Think he'll make it?"

Emmet looked at Red Moon.

"We owe it to him to try," he said.

"Mrs. Youngblood, it's morning," Jefferson said.

Asleep in the rocking chair, Amy opened her eyes and immediately looked at Duff.

"How is he?" she asked.

"Resting comfortably, I'm happy to say," Jefferson said. "He's still very weak, but I think he'll make it."

Amy stood and stretched her back.

"Any idea how this happened?" Jefferson asked.

"He came for a visit," Amy said. "We had a picnic lunch, and then he rode his buggy back to town. About an hour later, he showed up here with that knife in his chest."

"I guess he'll tell us when he wakes up," Jefferson said. "In the meantime, your girls have made breakfast. I suggest you go have some."

Emmet's admiration for his brother grew as they continued to ride west to Lamar. He was exhausted and so was his pinto, and several times Emmet felt himself drift off to sleep, but Jack just kept riding with Red Moon's horse in tow.

Jack never seemed to get tired or even hungry, and Emmet felt if he set his mind to it that Jack could ride for a week without stopping.

As the sun beat down on the back of his neck, Emmet felt himself start to drift. He forced his eyes to stay open, but it was no use and they slowly closed.

When Emmet opened his eyes, Jack had the pinto in tow as well as Red Moon's horse.

"Jack. Stop," Emmet said.

"I have to get to my office," Jefferson said. "But I'll be back later this afternoon to check on him. In the meantime, should he wake up, give him broth and water and bread, if he can hold it down. If he needs to use the privy, don't let him out of bed. Give him a basin."

"I've seen to sick men before," Amy said.

She returned to her bedroom and took a seat in the rocking chair. Duff was no longer sweating, and his breathing was softer, no longer raspy.

Maria entered the bedroom. "Chao-xing and the girls went fishing for trout," she said. "How is he?"

"Better," Amy said.

"Can I fix you something to eat?"

"Coffee and maybe some toasted bread."

"How about I toss in some scrambled eggs?"

"All right."

Maria turned to the door, paused, and looked back at Amy.

"When he is well, you're going to have a man on your hands," Maria said. "Even if you don't want one."

Emmet slept for two hours. When he awoke, Jack had hot food on the fire and fresh coffee.

Jack filled a cup and handed it to Emmet.

"He woke up for a bit," Jack said.

Emmet looked at Red Moon.

"He chanted his Sioux death song and fell back asleep," Jack said.

"I was thinking of chanting that myself," Emmet said.

"Get some food in you, and you'll feel better," Jack said. "I figure to make Lamar by ten tonight if we don't have to make too many more stops."

"Don't you ever get tired?" Emmet asked.

Jack grinned. "It's a hell of a life, being a marshal," he said.

Emmet sighed. "All things considered, I'd rather be a lawyer," he said.

Amy was feeding Duff beef broth with slices of crusty bread when Marshal Cal Witson arrived at the house.

Maria showed him into the bedroom.

"Mrs. Youngblood, Judge Parker sent me to see about Mr. Duff," Witson said.

"Hello, Marshal," Amy said. "And as you can see, Mr. Duff is very much alive."

"I see that," Witson said. "And I wonder if Mr. Duff has the strength to tell me what happened."

Duff looked at Amy. "May I sit up?"

"I'll help you, but if you bust your stitches, I'll thump your skull," Amy said.

Witson hid his grin.

Amy helped Duff to sit up.

"I had just left Mrs. Youngblood and was driving my carriage home when I met this fellow on the road," Duff said. "He said his horse went lame and he needed a ride to town. No sooner was he in the buggy than he shoved a knife in me. I believe he took my wallet as well. I think I walked back here, but I'm not sure."

"Lucky for you your wallet has your name on it in gold letters," Witson said.

"How did you know that?" Duff asked.

"This shifty-eyed fellow began flashing money in the Regal Saloon, and the bartender spotted your name on his wallet," Witson said. "He called for the town sheriff. We got him in the courthouse jail waiting on charges."

"My buggy?" Duff asked.

"Found about a mile outside of town," Witson said. "The fellow claims he found your wallet just lying in the road."

"I guess I'm lucky to be alive," Duff said.

"That you are, Mr. Duff," Witson said. "We'll keep him in jail until you're well enough to press charges."

"That's enough talking for now, Marshal," Amy said. "Come out to the kitchen and have something to eat."

"Thank you kindly, Mrs. Youngblood, I believe I will," Witson said.

"Emmet, are you awake?" Jack said.

"I'm not sure," Emmet said.

"Look directly to the west," Jack said.

Emmet looked west and saw tiny red dots on the horizon.

"Lamar?" he said.

"Can't be more than a mile or two," Jack said. "Does your horse have anything left in her?"

"Enough."

"Come on then," Jack said.

Jack raced his horse and kept a tight hold on Red Moon's. Emmet followed closely. They reached the fringe of Lamar in less than ten minutes. The streets were dark and deserted. The lights they had seen from a distance came from lanterns mounted on storefronts.

"The whole damn town is asleep," Jack said.

"Maybe they're . . . ?" Emmet said.

Jack pulled his Colt and started firing bullets into the dirt. "I'm United States Marshal Jack Youngblood, and we got a hurt man here that needs immediate attention," he yelled as he fired off six shots.

"Subtle," Emmet said.

Windows started to open; heads came out; lanterns in bedrooms lit up.

"But effective," Jack said as he reloaded the Colt.

"Who's out there?" a voice in the dark cried out.

"Are you people deaf?" Jack shouted. "I'm a US marshal, and I got a hurt man here needs doctoring."

"Bring him to the barbershop," a voice called out.

"There," Emmet said. "That barber pole."

Jack carried Red Moon into the back room of the barbershop and placed him on the table.

The barber's name was Amos Smith, and he'd been a surgeon during the Civil War. Afterward, he traveled west and settled in Colorado, but gave up his practice and settled in as a barber.

"He has a bullet in his lung," Smith said.

"We know," Jack said. "That's why we brought him to you."

"You boys will have to assist me," Smith said.

"What do you want us to do?" Emmet said.

"Go out front and boil a pan of water on the woodstove," Smith said.

"I'll do that," Jack said.

"Let me get my bag and instruments," Smith said.

Smith proved to be a very capable surgeon. After putting Red Moon under by placing a cheesecloth over his nose and using a dropper to place several drops of liquid onto the cloth, he went to work.

Smith turned to Emmet. "When I tell you to put a few drops on the cloth, I want you to use the dropper, but not until I tell you to, and then only a few drops."

"What about me?" Jack asked.

"You keep the hot water coming," Smith said. "Otherwise, you just stand there looking big."

By sunrise, Red Moon was resting comfortably in a bed in the room behind the barbershop and Emmet, Jack, and Smith were having breakfast at the lone café in town.

"Ambushed, you say," Smith said as he dipped bread into his runny eggs.

"He paid for it," Jack said.

"Will Red Moon make it?" Emmet asked.

"He will," Smith said. "He's a tough old bird."

"Do you have any law in this town?" Emmet asked.

"We only have three hundred residents," Smith said. "If we need the law, we'll ride over to Pueblo and see the county sheriff."

"How long will it take for Red Moon to recover?" Emmet said.

"Months, I'm afraid," Smith said. "He's welcome to stay here until he's fit to travel."

"We need a tracker," Jack said. "Where's the nearest railroad?"

"Pueblo," Smith said. "It's a full day's ride."

"What are you thinking, Jack?" Emmet asked.

"Take the railroad to Denver, see the army, and ask them for a tracker," Jack said. "Otherwise we're done."

"That's the same as starting over," Emmet said.

"Do you want to tell Judge Parker we gave up if we still have options?" Jack said.

"I do not," Emmet said.

"Then we go to Denver and secure another tracker," Jack said.

"Tomorrow," Emmet said. "Right now our horses need rest and, frankly, so do I."

Jack looked at Smith. "Is there a hotel in town?"

"No, but the widow Walsh takes in lodgers," Smith said. "You can check your horses at the livery at the end of the street."

Anna Walsh owned a three-story home at the edge of town on the north side. It was large and comfortable, and she presently had eight residents who paid ten dollars a week for board and an extra ten for meals twice a day if they desired. Most did for the convenience.

Jack slept for a solid six hours and was drinking coffee and whittling on a stick on the front porch when Anna came out and joined him.

"It's a fine afternoon," Anna said.

"Yes, it is," Jack said.

"My husband was a lawman," Anna said. "Down in Texas. I kept trying to get him to quit, but he said he didn't know how to do nothing else. You remind me of him in that regard. Is that how it is with you?"

"I expect so," Jack said.

"We had us a town drunk, but I expect every town does," Anna said. "Harmless fellow he was, right up to the point he stuck a pitchfork into my husband's chest when my husband went to wake him in the livery. He said later he had no idea why he did that. He apologized to me right before they hung him."

"I'm sorry," Jack said.

"Do you have a woman?"

"I do."

"Then what the hell are you doing being a lawman when you should be a husband?" Anna said.

Before Jack could reply, Smith approached the porch.

"Your friend is awake," he said.

"I best wake my brother," Jack said.

"You boys saved my life," Red Moon said. "But I'm afraid I'm useless to you in this condition."

"We're just glad you pulled through," Emmet said.

"We're headed up to Denver to see the army about another tracker," Jack said.

"Charlie Light Foot," Red Moon said. "Full-blooded Navajo. He's their chief scout and as good as me."

"From where we were, how long did you figure before we caught them?" Jack asked.

"They had ten days on us, but that's if they stayed the course," Red Moon said. "You'll have to backtrack once you secure Light Foot and start over."

"Well," Emmet said. "That's what we are going to do then."

At the livery, Jack and Emmet checked their horses. Jack's massive horse was fit and ready to ride, but Emmet's pinto needed more rest.

Jack rubbed the pinto's neck. "She's a game little thing, I'll give her that. But she won't be up for another twenty-mile ride until morning."

"Neither will I," Emmet said.

"I doubt there's one interesting thing to do in this town," Jack said. "Except eat."

In the morning, Jack and Emmet said goodbye to Red Moon before leaving for Pueblo.

"He'll be well taken care of until he's able to ride," Smith said.

Emmet gave Smith two hundred dollars for his time and expenses for caring for Red Moon.

"If you need more, send a telegram to Judge Parker in Fort Smith," Emmet said.

"That's more than enough," Smith said.

"Well, let's go if we're going," Jack said to Emmet.

CHAPTER SIXTEEN

Chao-xing, Mary, and Sarah were turning the soil in the front yard garden when Chao-xing noticed a wagon headed their way.

"Mary, go get your grandmother," Chao-xing said.

Amy and Maria came out to the porch as the prisoner wagon arrived. Marshal Witson was at the reins. One man was in the cage. Witson jumped down and approached the porch.

"Sorry for this disturbance, Mrs. Youngblood, but Judge Parker insisted I bring this bird out here to see if Mr. Duff can identify him as the man who stabbed him," Witson said.

"Is there any news from my boys?" Amy asked.

"No, I'm afraid not," Witson said.

"It will take some doing to get Mr. Duff out of bed," Amy said. "Come have a cup of coffee while we get him to his feet."

Witson came up to the porch.

"Maria, have Mary bring the marshal some coffee," Amy said.

Witson drank a cup of coffee and waited on the porch with Mary and Sarah until Amy and Duff appeared on the porch. Duff walked slowly and used Amy's shoulder for support, but he made it all the way onto the porch. Maria and Chao-xing stood behind him until Duff reached the railing and placed his hands on it to steady himself.

Witson stood up. "Mr. Duff, I'm Marshal Witson," he said. "Can you identify the man in the wagon for me?"

"I don't think I can make it down the stairs," Duff said.

Witson nodded and went down to the wagon. He opened the cage door and said, "Out, you varmint."

The man slowly climbed out of the cage. His ankles and wrists were in shackles.

"Walk to the porch so he can get a good look at you," Witson said.

The man clanked his way to the porch.

Duff looked at him.

"Why?" Duff asked.

The man shrugged. "It's my nature to commit such acts," he said.

"All right, back in the cage," Witson said. "Mr. Duff, we'll hold him until you're fit enough to appear in court."

Jack and Emmet rode at a quick and steady pace and reached Pueblo in six hours. A bustling, iron-mining town of five thousand residents, Pueblo was situated near the Arkansas River where iron ore was shipped by river and by railroad north to Denver.

The railroad station was located on the western fringe of town, and they stopped there first to check schedules. A train bound for Denver was scheduled to leave in thirty-five minutes.

"If the train is on time, we'll be in Denver by seven tonight," Emmet said. "We'll telegraph Ma and the girls and also the judge. We can ride to the army tonight or in the morning."

"Tonight," Jack said.

Emmet cocked an eye at Jack. "You're passing up a soft bed and a good steak?"

"Denver is a town full of temptations, and I'm trying to walk a straight path until we get home," Jack said.

Emmet grinned. "I do believe when we get home, you really are going to marry that girl," he said.

"Needle me some more and see what happens," Jack said.

"Nobody is needling you, Jack," Emmet said. "I just can't see you with a ring through your nose, is all."

"Why not? You got one through yours," Jack said.

"Yes, but I like it," Emmet said.

"Be quiet before I bust your head," Jack said.

Grinning, Emmet took out his pipe and struck a match.

"I thought, as a newspaper man, I've heard just about everything," Duff said. "The man said it was his nature to rob and kill other people."

Duff and Amy were seated in chairs on the porch. Each had a cup of coffee.

"My husband used to keep it all bottled up inside, the things he had to do as a lawman," Amy said. "Every once in a while he would tell me things, terrible things I didn't really want to hear, but I listened anyway. The world is full of evil, I'm afraid. The best we can do sometimes is survive it."

Duff sighed.

Amy reached over and took his hand.

Inside the house, kneeling at the window, Mary and Sarah watched and listened.

"I think Grandma has a beau," Mary whispered.

Standing behind the girls, Maria said, "Let's play the counting game."

Mary and Sarah turned and looked at Maria and Chao-xing. Chao-xing held a broom.

"One," Chao-xing said.

While Jack and Emmet waited for the train to arrive, a man pushing a cart came onto the platform. He pushed the cart to them and stopped.

"You boys look hungry," he said. "If you're riding the train to Denver, they don't serve food. I know. I ride it all the time."

139

Jack looked at the sealed brown bags in the man's cart.

"What's in the bags?" Jack said.

"Popcorn, my dear marshal," the man said.

"What's popcorn?" Jack asked.

"Why, it's a healthy and delicious food you can eat anywhere," the man said. "Even on a train."

"What's in it?" Jack asked.

"Corn," the man said.

"That's it? Just corn?" Jack said.

"I ate plenty of it at school in Boston," Emmet said. "How much a bag?"

"Five cents."

"Give us five bags," Emmet said.

Once the horses were secure in the boxcar and the train was underway to Denver, Emmet gave Jack a bag of the popcorn.

The bags were fastened close by a relatively new device called the staple.

"What's these little pieces of metal?" Jack asked.

"Those are called staples, Jack," Emmet said. "They've been around for ten years or so. The judge uses them to hold documents together."

Jack ripped open his bag and looked at the popped kernels of corn. "This doesn't look like no corn I ever saw," he said.

"It's popped with . . . just be quiet and eat it, Jack," Emmet said. "I'm going to read my law book."

After dinner, once the girls were in bed and the kitchen was quiet, Duff sat at the table with a notepad and pencil and wrote by the light of a lantern.

Amy, wearing a robe, came to the table and sat next to him.

"It's getting late and you need your rest," she said.

"I know, but I feel awake and excited," Duff said.

"What are you writing?" Amy asked.

"A column for the paper," Duff said. "And it's given me a wonderful idea."

"About what?"

"Crime," Duff said. "I'm going to dedicate one page in the paper every week just to crime reports. I'm going to call it *Crime Watch*. I'd like you to help."

"Help? How?"

"Information gathering. Writing. It won't take time away from your teaching when school is in session, and I'll pay a salary," Duff said.

"A salary?" Amy said.

"Of course," Duff said. "I don't expect you or anyone else to work for free."

"Right now, all I'm concerned about is getting you to bed so you can rest, or the only thing I'll be writing about is your funeral," Amy said.

Duff sighed.

"All right, but we'll talk about this in the morning," he said.

"Right tasty snack, that popcorn," Jack said as he led his horse off the railroad platform in Denver.

Directly behind Jack, Emmet led his pinto.

"We can ride to the fort first," Emmet said. "We can find a hotel later if you'd like."

Jack and Emmet mounted their horses and rode east toward the army fort. "Just follow the telegraph lines. They lead directly to the fort," Jack said.

"How far?"

"Maybe thirty minutes. This town's got a hotel eight floors high," Jack said. "And more than thirty saloons. Denver's a city grown up around the gold rush, but if you ask me, the only people getting rich are the ones selling mining equipment."

"Why does everything smell funny?" Emmet asked.

"That's right, you never been," Jack said. "First time I came out here was with Witson a few years back to pick up a prisoner. My horse was restless from being on the train; I took him for a run, and he damn near fainted."

"Fainted?"

"This whole town is built a mile above sea level," Jack said.

"The thinner air, of course," Emmet said.

"You get used to it, so after a time things seem normal," Jack said. "But I wouldn't go running our horses just yet."

They followed the telegraph lines directly to the large army post northeast from Denver. The sixteen-foot-high fence surrounding the large fort was patrolled by four armed soldiers.

The gates, as high as the fence, were open and manned by two armed soldiers.

Jack and Emmet dismounted at the gates by the two soldiers.

"I'm United States Marshal Emmet Youngblood and this is Marshal John Youngblood," Emmet said. "We would like to see the post commander."

Colonel Greenhill sat at his desk and looked at Jack and Emmet.

"I'm afraid that Charlie Light Foot is away with a squad far south of here," Greenhill said. "I don't expect them back for weeks."

"Well, I don't fancy sitting around for two weeks while murdering cattle thieves roam free," Jack said. "Have you any other trackers we can borrow?"

"No, but I have something else that might interest you," Greenhill said.

The fort stockade was the last building against the north wall. It was long, squat, and held six cells with iron bars. Just one cell was occupied.

The sergeant of the guard led Greenhill, Emmet, and Jack into the guardhouse. Wall-mounted lanterns provided light, but not enough to see inside the cells clearly. At the sixth cell, Greenhill said, "Prisoner, stand and approach the light, please."

Jack and Emmet watched as a figure stood from the cot and walked to the bars. They were surprised to see that a Comanche woman was the prisoner.

"Any idea who this woman is?" Greenhill asked.

"I do not," Emmet said.

Jack shook his head.

"This is Doli, the wife of Comanche outlaw Two Hawks," Greenhill said.

Jack squinted at her.

"Son of a bitch," he said.

"Had supper yet?" Greenhill asked.

"Had some popcorn on the train," Jack said.

"Popcorn?" Greenhill said. "Sergeant, tell the cook to open the officers' mess and to cook four steaks. Then escort Doli to the mess."

"Yes, sir," said the sergeant.

Jack sat opposite Doli at Greenhill's table. She knew her way around a knife and fork.

"Do you speak English?" Jack asked her.

"Of course I speak English, you overgrown imbecile," Doli said. "I also speak French, Spanish, Comanche, Apache, and Sioux. Do you speak English? Because you sound as dumb as you are big."

Emmet, seated next to Jack and opposite Greenhill, grinned.

"What's this all about, Colonel?" Emmet asked.

Doli glared at Jack. "Idiot with the sense of a goat," she said in Spanish.

"What?" Jack said. "What did you say?"

"She said you have nice table manners for a man so large," Emmet said.

Jack looked at Doli.

She smiled.

"And you smell just as bad," she said in French.

"I want you to read these telegrams," Greenhill said. "The first one I sent to Judge Parker in Fort Smith yesterday morning. The second is his response."

Greenhill handed Emmet a sheet of paper.

Emmet read the telegrams. "Is this on the level?"

"Very much so," Greenhill said.

"What?" Jack asked.

Doli grinned at Jack. "For so big a man, I bet you are a little boy between the legs," she said in Comanche.

Understanding Comanche, Emmet grinned.

"What?" Jack said. "What did she say?"

"Nothing. Forget it," Emmet said.

"Colonel, what's this all about?" Jack said. "Why is she here?"

"After Two Hawks and his army attacked the outpost at Fort Smith last year, he and a small following have been living in the mountains north of here," Greenhill said. "Right under our noses. There is a trading post just north of Boulder beside the mountains that is friendly with many native tribes. Doli makes regular visits to this trading post for supplies and such. Doli, why don't you tell the marshal the rest."

"Your woman probably looks like a pig and smells like a cow," Doli said to Jack in Spanish.

"In English, please," Greenhill said.

Doli smiled at Jack. "My husband enjoys coffee with sugar," she said. "I go once a month to the post to get them for him. I also get the English newspapers that he likes to read. He read a story about the stolen herd and nine murdered men from the reservation in Fort Smith. He sent me to see Colonel Greenhill to send a telegram to Judge Parker to volunteer his services to find the guilty men. He requested Emmet Youngblood to come to the army fort in Denver to meet with him."

"Just Emmet?" Jack asked.

Doli smiled. "Yes."

"This is crazy," Jack said. "Why would Two Hawks want to help us?"

"He enjoys killing white men," Doli said.

"You're crazy if you think we're—" Jack said.

"Where is he?" Emmet asked.

"You will never find him unless I take you to him," Doli said.

"For his help in tracking the men who killed the nine from the reservation, what does Two Hawks want in return?" Emmet said.

"Emmet, you can't be—" Jack said.

"He wants to live in peace. He wants to know that we are no longer wanted by your law," Doli said.

"Amnesty," Emmet said. "He wants amnesty."

"Amnesty? What is that word in Comanche?" Doli asked.

"There isn't one," Emmet said. "Amnesty means that, in exchange for his help, the law will forgive his crimes."

"Yes, that is what he wants," Doli said. "Amnesty."

"Emmet, you're not seriously considering this?" Jack said.

Emmet handed Jack Judge Parker's telegram. It read *Give Two Hawks what he wants in exchange for his help.*

"Shit," Jack said.

"That word I understand." Doli smiled at Jack. "And you smell just like it," she said in French.

"Can Two Hawks track the men responsible for killing those men and stealing the reservation herd?" Emmet asked.

"He can," Doli said. "But you can't. We both know that."

"We'll find us another tracker," Jack said.

Doli smiled at Jack. "Who?" she asked. "From where? And if

you could, how much time will you lose?"

Jack looked at Emmet.

Emmet nodded.

"Damn," Jack said.

"When can we leave?" Emmet asked.

"Tomorrow morning," Doli said. "It's two days' ride. That is all I will tell you for now."

"How do we know we aren't walking into a trap?" Jack asked.

"You don't," Doli said. "But I will tell you this. My husband lives by his word. He will keep his end of the bargain. Will you?"

Emmet nodded. "I have Sioux and Apache blood in my veins," he said in Comanche. "Two Hawks knows I will keep my word, or he wouldn't have sent you for me."

Doli looked at Jack. "And the big dumb one, does he feel as you?" she said in Comanche.

"Jack is a great lawman and will abide by what Judge Parker ordered," Emmet said in Comanche. "But it is wise to stay on his good side."

Doli nodded. "Then we leave in the morning," she said in English.

"Now that we've settled this, I had the cook prepare chocolate ice cream for dessert," Greenhill said.

"What's ice cream?" Jack asked.

"Imbecile," Doli said in Spanish.

Jack stared at her. "Do not provoke me past my breaking point," he said in Chinese. "That would be unwise and very unhealthy."

Stunned, everyone looked at Jack.

"What language is that?" Doli asked.

"Damn," Emmet said.

Greenhill put Emmet and Jack up for the night in quarters

reserved for guests. It was a comfortable room with two large beds.

In his bed, Emmet smoked his pipe and read his law book by lantern light.

Jack sprawled out on his bed, looked at the ceiling, and smoked a cigarette.

"Emmet?" Jack said.

"Yeah?"

"How do we know we can trust Two Hawks?" Jack asked.

Emmet rolled over and looked at Jack.

"Two Hawks is a full blood Comanche War Chief," Emmet said. "He would rather die than break his word. The only exception is if we break ours."

"I guess we'll just have to trust him," Jack said.

"By the way, when did you learn Chinese?" Emmet asked.

"Chao-xing teaches me," Jack said.

"She will make a fine wife, Jack," Emmet said.

Jack blew a smoke ring at the ceiling.

"We best get some sleep," Jack said.

Chapter Seventeen

Greenhill saw them off at the gate.

"Thank you for the supplies, Colonel," Emmet said. "If I could ask you to send these telegrams for me, I'd appreciate it."

"I'll send them myself," Greenhill said.

"Thanks," Emmet said. "Doli, lead the way."

With Doli riding point, they traveled northwest and into the foothills of the Rocky Mountains. They rode without speaking until noon, when they broke for lunch and to rest the horses.

Jack made a fire and put on some food and coffee.

"You are the one who would become the lawyer," Doli said to Emmet as they ate beside the fire.

"Hopefully," Emmet said.

"It takes much learning," Doli said.

"Very much," Emmet said.

"When you get this learning, you will quit being a lawman?" Doli said.

"In a sense, a lawyer is a lawman," Emmet said. "For the court. I plan to work for Judge Parker and make sure those living on the reservation don't get cheated."

"I would say it is a little late for that," Doli said. "Wouldn't you?"

"I'm not saying I can repair all the damage that's been done, nobody can," Emmet said. "But maybe I can help."

"Last year, the Mexican woman Two Hawks captured, she was yours?" Doli asked.

"Yes."

"What happened to her?"

"She is now my wife," Emmet said.

"Then I am glad Two Hawks wouldn't let me kill her as I wanted," Doli said.

"That makes two of us," Emmet said.

"Let's pack up and get moving," Jack said.

By late afternoon, Doli rode them deep into the foothills and directly to the mountains.

"Tomorrow we will reach the trading post," Doli said. "It is the only store between Denver and Boulder along the mountains."

"What's in Boulder?" Jack asked.

"White men," Doli said.

"All white men aren't bad, you know," Jack said.

"That's depends on what color skin you're wearing," Doli said.

Late in the afternoon, Doli led them to a small mountain stream and dismounted.

"By noon tomorrow we will reach the trading post," Doli said. "Build a fire. I am going to take a bath."

"A bath? Now?" Jack said.

"Because you smell like a wet dog is no reason I should," Doli said and walked to the stream. She removed her boots and then, without hesitation or inhibition, pulled her dress over her body and tossed it aside.

Jack stared at Doli as she waded into the stream.

"Jack," Emmet said.

"What?"

"Give her some privacy," Emmet said.

"Did you see what she . . . ?"

"No, and you shouldn't either," Emmet said. "Tend the horses while I make a fire."

With just her head above water, Doli said, "Do you have a bar of soap?"

Night settled in around them as they ate supper beside the fire.

Doli looked at Jack. "I have heard that you have killed many men," she said.

"I have," Jack said.

"Because the law says you can?" Doli said.

"Because they broke the law and weren't willing to pay for their crimes in court," Jack said.

"So you made them pay?" Doli said.

"In a sense," Jack said.

"Then explain to me how you are different than Two Hawks," Doli said.

"I didn't deliberately set out to kill a man," Jack said.

"Neither did Two Hawks."

"Enough of that," Emmet said. "Doli, when we reach Two Hawks, how many men does he have with him?"

"Two," Doli said. "Are you afraid?"

"No. I just like to know what we're dealing with," Emmet said.

"Two Hawks doesn't plan to take his men with him when he leaves to scout for you," Doli said.

"Then why have them?" Jack asked.

"Ask Two Hawks," Doli said.

"I will," Jack said. "And a few other things, as well."

Emmet looked at Jack. "You hold that Irish temper of yours, Jack."

"Yeah, yeah," Jack said.

"I mean it," Emmet said. "If Two Hawks is willing to track for us, it might be the only chance we have at this point of catching those men."

Jack tossed his plate to the ground and stood up. He walked to the stream and rolled a cigarette.

Emmet looked at Doli. "And you quit aggravating him," he said. "My brother has a limit as to what he'll take, and you're pushing it."

"He is fun to tease," Doli said.

"You won't think it's so much fun if you're on the wrong end of it," Emmet said. "Now leave him be until we reach Two Hawks."

Doli nodded. "I will leave him be," she said.

"Good."

The trading post was a log cabin set against a hillside. It carried most dry goods and had a bar on one end. A small corral with a few horses in it stood to the right. A few men dressed as mountain men were on the porch, drinking whiskey from a jug.

Emmet, Jack, and Doli rode to the corral and dismounted.

"Water the horses," Emmet said. "I'll go in and pick up a few things."

"Get coffee, sugar, and the newspapers for Two Hawks," Doli said. "And tobacco for his pipe."

Jack led his horse and the pinto to the water trough. Doli followed with her horse.

Emmet went to the porch, walked past the two men, and entered the post.

The two men on the porch looked at Doli.

"Right nice looking squaw," one of them said.

The other snickered.

"Looks like she's got herself two bucks," the other man said. "And from the looks of her, she can handle a few more."

"Hey, squaw, how 'bout you come up here and show us what you got?" the first man said.

"And we'll show you what we got," the second man said.

Both men snickered as they pulled on the jug.

Doli looked at Jack. His back was to the men, and his face appeared hard and tight. She wondered: if she was white would he allow the men to speak to her that way?

One of the men stood, unbuttoned his pants, and began to urinate over the porch railing. "Hey, squaw, this is for you," he said.

Jack turned and looked at the man. Doli saw the look in his eyes and waited to see what Jack would do.

Jack stood motionless for a moment as he watched the man urinate.

Then, with speed that defied so large a man, Jack walked to the porch, reached up, grabbed the man by the shirt, and flung him over the porch and to the ground.

The man landed with a loud thud. Immediately Jack picked him up and pummeled the man until the man fell, unconscious.

The man on the porch had a rifle. He stood and aimed it at Jack as Jack climbed the porch stairs.

"Now you hold it right there," the man said.

Jack ignored the rifle aimed at him, slapped it away, and grabbed the man. In one quick motion, Jack flung him over the railing to the ground.

Jack hopped over the railing and simply kicked the man until he was unconscious.

Without saying a word, Jack returned to his horse.

Doli looked at him.

Emmet appeared on the porch with an armload of supplies. He walked down the stairs and glanced at the two unconscious men.

"What happened here?" Emmet asked.

"They aggravated him," Doli said.

★ ★ ★ ★ ★

Jack and Emmet rode behind Doli as she took them higher into the mountains.

Emmet broke away and rode next to Doli.

"How much farther?" he said.

"An hour at most," Doli said.

"What happened back there at the store?" Emmet asked.

"He defended my honor," Doli said.

"I see," Emmet said.

"He has the blood," Doli said.

"Our mother is part Sioux and Apache," Emmet said. "She's half Irish, and our father was all Irish. Jack has the blood, all right. And when it's up, stand out of his way."

Doli nodded. "Would you have defended my honor?"

"Yes, but I would have taken a more delicate approach," Emmet said.

"He just simply beat them senseless," Doli said.

"That he didn't kill them is Jack's way of being delicate," Emmet said.

Doli smiled and then pointed ahead. "Through that narrow pass," she said.

They rode single file through a long and narrow pass that emptied out to a lush meadow of wildflowers and tall grass.

Smoke rose up in the distance.

As they rode closer, they could see three tipis. Several horses were tethered to ropes anchored to the ground.

"Follow, but not too close," Doli said.

She raced her horse ahead, dismounted beside Two Hawks, and embraced him warmly.

"How were you treated?" he asked.

"Very well," she said. "I had fresh steak at the fort and ice cream."

Two Hawks nodded. "And them?"

"They are men of honor," Doli said.

"I wouldn't have sent for them and entrusted them with your life if they weren't," Two Hawks said.

Doli nodded and entered a tipi. She returned, holding a baby and with a white man by her side, as Jack and Emmet arrived.

"Emmet Youngblood," Two Hawks said.

Emmet dismounted. "Two Hawks," he said.

Jack stayed mounted and looked at Two Hawks.

Emmet looked at the white man beside Doli. He was oddly dressed, in mountain gear with slick rubber boots on his feet.

"Who are you?" Emmet asked.

"Name is Coors. From Golden."

"Not with an accent like that, you aren't," Emmet said.

"By way of Prussia," Coors said.

"What are you doing here with Two Hawks?" Emmet asked.

"I make beer," Coors said. "In Golden. I own the Golden Brewery."

"But what are you doing here?" Emmet said.

Quietly, Two Hawks moved away from his two men and approached Jack, who was still in the saddle.

"Oh, well, I've always believed that to make perfect beer, you need perfect water," Coors said. "I've been searching for the perfect stream for years now. I believe I found it when my horse took a fall and I had to shoot him. I'm afraid on foot, I became terribly lost. These gentlemen rescued me."

"Rescued you?" Emmet said.

On his horse, Jack looked at Two Hawks. "Something you want?"

"I am admiring your fine animal," Two Hawks said.

Jack slung his right leg over the saddle and slid to the ground. Two Hawks was a large and powerful warrior, but Jack towered over him by a good head or more.

"Give me one reason why I don't kill you where you stand and your two men?" Jack said and looked at Uday and Little Buffalo. "Yeah, I remember you two."

"I will give you one reason," Two Hawks said. "Judge Parker. If he didn't agree to my terms, you would not have come here."

"Maybe I agreed just so I could have the pleasure of killing you myself," Jack said.

"Jack, that's not true and you know it, so stop blowing smoke," Emmet said. "We're here to do a job and . . ."

Jack glared at Two Hawks. "All those innocent people you killed, huh," he said.

"Innocent?" Two Hawks said. "Innocent of what? My people lived here free five hundred years before your Columbus. You whites think you own the world. You come and take by force what isn't yours, and then you act surprised when those who were here first fight back for what is theirs. Innocent, you say? The only thing that surprises me about you whites is how shocked you are when I kill them."

Emmet sighed. "Two Hawks, let's talk."

Emmet and Two Hawks sat close to the fire as they ate off tin plates. Doli had made coffee, and they drank from cups.

"We lost the trail in a pass in Mount Sunflower," Emmet said. "Our tracker, Red Moon, was ambushed by a drifter, and we took him to Pueblo."

"Mount Sunflower is in Kansas," Two Hawks said.

"Red Moon believed they were headed northwest to some secret hiding place," Emmet said.

"Northwest to where?" Two Hawks said. "Who would buy a herd without papers? It would take a great deal of time to change the brands on so many."

"That's how I see it," Emmet said. "My guess is they have a place to hole up and take their time changing brands, and then will take them into Canada."

Two Hawks nodded. "I'm searching for the word," he said. "Prearranged. They must have had an agreement with a buyer in Canada before stealing the herd."

"That's how I see it," Emmet said.

"Have you fresh pipe tobacco?" Two Hawks asked.

"Yes."

"Let's smoke."

In a tipi with Coors, Jack lit a cigarette from the fire in the center and said, "What did you mean, you were looking for the perfect water?"

"The clearest water I could find," Coors said. "The better the water, the better the beer. I believe I found what I'm looking for, if I can locate it again."

"Mr. Coors, you're crazy," Jack said.

Coors grinned. "I've been told that before," he said. "I expect I'll be told it again."

"How is it these folks found you?"

"I was wandering around lost and there they were," Coors said. "They said they were headed to a place, took me with them, and here I am."

"Unharmed?" Jack said. "That doesn't sound like Two Hawks."

"I assure you, they've harmed me in no way," Coors said. "In fact, I probably wouldn't be alive if they hadn't come along."

Jack sighed.

"Well, they said we're leaving early in the morning," Coors said. "I'm going to get some sleep."

"You know what happened to Yellow Sky was nobody's fault," Emmet said. "People get sick and people die, and there is nothing we can do about it. My wife died giving birth. There is nobody to blame for things like that."

"My people live on a reservation and not the land they were born on. Who is to blame for that?" Two Hawks said.

Emmet puffed on his pipe.

Two Hawks puffed on his pipe.

"The people in Washington are not honest," Two Hawks said. "Their word is useless. They are infected with greed and power, and to them, my people are fleas on a buffalo's back."

"I'm sorry to say that I agree with you, but not all white men are like that," Emmet said. "Nobody cared more or loved your people more than Henry Teasel, and there are others like him."

"I was sorry to hear what happened to Henry," Two Hawks said. "He was good to my people."

"Straight-up answer, can you track these outlaws?" Emmet said.

"Yes."

"Judge Parker will keep his word," Emmet said.

"I would not have asked for it otherwise," Two Hawks said. "And the word of your brother?"

"Ask Doli about the trading post," Emmet said.

Doli was naked inside her blanket with her infant son in her arms when Two Hawks entered the tipi and closed the flap.

"What happened at the trading post?" he asked in Comanche.

Doli rolled over and looked up at Two Hawks.

"The small one went into the trading post for supplies," Doli said in Comanche. "We waited outside and watered the horses. Two men on the porch started to call me names. Squaw and such. One of them took out his manhood and started to piss in my direction."

"Piss?" Two Hawks said.

"Yes," Doli said. "And the big one, he never said a word. He simply walked to the two men and beat them unconscious."

"He defended your honor?" Two Hawks said.

"It surprised the hell out of me, too," Doli said.

Two Hawks stripped naked and then got beside Doli under the blanket.

"Tell me about the ice cream," he said.

CHAPTER EIGHTEEN

After breakfast, Two Hawks told Uday and Little Buffalo to take Coors to Golden and then return to their camp with Doli and his infant son.

"Please come visit me in Golden," Coors told Two Hawks.

"I doubt I will ever get to Golden, but if I do, I will visit," Two Hawks said.

Jack and Emmet were already mounted when Two Hawks mounted his horse and joined him.

"How far to Boulder?" Emmet asked. "We can take the railroad there back to Denver and save us days in the saddle. And buy you some new clothes."

"What is wrong with my clothes?" Two Hawks asked.

"Not a thing," Emmet said. "If you were leading a war party."

"Who says that I'm not?" Two Hawks said and dashed his horse ahead.

Around noon, they rested the horses for one hour. They ate a cold lunch of biscuits and jerky with water.

As Jack rolled a cigarette, he looked at Two Hawks. "Tell me something," he said. "Not a year ago, you were hell bent on killing every white man you set eyes upon. What changed your outlook?"

"Reality, mostly," Two Hawks said. "The telephone, the light bulb, more and more railroads across the country. I read all your newspapers. I read a story recently about a man in

Germany who claimed to have invented what he calls the horse-less carriage. They say by the time my son is fifteen years, they will be everywhere. My people can't fight your people and hope to survive any longer."

"We all feel that way at one time or another," Emmet said. "Who knows what the world will look like by the time my daughters are my age? I suspect it'll be entirely different than at this moment, but however it looks, we'll have to adapt to it or we'll die."

"How does a horseless carriage work exactly?" Jack asked.

"The story didn't say, just that it will run on what it called combustion," Two Hawks said.

"Well, I don't see how man can exist without a horse," Jack said.

"Twenty years ago it took six months to go from New York to California by covered wagon," Emmet said. "Now you can do it in ten days on the railroad."

"And miss a lot of beautiful country in between," Jack said.

"The price you pay for progress sometimes is a lack of beauty," Emmet said.

"Speaking of progress, we best make some," Jack said.

They reached Boulder by four in the afternoon. A train was scheduled to leave for Denver at five.

Several dozen people waiting for the train glanced uncomfortably at Two Hawks as he sat on a bench outside the station. Emmet and Jack sat with him on the bench after Emmet purchased tickets.

"Do you see all these people?" Two Hawks said. "If I weren't in the company of two lawmen, they would run for the hills at the sight of me."

"Pay them no mind," Emmet said.

Two Hawks glared at a woman holding a baby and growled.

The woman scurried to the other end of the platform.

Two Hawks grinned as he took out his pipe.

Shortly after the train left the station, the conductor entered the car Emmet, Jack, and Two Hawks were seated in to punch tickets.

"He can't ride in here," the conductor said as he looked at Two Hawks. "Company policy."

"Your policy stinks," Jack said.

"I don't make policy, Marshal," the conductor said.

"Where do you suggest he ride?" Emmet asked.

"He can ride in the boxcar," the conductor said.

"With the horses and mules?" Jack said.

"This man is our prisoner," Emmet said. "If he rides in the boxcar, we have to as well, in order to keep an eye on him."

"Prisoner, huh?" the conductor said. "It's only an hour or so to Denver. Why don't I put you up in the executive car, seeing as how it's empty on this run."

"Executive car?" Jack said.

"Follow me," the conductor said.

The executive car was as fine as any first-rate hotel room in New York or San Francisco. It was decorated with fine leather chairs and sofa, red lanterns, and even had a full liquor cabinet.

Jack filled three glasses with excellent bourbon and he, Emmet, and Two Hawks enjoyed a quiet and uneventful ride to Denver.

Colonel Greenhill sat behind his desk and looked at Two Hawks.

"This time last year, you were the most hunted man in the country," Greenhill said.

"Things have a way of coming around, Colonel," Two Hawks said.

"Thanks to Judge Parker, they surely do," Greenhill said.

"I will abide by the agreement," Two Hawks said. "Will your government?"

"Unless you give us a reason not to, we will," Greenhill said. "Now, there has been a new development since you left. A herd of four hundred from the Chisum Ranch was stolen en route to the army in Dallas. Six cowboys were killed in the process. I took the liberty of wiring Judge Parker, and here is his reply."

Greenhill handed Emmet a telegram.

Emmet read it and looked at Jack.

"Looks like we're going to the Chisum Ranch," he said.

"Fresh tracks will be easier to follow than the tracks in Mount Sunflower," Two Hawks said.

"Colonel, I suggest you swear in Two Hawks as an official army scout," Emmet said. "The rank of Sergeant Major should do nicely."

Greenhill sighed. "Two Hawks, raise your right hand and repeat after me. Then report to the quartermaster to draw a uniform."

"Colonel, do you have a schedule for the railroad?" Emmet asked.

"I do. Next train to Roswell leaves at eight tomorrow morning," Greenhill said.

"Then we have time for a hot meal and a bath," Emmet said.

"You can sit at my table for evening chow," Greenhill said.

The evening meal consisted of beef stew, salad, and fresh loaves of crusty bread with coffee or milk.

"The army doesn't lack for food, does it, Colonel?" Two Hawks said.

"No, it does not," Greenhill said. "Wars are won and lost on an army's stomach."

"Tell me, Colonel, am I drawing pay?" Two Hawks asked.

"A scout's pay with your rank is forty dollars a month,"

Greenhill said. "I can advance you the money if you'd like."

"Keep it, Colonel," Two Hawks said. "I'm not doing this for the pay."

"No, I suppose you're not," Greenhill said.

"Colonel, I'm wearing my last clean shirt," Emmet said. "May we use the fort laundry?"

"Of course," Greenhill said.

"Colonel, were there any other details about the latest rustling?" Jack asked.

"The cowboys set out for Dallas," Greenhill said. "They made it forty miles due west of the Chisum Ranch before they were attacked and the herd stolen. A squad of soldiers from Santa Fe was dispatched and tracked the herd to the northern section of the Rio Grande, where they lost the trail. Maybe by now there is more information, but if there is, it will have to wait until you see Miss Chisum."

"I expect she is not a happy woman about now," Jack said.

"No, she is not," Greenhill said.

"Colonel, have you any ice cream?" Two Hawks asked.

Greenhill sighed. "Vanilla and chocolate. Which would you like?"

"Both," Two Hawks said.

Emmet and Two Hawks sat on the porch of the guest housing and smoked their pipes and drank coffee.

"The Grande goes well into Colorado, and it is down this time of year," Two Hawks said. "The people behind this know the country. They are well organized and well equipped."

"Too well organized," Emmet said.

"What do you mean?" Two Hawks asked.

"How did they know about the thousand head going to the reservation, or the six hundred outside of Dodge or this latest herd?" Emmet said.

"A spy?" Two Hawks said.

"There would have to be more than one of them for the news to get around so quick," Emmet said. "Even Jesse James and the Dalton boys were not so well organized—as they found out in Minnesota."

Jack approached the porch and took a chair. "I sent the telegrams to Ma and Judge Parker. They should have them by morning."

Two Hawks puffed on his pipe as he thought for a moment. "I know your mother," he said. "She is a good woman. She carries the faith, as did Yellow Sky. I am sorry she was injured last year when my people attacked your home."

"She could have died, and so could Chao-xing. And the children, for that matter," Jack said.

"There is no point talking about it now," Emmet said. "We have a job at hand to do, and we best keep our thoughts on that."

Jack looked at Two Hawks. "You better be the tracker Red Moon was," he said.

Emmet stood up. "I'm going to the privy and then to bed. Morning chow is served at five-thirty around here. I suggest you get some sleep, or go hungry come morning."

Emmet stepped off the porch and went around back to the outhouse.

"He is a sensible man, your brother," Two Hawks said.

"If you do anything to put him in danger, I will kill you where you stand," Jack said. "Just so we're clear on that point."

"You still don't understand, do you?" Two Hawks said.

"Enlighten me," Jack said as he rolled a cigarette.

"This is my land, my country. You stole it from me," Two Hawks said. "I should thank you for that?"

Jack struck a match and lit the cigarette.

Two Hawks stood and entered the guesthouse.

"Hell," Jack said.

CHAPTER NINETEEN

Amy rode to town in Duff's buggy, although she insisted on handling the reins. Maria, Chao-xing, Mary, and Sarah followed in Amy's buggy.

Chao-xing took the reins. Maria sat beside her. Going on four months now, Maria's stomach showed a nice bump where it used to be flat.

"When are you having the baby?" Mary asked from behind Maria.

"It should come around late November or early December," Maria said.

"Is it a boy baby or a girl?" Sarah asked.

"I honestly don't know," Maria said. "There is no way to tell. We'll just have to wait and see what pops out."

"Are you afraid?" Mary asked. "I heard it's supposed to hurt."

Maria grinned. "No, I'm not afraid. If it hurts, it's the way nature intended it to be," she said.

"What about you, Chao-xing? Why don't you have a baby?" Sarah asked.

Chao-xing looked at Maria, and both women smiled.

"Perhaps you should ask your Uncle Jack that question when he gets home," Chao-xing said.

"I will," Sarah said. "Although I don't know what he has to do with it."

Chao-xing and Maria laughed.

"Quite a bit, I'm afraid," Chao-xing said.

"I don't know what you . . ." Sarah said.

"That's enough questions for now," Maria said. "We're almost in town."

Before he mounted his horse, Two Hawks looked at Emmet and Jack.

"How do you like my uniform?" Two Hawks asked.

"It's a right nice fit," Emmet said. "Sergeant Major."

"Perhaps I should take the colonel's offer for pay and buy a sidearm," Two Hawks said. "I feel naked unarmed."

Jack opened his saddlebags, dug out his spare Colt and holster, and tossed it to Two Hawks.

"I expect it back in the same condition it was given," Jack said.

"Let's say goodbye to the colonel," Emmet said. "We have a train to catch."

In front of Greenly's General Store, Amy said, "Girls, I am taking Mr. Duff to his newspaper and then home. Do your shopping, and I'll be back in two hours. I don't want to ride home in the dark."

Amy cracked the reins and drove the buggy three blocks to Duff's newspaper.

She got down first, lent a hand to Duff, and he stepped down to the street. He winced a bit as the stitches tugged, and he paused to catch his breath.

"Another week in bed would have served you well," Amy said.

"I'm fine, Amy," Duff said. "And weeks behind in work as it is."

He unlocked the door and looked at the pile of mail that had been dropped through the mail slot. As he picked up the mail,

Duff said, "Have you given my proposal to write for me consideration?"

"I have, and I'll do it on one condition," Amy said.

"And that is?"

"I use a pen name," Amy said. "People might take the stories more seriously if a man were writing them than if Amy Youngblood wrote them. Don't you agree?"

"Sadly, yes," Duff said. "We shall begin tomorrow."

"Tomorrow is Sunday."

"So it is," Duff said. "Then maybe you can drive me home. I'll make us some tea, and we can scan through all this mail?"

As Two Hawks looked out the window of the train, he said, "I notice that, wearing this uniform, no one questions where I sit. Take it off, and I'm just another savage."

"Take it off and you'll be naked, and I'd have to arrest you for indecent exposure," Jack said.

Emmet, his nose in his law book, glanced up at Jack and grinned.

"We will need a good mule and supplies once we reach Roswell," Two Hawks said.

"We have a mule," Emmet said. "And you're sitting next to him."

Jack placed his hat over his eyes and said, "Funny. Wake me when we reach Roswell."

"I'm afraid things got a bit dusty while I was away," Duff said.

He lit a lantern in the living room.

Amy glanced at the large collection of books in the bookcase against the wall.

"Make yourself comfortable while I put on the kettle," Duff said.

While Duff went to the kitchen, Amy scanned the collection

of books. Duff was a voracious reader, to say the least. Twain, Verne, Plato, Shakespeare, and dozens of other classics filled the shelves.

After a time, Duff returned with a tray that held a teapot, cups, sugar, and spoons. "I'm afraid I don't have fresh milk," he said.

He set the tray on a table and looked at Amy.

"Are you feeling ill?" he asked.

"Why do you ask?" Amy said.

"Your cheeks are rather flushed."

"How old are you, Stanly? Sixty-two?"

"Yes, but . . . ?"

"I will turn sixty-one shortly," Amy said.

"I don't . . ."

"We are running out of time," Amy said.

"I'm afraid I don't understand," Duff said.

"Take me to your bedroom, Stanly," Amy said.

Duff stared at her.

"Now," Amy said.

"Right now?"

"Yes, Stanly, right now," Amy said.

Sheriff Pietrie met Emmet, Jack, and Two Hawks on the station platform in Roswell.

"Got your wire this morning," Pietrie said.

"I expect Miss Chisum is none too happy right about now," Emmet said.

"Mad as a wet hen covered in oil," Pietrie said.

"Did you ride to the Grande with the army?" Jack asked.

"I did," Pietrie said. "Even crossed it with the army, but it was no use. We lost the trail in the Grande, and they had too much head start on us. This your tracker?"

"Sergeant Major Two Hawks," Emmet said.

Pietrie looked at Two Hawks. "Good luck to you, sir. You'll need it."

"How far to the Chisum Ranch?" Jack said.

"Head north and ride for about an hour," Pietrie said. "You'll see it."

Still in bed, Duff watched Amy lace up her shoes.

"I didn't disappoint you, did I, Amy?" Duff asked.

Amy paused and turned to Duff.

"Heavens, no," she said. "Why would you think something like that?"

"My experience since my wife died has been quite limited," Duff said. "None, I'm afraid."

"We're both a bit rusty in that department, Stanly," Amy said. "But if my girls weren't waiting for me, I would stay and do it again. As it is, I'm late. Now don't go opening those stitches, and I will see you tomorrow at church."

Sally Chisum wore dark pants with a white blouse and boots as she served lemonade on the porch of her ranch house.

"Miss Chisum, we understand that the four hundred head were on the way to Dallas when they were rustled and your men killed," Emmet said. "About forty miles west of your ranch?"

"Not west of. Still on," Sally said as she sat next to Jack.

"I'm afraid I don't understand," Emmet said.

"Ride forty miles west, and you're still on my property," Sally said.

"Who discovered your men?" Emmet asked.

"I have a dozen or more men who do nothing but ride the ranges, pick up strays, and kill wolves and such," Sally said. "They ride in pairs and came across the site the next day. Otherwise, it would have been two weeks before Dallas reported the herd late."

"Why would Dallas know the herd was late?" Jack asked.

"It's customary to telegraph the Cattlemen's Association with the expected time of arrival," Sally said. "All brands are registered, as you know, and by wiring, it cuts down on rustlers trying to pass off stolen brands at auction."

"It fits," Jack said.

"What fits, Marshal?" Sally said.

"We have a theory that eventually the rustlers will cross into Canada and sell one large herd to a buyer," Emmet said.

"An operation like that would require twenty or more men good with a rope and cattle," Sally said. "Not to mention a range large enough to accommodate a large herd while brands are being altered."

Sally looked at Two Hawks.

"What do you say, Sergeant Major?" she asked.

"You make good lemonade," Two Hawks said.

Sally stared at Two Hawks.

"I have been tracking man and beast since I first learned to walk," Two Hawks said. "They may have a head start on us, but I will find them. You can bet your last acre of land on that fact."

Sally nodded. "I believe you, Sergeant Major," she said. "My cook will have supper ready in one hour. You gentlemen can freshen up in the bathroom. I have indoor plumbing for your convenience."

Amy took the reins and drove the buggy home. Maria sat beside her while Chao-xing and the girls occupied the back seat.

"How was your visit with Mr. Duff?" Maria asked.

"Fine," Amy said.

"Eventful?" Maria said.

Amy looked at Maria. "Why do you ask?"

Maria leaned over and whispered in Amy's ear. "Your shoes

are on the wrong foot."

Amy grinned. "I wondered why my feet hurt," she said.

Jack, Emmet, and Two Hawks stared at the indoor toilet that consisted of a large tank, a chain, and a seat with a lid.

"You ever see anything like this?" Jack asked.

"Not even when I was in school in Boston," Emmet said.

"What is it, and how does it work?" Two Hawks said.

"Gentlemen, is there a problem?" Sally's butler asked as he entered the bathroom.

"We're . . . we . . . what is that?" Jack said and pointed to the toilet.

"That is an indoor toilet, Marshal," the butler said.

"Toilet?" Jack said.

"From London, England," the butler said. "It is called the Crapper and works on gravity-fed water from a tank on the roof. It's quite old in theory, going all the way back to the ancient Romans."

"How does it work?" Emmet asked.

"It's quite simple, really. You sit, do your business, and when done, you pull the chain on the tank. Gravity does the rest."

Two Hawks looked at the toilet. "I'll be damned."

"Dinner is in the formal dining room in fifteen minutes," the butler said.

"Although my uncle never married, he loved to host large family dinners," Sally said from her seat at the head of the table. "I spent many a summer living here growing up, but I never dreamed that one day I would be the one to carry on his legacy."

The table had chairs for sixteen, although Jack, Emmet, and Two Hawks sat near Sally.

"Miss Chisum, may I be so bold as to ask you a question?" Emmet said.

Eating soup, Sally smiled and put the spoon down. "Mr. Teasel asked the same question," she said. "It is true that my uncle befriended Billy the Kid, and he spent many days and nights here and at the summer camp by the lake. I have a tin plate of Billy playing croquet at the lake around here somewhere. Someday I will have it developed."

The butler entered pushing a serving trolley and served thick steaks with potatoes and gravy.

"I was terribly upset to hear about Mr. Teasel," Sally said. "I wired Judge Parker and returned the twenty thousand to the bank in Fort Smith."

"That was very generous of you, Miss Chisum," Emmet said.

"Now may I ask you a question?" Sally said. "What are you prepared to do about these rustlers?"

"Track them and bring them to justice," Emmet said.

"I realize that," Sally said. "What I mean is, how far and how long are you willing to go? If your pursuits don't bring results after a month, two months, will you quit and wait for the next herd to disappear?"

"Miss Chisum, you sound like you have something on your mind," Emmet said.

"I have contacted Pinkerton's in Chicago," Sally said. "A representative will arrive next week sometime to discuss details."

"Miss Chisum, you are certainly free to hire whoever you wish," Emmet said. "It won't prevent us from doing our job. However, this matter is a federal investigation, and any information Pinkerton's might uncover must be shared with the federal government."

"That is understood," Sally said. She looked at Two Hawks. "What do you say, Sergeant Major?"

"Have you any ice cream?" Two Hawks asked.

"Why, yes, we do," Sally said.

★ ★ ★ ★ ★

After supper, Jack, Emmet, and Two Hawks drank coffee on the front porch and watched the late June sun slowly set.

Jack rolled a cigarette. Emmet and Two Hawks smoked their pipes.

Lost in thought, Emmet sighed softly.

"Something bothering you, little brother?" Jack asked.

"Yes, but I don't know what," Emmet said. "Just something nagging at me."

"About Pinkerton's?" Jack said.

"No. Miss Chisum has the right to spend her money as she sees fit," Emmet said.

"You ain't homesick, are you?" Jack asked.

"Of course, I'm homesick," Emmet said. "You think I fancy another month of sleeping on the ground when my wife and a warm bed are home waiting for me?"

The question went unanswered, as the porch door opened and Sally came out holding a cup of coffee. She sat next to Jack.

"My foreman picked out our best mule for you, and I had my butler put together one hundred pounds of supplies," she said. "Will that do?"

"More than," Emmet said. "Thank you."

Sally looked up at the fresh night sky. "I love watching the stars come out. I have since I was a child," she said.

"It's a beautiful sky," Emmet agreed.

"Gentlemen, I believe I will turn in," Sally said. "I'll see you off in the morning."

"Excellent idea," Emmet said.

"Go on up. I want to sit a minute," Jack said.

Alone on the porch, Jack rolled another cigarette. He wouldn't admit it to Emmet, but he was homesick himself.

He didn't think it was possible to miss Chao-zing as much as he did, and thoughts of her dominated his dreams.

He vowed to be a better man to her once he returned home. He wondered if there was some other way to make a living that would keep him home, but if there was, he couldn't think of one.

Clerk in a store? What a miserable existence.

Cowboy for twenty-five dollars a month? Not likely.

It seemed all he was cut out to do in life was be a lawman.

How many more long trips away from home would Chao-xing tolerate before she decided she wasn't cut out to be the wife of a lawman?

The thought of her walking out on him rocked Jack clear to the bone.

He was determined not to let that happen.

The question still remained.

How?

CHAPTER TWENTY

Sally had the cook prepare a full breakfast before dawn and by sunrise Jack, Emmet, and Two Hawks were ready to ride.

"There's a fellow you might consider hiring," Emmet told Sally. "He's what they call a stock detective. He's good tracker and knows his way around cattle. Name is Tom Horn."

"I will look into that," Sally said.

Two Hawks took the lead, and Jack held the mule in tow. Emmet rode beside Jack.

"We'll need to make twenty miles or more today," Jack said.

Emmet nodded.

"Still working on what's bothering you?" Jack asked.

"I'm giving it some thought," Emmet said.

"Don't let it bother you too much," Jack said. "This is a bad bunch we're after, and it will get bloody. You'll need to keep a clear head or someone might shoot it off."

After church, Amy announced that everyone was going for a picnic by the creek near home.

Judge Parker handed her a telegram, and she read it aloud before they entered their buggies.

"Roswell in New Mexico," Amy said. "That's one town I've never heard of."

Duff drove Amy in his buggy, and the girls followed in Amy's.

The picnic consisted of fried chicken, fresh fruit, apple pie, and buckets of lemonade. Duff, Sarah, and Mary fished in the creek and caught several trout large enough for a nice supper.

The attack came so suddenly that for several seconds Mary was unaware that a large rattlesnake had bitten her on the left arm. She sat on a pile of rocks near the stream to scale the fish and dropped the knife. When she reached under the rocks for the knife, the sleeping snake awoke and struck out of fear.

Mary stood with the snake dangling from her left arm and screamed.

Duff reacted first. He ran to Mary, grabbed the snake by the head, and flung it into the creek.

Mary began to cry as he lowered her to the ground and pulled out his pocketknife.

"Maria, Chao-xing, take the buggy and go for Doctor Jefferson," Amy said. "Take Sarah with you."

"I'll need a piece of cloth," Duff said.

Amy ripped off a piece of her skirt and knelt beside Duff.

Mary's face was beaded with sweat and her eyes were glassy.

"Hold her down. Tight," Duff said.

As Amy held Mary, Duff used his pocketknife to slice open the puncture holes and bleed the wound. As the wound bled, Duff sucked as much venom from it as he could.

"Give me the cloth," he said.

Duff wrapped the strip of cloth around Mary's upper left arm and tied it as tightly as possible. Then he lifted her and carried her to his buggy. Amy climbed in beside him and took the reins.

"Quickly," Duff said.

Around noon, Emmet, Jack, and Two Hawks rested the horses and mule for one hour. They ate a cold lunch of biscuits and water.

"I used that Crapper toilet," Jack said.

"And?" Emmet asked.

"Most disgusting thing I've ever seen," Jack said.

"Nobody ever said progress would always be pretty," Emmet said.

"Speaking of progress, we need to make twenty miles before dark," Two Hawks said. "So we can reach the site where they stole the herd by midday tomorrow. That will give us the chance to cross the Rio and scout ahead."

"Are you sure you can track them?" Jack asked.

"I can track them," Two Hawks said. "I learned to track almost before I could walk. Tracking is a part of our life. I can track them."

"Say you are right and you track them to wherever, what then?" Jack said. "You seem to have given this a lot of thought; you must have something planned for afterward."

"Amnesty is my plan," Two Hawks said. "The opportunity to raise my son as a man without having to worry that every day someone might show up to claim the reward for my life. I knew I would have to give my word, but only to someone whose word is also good. I knew Judge Parker and Emmet have such a word."

"I'm not sure how to take that," Jack said.

"Had you been alone, you would not have given your word," Two Hawks said. "You would have simply tried to kill me."

"If you fail to live up to your end of the agreement, don't think I can't or won't still kill you," Jack said.

"This is not a time for threats, Jack," Emmet said.

"Who said I was making one," Jack said. "Let's mount up, we're wasting daylight."

Doctor Jefferson came out of the bedroom holding his doctor's bag and entered the living room where everyone was gathered.

"She'll burn tonight for sure, but she won't lose the arm," he said.

"Oh, thank God," Amy said.

Jefferson looked at Duff. "You look a bit feverish, Mr. Duff. How much poison did you swallow?"

"I'm not sure," Duff said.

"No doubt you saved the child's life, but you'd better let me have a look at you," Jefferson said.

Jefferson felt Duff's neck and said, "A bit swollen. Better stay the night so Amy can keep an eye on you. In the meantime, I suggest hot soup with bread when Mary wakes up. A bit of that wouldn't hurt you none either, Mr. Duff."

"Is my sister going to be okay?" Sarah asked.

"In a few days she'll be good as new, thanks to Mr. Duff," Jefferson said.

Late in the afternoon, Two Hawks rode ahead to scout the route taken by the herd.

Emmet and Jack rode side by side with the mule in tow.

"You were a bit hard on Two Hawks earlier," Emmet said.

"A bit hard?" Jack said. "Did you forget last year?"

"I did not," Emmet said.

"He killed settlers and soldiers for no reason," Jack said. "People that have no good reason to be dead."

"He had a reason," Emmet said. "And we gave our word, as did the judge."

"You gave your word," Jack said. "I gave nothing."

"Do you want to go home?" Emmet asked.

"What kind of stupid question is that? Of course I want to go home."

"Right now that man is our best chance of tracking these outlaws," Emmet said. "You think on that, big brother, next time you miss Chao-xing."

Jack scowled at Emmet.

"You see that I'm right, don't you?" Emmet said.

"It doesn't mean I have to like it," Jack said.

Emmet looked in the distance.

"Two Hawks is coming, and he's bringing company," Emmet said.

After supper, Amy and Duff took coffee on the porch.

"How do you feel?" Amy asked.

"A bit of a sore throat, but otherwise fine," Duff said.

"That was a very brave thing to do," Amy said.

"I didn't think about it," Duff said. "The child needed help."

Amy stood up. "I think my horse might have a sore leg from running so hard," she said. "Perhaps you could take a look at it."

She left the porch and glanced back at Duff.

"I know nothing about sore horses, I'm afraid," Duff said.

"Come take a look anyway," Amy said and walked toward the barn. "You might see something else you like."

"Oh," Duff said and stood up.

Amy paused and looked at Duff.

"Coming?" she said.

"Hell, yes," Duff said and rushed off the porch.

Two Hawks returned with three of Sally Chisum's range cowboys. They were grateful for a hot cup of coffee and a plate of hot food. One of the cowboys was half black and half Cherokee. His name was Bill Pickett. The other two were Mexican.

Emmet looked at Pickett. "How old are you, son?"

"Fifteen or sixteen," Pickett said. "I ain't rightly sure."

"Can you read?" Emmet asked.

"No, sir," Pickett said. "My mother was born a slave down in Texas. My daddy was Cherokee."

"Miss Chisum hired you, knowing you can't read?" Emmet asked.

"Yes, sir," Pickett said. "I real good with a rope. She say if I do a good job for her, she'll have me some schooling when the season ends."

"Do you boys know where the herd was stolen?" Jack asked.

"Yes, Marshal," one of the Mexican cowboys said. "If you leave at sunrise and ride west toward the river, you should reach it by noon."

"Are you after them that did it?" the second Mexican cowboy asked.

"We are," Jack said.

"The grass has growed some since last week," the first Mexican cowboy said. "You can't tell now but there must have been a dozen to maybe fifteen riders that stole the herd."

"You find them, you hang them for sure," the second Mexican cowboy said. "Those boys they kilt were top hands and my friends."

"You boys staying the night?" Emmet asked.

"You got something for breakfast?" the second Mexican asked.

"We do," Emmet said.

"Then we staying the night."

After their visit to the barn, Amy and Duff sat on the porch where the night air was much cooler than inside the house.

Maria came out and joined them.

"Mary's fever is nearly gone," Maria said. "I will sleep in her bed with her tonight. Chao-xing is with Sarah."

"Speaking of sleep, you better get some," Amy said. "Your baby needs as much rest as you do."

Showing greatly now, Maria rubbed her swollen stomach. "Tell that to the baby," she said. "Half the night is spent kicking."

"Do me a favor and make up the guest room for Mr. Duff," Amy said.

"Will you allow me to make breakfast?" Duff asked.

Amy looked at him.

"I'm a fair hand in the kitchen," Duff said.

"Agreed," Amy said.

"Don't stay up too late," Maria said. "And you might want to brush the straw from your hair."

After Maria went into the house, Amy and Duff looked at each other and burst into laughter.

A million stars were visible overhead.

Each man was lost in thought as he waited for sleep.

"This is a bad bunch you're after," one of the Mexican cowboys said softly. "One of my friends, they put a gun to the back of his head and shot him. Why do something like that? They had the herd, why shoot a man in the back of the head? Yes sir, this is a bad bunch you're after."

With his eyes closed, Two Hawks said, "When we catch them, I will return the favor."

CHAPTER TWENTY-ONE

Two Hawks scouted ahead and located the area where the herd was stolen. Five freshly dug graves sat near the Rio Grande River.

The disturbed banks of the river told him exactly where the rustlers crossed.

He crossed the wide shallow river and inspected the Colorado banks. The murderers kept the herd in the water to avoid detection.

Two Hawks crossed the river again and found a shady spot under a tree to wait for Emmet and Jack to arrive.

He stuffed and lit his pipe and waited.

After about an hour, they arrived. They dismounted, and Emmet looked at the graves.

"Good God," Emmet said.

"They crossed here and followed the river north into Colorado," Two Hawks said.

Jack gathered some wood to build a fire.

"We best eat and rest the horses for a while," he said.

Emmet removed cookware from the mule and put on a pot of coffee, beans, and bacon.

"No telling how far we'll need to go," Emmet said. "We best check the map and see where we can resupply when necessary."

As they ate, Emmet checked the maps.

"Directly north it's a day's ride to Alamosa," Emmet said. "They would have taken the herd west to avoid a town."

"I don't need a map to know that," Two Hawks said.

"I know, but I'm thinking we can make a quick stop for supplies and send a few telegrams," Emmet said.

Two Hawks shrugged. "I could use some fresh pipe tobacco," he said.

Once the horses were well rested, they mounted up and Two Hawks led the way into the Rio Grande. The trail led directly north for several hours until Two Hawks found the location along the banks where the herd had emerged.

The grass had grown considerably since the four hundred head of cattle walked upon it, but Two Hawks had little trouble picking up the trail.

"Give the horses a break for a few minutes," Emmet said.

While the horses and mule took advantage of the tall, sweet grass, Emmet studied the maps.

"One of us can make Alamosa by sundown and send the telegrams," Emmet said.

"One of us?" Jack said.

"You're the better tracker, Jack," Emmet said. "You should be able to catch up to us by sundown tomorrow."

"Don't forget to get supplies and tobacco for my pipe," Two Hawks said.

Jack glared at Two Hawks. "Write out the telegrams, and I'll be on my way before a certain someone asks for a bag of candy," he said.

Jake's large and powerful horse reached Alamosa in three hours. A town of about a thousand people, it grew quickly when the railroad built a station several years back as a gateway to supply and repair its trains.

As he rode into town, Jack passed large warehouses that were filled with parts for various trains.

There was a slight aroma of coal in the air, but if the people on the streets noticed it, they didn't seem to care.

He dismounted and walked his horse along the streets, ignoring curious glances from citizens.

Two Hawks inspected the northwestern banks of the Rio Grande River while Emmet stayed mounted with the mule in tow.

"They reentered the river here," Two Hawks said. "We have an hour of daylight left. I'll scout ahead while you make camp."

While Two Hawks entered the river and rode off, Emmet built a fire, put on food and coffee, and then tended to his horse and the mule.

Two Hawks returned at sunset.

"They left the river several miles from here and headed northwest," he said as he dismounted.

"If they're headed out of Colorado, there are at least five or six more rivers to cross," Emmet said.

Two Hawks removed the saddle from his horse and set it aside. "They know how to move a herd," he said. "They had ten or eleven days on us. We will have to travel fast to catch them."

"Sit and have some food," Emmet said.

Two Hawks sat, and Emmet dished out a plate of food for him and then one for himself.

"We have some riding to do," Two Hawks said.

"Yes, we do," Emmet agreed.

"Will your brother be able to find us?"

"Jack, he'll find us," Emmet said. "He's a fair tracker in his own right."

"He'd better be," Two Hawks said. "The western side of the Rockies is no country for a tenderfoot."

Emmet grinned. "Jack is anything but a tenderfoot."

Jack walked his horse to the sheriff's office. The sheriff was out of town, but a young deputy was on duty.

"Marshal, are you here about the robbery?" the deputy asked.

"No. What robbery?" Jack asked.

"Some thieves broke into a warehouse and made off with a wagonload of railroad property," the deputy said. "The sheriff and railroad police are out with a posse."

"As sad a bit of news as that is, I'm passing through on a more pressing matter," Jack said. "What do you got for hotels in this town?"

"Six of them along Main Street," the deputy said. "We get a lot of railroad people stopping through."

"Which is the best?"

"The Alamosa."

"Thanks."

Jack located Main Street, passed several crowded saloons, and found the Alamosa Hotel at the end of a long block. It had its own livery, and he left his horse and saddle with the stable boy and carried his saddlebags and rifle into the hotel.

The lobby was fairly plush and crowded with what Jack considered dudes in suits. Most had the attention of professional girls. A clerk at the desk smiled at him as he approached the desk.

"What can I do for you, Marshal?" the clerk asked.

"I need a room for tonight and a bath," Jack said.

"We have one on the third floor," the clerk said. "Three-o-six."

"Have my saddlebags and Winchester brought up, and I'll be back in one hour for the bath," Jack said.

After registering, Jack left the hotel and walked several blocks to the telegraph office. "I'd like to send these telegrams. You can have the reply delivered to the Alamosa Hotel to Marshal Young-blood," he told the operator.

Across the street from the telegraph office, Jack entered a

large general store and placed an order for forty pounds of supplies for the morning.

He returned to the hotel and picked up the room key.

"Your bath is ready, Marshal," the clerk said. "Take the stairs on the third floor at the end of the hall."

"Thanks," Jack said.

He went to his room, dug out a clean shirt, socks, and underwear from the saddlebags, and took them up one flight to the bathhouse.

He stood in the hall and looked at the eight private rooms.

A door on one room opened and a blond woman wearing a robe said, "Did you order a bath?"

"I did," Jack said.

"It's ready."

Jack entered the room and the woman closed the door. A large, ornate tub was centered in the room. Two red lanterns hung from the walls, and a third was on a table.

"Would you like a shave?" the woman said. "No extra charge."

"I would," Jack said.

"Go ahead in and I'll be right back," the woman said.

After the woman left the room, Jack stripped down and got into the tub. The hot water was scented with oils and bubble bath.

He rested his head against the rim and waited for the woman to return. She came back carrying a tray that held soap mug, brush, and razor.

"Go ahead and wet your face," she said.

Jack dunked under. When he came up, the woman was lathering up the brush in the soap dish.

"When they told me I had a special guest, I thought it was just another railroad executive," she said. "They didn't tell me it was a US marshal. Close your eyes now, hon."

Jack closed his eyes and she lathered his beard. Then she

removed her robe, climbed into the tub, and sat on his lap.

Jack opened his eyes and looked at her pointed breasts.

"What are you doing?" he said.

"Shaving you," the woman said. "Now hold still or I'll draw blood."

Jack held still as she scraped the stubble from his face and neck. With each stroke of the razor she wiggled just a tiny bit on Jack's lap.

"Chin," she said.

Jack tilted his chin and closed his eyes.

She scraped his chin and wiggled herself just a bit lower.

This was a test, Jack told himself. Of his fortitude and character as a man. He took a deep breath and opened his eyes.

The woman smiled at him.

"All done," she said. "Is there anything else I can do for you?"

"You can get off my lap," Jack said.

She wiggled on top of him. "I'm just getting warmed up," she said.

"Miss, I'm spoken for," Jack said. "Please get off my lap."

"You're serious?" she said.

"I am."

The woman stood, got out of the tub, and picked up her robe. "I thought your kind no longer existed," she said.

"What kind is that?" Jack asked.

"Honorable. Good for you, Marshal," the woman said. "Would you like you dirty clothes cleaned?"

"I would. Thanks."

The woman smiled. "You're welcome."

Emmet and Two Hawks smoked their pipes as they rested against their saddles. It was a moonless night, and the stars were out by the millions.

"Tell me about your wife, the Mexican woman," Two Hawks said.

"I met her just a short time before you attacked the church complex she and the priest were building," Emmet said. "I knew the moment I set eyes on her she would be my wife."

"Doli wanted to kill her," Two Hawks confessed. "She thought I took her to make her my own. She didn't understand about leverage in a conflict."

"Doli seems like a true Comanche spirit, and she gave you a fine, beautiful son," Emmet said.

"She and the baby are the reason my heart has turned, the reason I am doing this," Two Hawks said.

"I guess in any culture a woman and a baby can turn a man's heart," Emmet said.

"What of your brother's woman?" Two Hawks asked.

"Damnedest thing I've ever seen," Emmet said. "This tiny Chinese woman has a grip on him like a blacksmith's vice. Besides my mother, Chao-xing may be the only person who can put fear into Jack."

Two Hawks grinned and looked at the stars. "You, me, and your brother, we are the warriors, but we are not in charge," he said.

Emmet puffed on his pipe. "No we are not," he said. "And I'll tell you something else. We're just fooling ourselves if we think we are."

After having a late supper in the hotel dining room, Jack took coffee on the porch where the night air was much cooler.

He was rolling a cigarette when the woman who'd shaved him came out with a mug of coffee and took a chair next to Jack.

"Can you spare one of those?" she said.

"Take this one," Jack said and rolled another. He struck a

wood match and lit both.

"Thanks," she said. "You know, Marshal, I really admire you staying true to your woman like that. Most men wouldn't. I know that for a fact."

"Mind me asking how . . ." Jack said.

"I wound up a whore in a railroad hotel?" the woman said. "I was raised poor and without an education. My folks died when I was sixteen, and a railroad pimp took me in. Ten, twelve years ago they were laying track across the country. Wherever there are large groups of men, there is a demand for women. When they built this hotel, I came to work for the railroad as entertainment."

"Entertainment?" Jack said.

"It's what the railroad executives call it," she said. "In a couple of more years I'll have enough money squirreled away to move west and settle in San Francisco as a lady."

The desk clerk suddenly appeared on the porch. "There you are," he said angrily. "Mr. Herrmann is waiting for you in room four, you stupid whore. Now get a move on or I'll slap you good."

Jack sat his cup on the railing, stood, grabbed the clerk by the shirt, lifted him, and tossed him off the porch and into the street.

"That's no way to speak to a lady," Jack said.

The woman grinned at Jack. "Goodnight, Marshal," she said.

"Goodnight, miss," Jack said.

After the woman stood up and entered the hotel, the clerk looked up at Jack.

"What did I say, Marshal?" the clerk said.

"She may be just a whore to you carpetbagger, but she's still a woman, and she has feelings," Jack said. "You best remember that."

"Yes, sir," the clerk said and meekly stepped up to the porch and entered the hotel.

CHAPTER TWENTY-TWO

An hour before sunset, Emmet pulled up. "My horse is played out," he said and dismounted.

"Make camp," Two Hawks said. "I'll scout ahead for a bit."

After Two Hawks rode off, Emmet removed the saddle from his pinto. He got a fire going, put on beans and bacon and a pot of coffee, and then tended to his horse. After a good brushing and a bag of oats, he inspected the pinto's legs and muscles. They rode thirty miles today through hills and hard country, and his pinto was tired.

Two Hawks returned at dark.

"They crossed the Colorado River headed west," he said as he dismounted.

"How many rivers is that since the Grande?" Emmet asked.

"Five at least," Two Hawks said.

Emmet dished out plates of beans and bacon with thick slices of cornbread.

"This is all too well organized for two-bit outlaws," Emmet said. "There's some planning behind this."

"Perhaps a Comanche is in charge," Two Hawks joked.

"Whoever is in charge has a purpose in mind," Emmet said.

"I heard Geronimo has left the reservation in Arizona," Two Hawks said. "Maybe he is behind this?"

"You and I both know Geronimo has no interest in money or cattle," Emmet said.

"I know," Two Hawks said. "I was being . . . what's the word?"

"Ironic?"

"Yes, ironic."

"What's really ironic is that a year ago, Jack would have killed you on sight or you him, and here we are riding together for the same purpose," Emmet said.

"We are not so different, your brother and I," Two Hawks said. "We are not afraid to fight for what we believe in or die for it."

"Jack is . . ." Emmet said.

Two Hawks held up his right hand and Emmet became silent. Slowly, silently, Two Hawks stood and drew his Colt pistol. He cocked it so slowly, the hammer barely made a noise.

Emmet looked at Two Hawks as Two Hawks stared past the fire into the darkness.

"Hello to camp," a voice called out from a hundred feet past the fire. "I am Deputy Sheriff Theodore Roosevelt, and I am unarmed and afoot. May I approach and have a cup of your coffee?"

"I'm United States Marshal Emmet Youngblood. With me is army scout Two Hawks," Emmet said. "Are you alone, Deputy?"

"Yes," Roosevelt said.

Emmet looked at Two Hawks and Two Hawks nodded.

"Come ahead," Emmet said and stood up beside Two Hawks.

Slowly, Roosevelt walked into camp with his hands up. He was a tall, young man dressed in buckskin pants and shirt. He wore round, rimless glasses and had a thick mustache.

"What in God's name are you doing out here alone?" Emmet asked.

"It's a very long story, Marshal," Roosevelt said. "Maybe I can tell it to you over a plate of food? I haven't eaten in two days."

Two Hawks opened his eyes and stared up at the stars overhead.

He kept still and kept his breathing shallow, and let his ears do the work.

He rolled over and gently nudged Emmet awake.

When Emmet opened his eyes, Two Hawks whispered, "Your brother is here."

The coffee was still warm in the pot and as Jack drank a cup and smoked a cigarette, Emmet fueled the dying fire with fresh wood.

Jack looked at Roosevelt. "Made a new friend, huh?" he said.

"Jack, this is Deputy Sheriff Theodore Roosevelt out of North Dakota," Emmet said. "He's . . . hell, it's a long story. You tell him, Theodore."

"Could you spare one of those?" Roosevelt asked.

Jack tossed Roosevelt his tobacco pouch and papers.

"North Dakota's a long way off," Jack said.

"Yes," Roosevelt said. "Traveling this far was unintentional, to be sure. I set out after four horse thieves who murdered a man and stole his horses. Left behind a wife and three children. That was about a month ago, I guess. I had no notion it would take me this long and far, but once I started out, I couldn't very well turn around. Two nights ago, they snuck up on me and woke me up and stole my horse, gun and food. I stumbled around for a while before I gave it up. Then I saw the campfire and walked in, and here I sit."

"It appears so," Jack said. "We'll leave you enough food and water to walk to Denver."

"Jack, Denver is near two hundred miles from here," Emmet said.

"Well what do you propose to do, lend him your horse?" Jack said.

"No, yours," Emmet said.

Jack looked at Emmet.

Emmet nodded.

"Best get some sleep," Emmet said.

"We'll continue tracking the herd," Emmet said. "You catch up to us when you can. Good luck, Deputy."

"Thank you, my friends," Roosevelt said from behind Jack. "I shall remember your kindness."

Jack tugged the reins, and his tall horse eased into a trot. If he was aware that he carried two riders, it didn't appear to bother him in the least.

They had little trouble backtracking Roosevelt's steps and rode most of the morning and into the afternoon before stopping to rest the horse for an hour.

"When they left me, they rode southeast toward the mountains," Roosevelt said.

"Four riders and a horse in tow shouldn't be too difficult to follow," Jack said.

And it wasn't. By four in the afternoon, Jack had picked up a fresh trail of four riders with one horse in tow.

"Your mount has slowed them considerable," Jack said. "Can't be more than four or five hours ahead of us."

After sunset, Jack spotted the red dot of a campfire in the distance.

"We'll rest here a while," he told Roosevelt.

They dismounted and ate slices of cornbread with jerked beef and water.

"We'll let them get drunk and comfortable and then take them," Jack said softly.

"Take them how?" Roosevelt said. "I'm unarmed."

"No more talk, Deputy Roosevelt," Jack said. "Sound travels great distances after dark. Go ahead and take a nap if you want. I'll wake you when the time comes."

While Roosevelt took a nap, Jack sat and watched the fire in the distance. He could hear voices and soft laughter. After a time the voices sounded drunk, and the laughter turned to giggling. Finally, the laughter and talking silenced.

Jack nudged Roosevelt.

"Deputy, it's time to move out," Jack said.

They mounted Jack's horse. Jack tugged the reins hard and the powerful horse raced forward.

Jack ran them toward the dying fire. A hundred yards from it, he pulled up, let Roosevelt off, and then dismounted.

"Grab my Winchester," Jack whispered.

Roosevelt removed the Winchester from the saddle and looked at Jack.

"Do what I do," Jack whispered.

Jack pulled his Colt, cocked it, and walked directly toward the sleeping outlaws.

Roosevelt followed.

Jack stopped at the fire. He counted four men in their bedrolls and five horses.

"Is that your horse, Deputy Roosevelt?" Jack said.

"It is."

Jack fired a shot into the ground, and the four outlaws bolted awake.

"Nobody move," Jack shouted.

Of course, the four outlaws jumped from their bedrolls and reached for their guns.

Jack shot one, then a second and third, and the fourth outlaw tossed his gun and put his hands up.

"Deputy Roosevelt, secure your prisoner," Jack said.

Roosevelt was frozen where he stood.

"Deputy, secure your prisoner," Jack said again.

"I'll . . . find some rope," Roosevelt said.

Jack approached the remaining outlaw. "Don't you know horse theft is against the law?" Jack said.

196

"Screw you," the outlaw said.

Jack smacked him in the face with the barrel of his Colt, and the outlaw went down.

As he looked at the fallen outlaw, Jack opened the gate on his Colt and removed the spent shells.

Roosevelt appeared at Jack's side. "I found some rope."

"Tie him up, so we can get some sleep," Jack said.

"What about the bodies?" Roosevelt asked.

"They're already asleep," Jack said.

"That was a fine breakfast you prepared, Deputy Roosevelt," Jack said. "According to my map, there's a town called Vail about a day's ride west of here. We can take your prisoner there, and I'll be on my way."

"What about the dead?" Roosevelt asked.

"I won't waste sweat burying them," Jack said. "Leave them for the buzzards. The filthy creatures got to eat, too."

Emmet and Two Hawks stood on the banks of the White River.

"They crossed here," Two Hawks said.

"We'll cross and rest the horses for an hour," Emmet said.

The water level was low, and the horses and mule had little trouble crossing. On the other side, they dismounted and built a fire.

As they ate beans and bacon with cornbread and coffee, Emmet checked his maps.

"After the Yampa River, it's a day's ride into Wyoming," Emmet said. "There's a town called Yampa on the north side of the river. If they have a telegraph, I'd like to check in and wait for Jack."

"Wyoming is big country," Two Hawks said. "A man can get lost in Wyoming, and so could a herd."

"I've never been to Wyoming," Emmet said. "But I doubt it's

their final destination."

"Last year I rode through the north part of Wyoming. They have what they call Yellowstone Park," Two Hawks said. "They call it a geyser. Boiling hot water shoots a hundred feet into the air every hour or so. White explorers found it about fifteen years ago and named it Old Faithful, but the Lakota and Crow have watched it for hundreds of years."

"I've seen photographs of it," Emmet said. "That will have to do for now."

Riding east toward the town of Vail, Jack held the outlaw in tow while Roosevelt held the three horses belonging to the dead men.

"Looks like company coming," Jack said.

A half mile east was an approaching prisoner wagon escorted by three men on horseback and one in the buckboard.

One of the riders broke away and road directly toward Jack.

"I'll be damned," Jack said.

"What?" Roosevelt asked.

The rider reached Jack, and the two men stared at each other until both broke out in wide grins.

"Deputy Roosevelt, this is Marshal Seth Bullock, the man who cleaned up Deadwood," Jack said. "Had your lunch yet, Seth?"

Two Hawks rode ahead and picked up the trail of the herd. They were headed northwest to the Yampa River.

He dismounted to inspect the tracks. He counted twelve distinct sets of horseshoes. As he knelt beside a set of tracks, he spotted buzzards circling in the sky a mile away.

Two Hawks mounted up and rode to the buzzards. They scattered and took to the air when he arrived and dismounted.

Two men lay dead on the ground. From their clothing, they

were Mexican. They'd had a dispute and engaged in a brutal knife fight. A long field knife stuck out from the rib cage of one of them. The other had a knife stuck in his upper right thigh at the groin. Both men died of their wounds.

Their saddles were left behind. Their horses were not.

Two Hawks lit his pipe and waited for Emmet to arrive.

About thirty minutes later Emmet, with the mule in tow, arrived and he dismounted.

"That's two less we have to worry about when we catch them," Two Hawks said.

Emmet looked at the two men on the ground.

"Jesus," he said. "That's no way for a man to die."

Roosevelt and Bullock seemed to hit it off immediately and were soon chatting like old friends over cups of coffee.

Jack learned a few interesting things of no consequence about Roosevelt as he listened to their conversation.

Roosevelt was from back east in New York City. He was interested in Republican politics and gave a speech in the nineteen eighty-four convention in Chicago. He was thinking of returning to New York to run for mayor in a few years, if his ranch and career as a sheriff failed.

"Well, Deputy Roosevelt, I leave you in Marshal Bullock's capable hands," Jack said as he mounted his horse.

"Be seeing you, Jack," Bullock said.

"Marshal Youngblood, I will forever be in your debt," Roosevelt said.

"Don't take this as an insult, Deputy Roosevelt, but if I was you I'd find a new line of work," Jack said and rode away.

"He's a good man," Roosevelt said to Bullock.

"Jack is as fearless as he is *loco*," Bullock said. "Another cup of coffee, Ted?"

★ ★ ★ ★ ★

Emmet wrote a note to Jack on a sheet of paper and stuck it between two rocks near the dead Mexican outlaws.

"We'll wait for Jack in Yampa," Emmet said to Two Hawks as he mounted his pinto.

CHAPTER TWENTY-THREE

Judge Parker's courtroom had room for thirty spectators. Every seat was occupied for the man who robbed and stabbed Stanly Duff.

Besides the court reporter and two deputy marshals, there was private seating for newspaper reporters.

The lone occupant in the private seating was Amy Youngblood. As Duff was the primary witness in the trial, he couldn't write the news story for the paper, so he asked Amy to cover the story for him.

She held a notepad and pencil at the ready as she waited for Judge Parker to call the trial to order.

Finally Parker banged his gavel and called the court in session.

The trial lasted barely an hour.

As a town, Yampa died as quickly as it was born. Situated in the foothills, the eight wood structures had burned to the ground, leaving behind charred fragments of wood and some fixtures.

"What do you suppose happened here?" Emmet said as he and Two Hawks walked among the remains.

"Wood structures close together," Two Hawks said. "One goes, and they all go. The people decided it wasn't worth rebuilding."

"We best make camp for the night," Emmet said. "Jack should be along by morning."

"I spotted some wild chickens a ways back," Two Hawks said. "Get a fire going. I won't be long."

Emmet built a fire and then brushed and fed his pinto. Before dark, Two Hawks returned with three wild chickens slung over his saddle.

Emmet built a large spit out of charred wood from a building and, by nightfall, he and Two Hawks were feasting on plump chicken breasts and legs.

"When we reach Wyoming, we will stop at Rock Springs and send a telegram home," Emmet said. "Do you have any way of contacting Doli?"

"Contacting her for what?" Two Hawks asked.

"To let her know you're all right."

"Doli is Comanche," Two Hawks said. "She will know I am all right when I return. If I don't return, she will know I am dead."

"My wife would be mad at me for months if I didn't send a telegram," Emmet said.

"Your wife is not Comanche," Two Hawks said.

Jack reached the spot where Emmet left him the note shortly before sunset.

"Yampa?" he said.

He looked at the two dead Mexican men, yanked the knife free from one of them, and held it up.

"Waste of a good knife," he said.

Duff read Amy's story at the printing press.

Amy stood by his side and watched until Duff lowered the paper.

"Remarkably well done," he said.

"Thank you, but now I must get home," Amy said.

"It's ten o'clock at night," Duff said.

"They must be worried sick," Amy said.

"But we haven't set the type yet," Duff said. "Help me put the paper to bed, and you can stay at my house."

"What will people think? What will my grandchildren think if I don't come home?" Amy said.

Duff sighed. "You're right, of course," he said. "My carriage is right outside. I'll take you home."

"How did you survive in the Rockies a year with everybody looking for you?" Emmet asked Two Hawks as they lay by the fire.

"It is not as difficult as you think," Two Hawks said. "The mountains are harsh in winter, for sure, but if you know how to survive them, they can be a beautiful and peaceful place to live."

Two Hawks rolled over and looked at Emmet. "Besides, the white man is too lazy to traverse the mountains in winter," he said.

Emmet closed his eyes and felt sleep start to take him. Slowly his eyes opened and he turned to look at Two Hawks.

"What haven't you told me?" Emmet said.

Two Hawks looked at Emmet.

"I gave you my word," Emmet said.

"And I gave you mine," Two Hawks said.

"You know something. What?"

"Nothing. Just a suspicion," Two Hawks said.

"A suspicion of what?" Emmet asked.

"I'm tired," Two Hawks said. "We will talk in the morning."

"We will talk now," Emmet said.

"Don't push me," Two Hawks said.

"What are you suspicious of?" Emmet said.

"Talk. That's all."

"Talk about what?"

"Nothing I can prove at the moment, so why talk about it?"

"You ride with a man, you give your word to a man, you better be honest with him," Emmet said.

Two Hawks stared at Emmet.

"Are you calling me a liar?" Two Hawks said.

"I think you are not telling me something," Emmet said and sat up. "That is the same thing."

"No, it is not."

Two Hawks sat up and punched Emmet in the face.

"Son of a . . ." Emmet said and punched Two Hawks in return.

They looked at each other, and in the next moment, both had grabbed the other and were rolling around on the ground. They punched, kicked, gouged, and bit each other until they broke apart and jumped to their feet.

They stood three feet apart and made eye contact in the dim light of the dwindling fire.

Both men were two hundred pounds and strong and showed mutual respect.

Two Hawks punched Emmet on the jaw, and Emmet fell to the ground. He got up quickly and retaliated with a punch to Two Hawks's face that sent him reeling to his knees.

Two Hawks stood, and then he and Emmet traded punch for punch until both were so exhausted, they fell into each other's arms and slumped to the ground and gasped for air.

From the darkness, Jack walked his horse to the nearly extinguished fire. An unlit cigarette was between his lips. He knelt and picked up a small stick, stirred the fire and then lit the cigarette with the stick.

As he stood, Jack said, "As entertaining as it was watching you two beat each other's brains out, mind telling me what it was about."

Emmet stood up and said, "What did you do, ride all night?"

"Some of us have real horses instead of ponies," Jack said.

"Funny," Emmet said as he reached into Jack's saddlebags for a bottle of whiskey. He removed his bandana, poured whiskey on it, and then dabbed at his cuts. When he finished wiping the cuts, he tossed the bottle to Two Hawks.

Two Hawks took a long swallow and then poured some whiskey on his right hand and wiped his cuts.

"Hell, I don't know," Emmet said.

Jack looked at Two Hawks. "You?"

"I'm hungry," Two Hawks said.

Jack went to his saddlebags, in which he had forty pounds of fresh supplies. He dug out a large round loaf of crusty bread and a pound of salted butter wrapped in waxed paper. He tossed the bread and butter to Emmet.

"I got three dozen eggs, five pounds of bacon, and ten pounds of coffee," Jack said. "And a pound of sugar."

Emmet sat next to Two Hawks while Jack added some wood to the fire and stirred the ashes to get it going again. Then he sat next to Emmet.

Emmet ripped off three hunks of bread and used his knife to lather on butter. He passed a hunk each to Jack and Two Hawks.

"For hundreds of years my people have spoken of a secret, holy place hidden in the mountains," Two Hawks said. "The location was discovered by the Lakota and guarded as sacred ground. The Lakota have become weak people given to whiskey. I have heard the talk that white men may have exchanged the location for whiskey."

"I've heard the stories of this secret place in the mountains," Emmet said.

"Say this place exists, what of it?" Jack asked.

"If you were an outlaw and a cattle thief, it would make a good place to hide stolen cattle," Two Hawks said.

Jack and Emmet exchanged glances.

"It would, wouldn't it?" Emmet said.

"I believe I am tracking these men directly to this place," Two Hawks said. "I felt that before I sent for you to make the deal with the judge."

"Why?" Jack asked.

"If this place exists, I will live out my days there with Doli and my son," Two Hawks said. "Away from white men my son will grow up Comanche."

"Help us, help yourself," Jack said.

"I learned that from white men," Two Hawks said.

"If what you're saying is true, outlaws and Indian are working together," Emmet said.

"It would appear so," Two Hawks said.

"When were you going to tell us all this?" Jack asked.

"When my suspicions were proven true," Two Hawks said.

"And if they weren't?" Jack asked.

"We'd have nothing to talk about," Two Hawks said.

"Well, where is this secret paradise supposed to be anyway?" Jack said.

"Some say it is in Utah. Others speak of Wyoming," Two Hawks said. "If they are headed there, I will find them."

"You'll find them regardless of where they are headed," Jack said. "Or the bargain with the judge is off. You'd best remember that."

Two Hawks looked at Jack. "You have taken my land, my home, and my hunting grounds. All that I have left is my word and, as long as I breathe, I will keep it."

"As long as we're all still breathing, let's get some sleep," Emmet said.

As he drove his buggy along the very dark road on the reservation to Amy's house, Duff suddenly stopped his horse with a tug of the reins. Two lit lanterns on the fenders of the buggy provided enough light to cut through the darkness.

"It's almost one in the morning, Stanly, why did you stop?" Amy said.

"Mrs. Youngblood, I . . ." Duff said.

"That sounds so formal, Stanly," Amy said.

"What I have to say is formal," Duff said. "I'm sixty-two-years-old and have been in love just twice in all that time. I lost my first love to illness. I don't want to lose the second because I waited too long. Mrs. Youngblood, would you consider becoming my wife."

Amy stared at Duff for many long seconds.

"Oh, dear God, I think I am going to say yes," Amy said.

CHAPTER TWENTY-FOUR

Two Hawks and Jack scouted ahead while Emmet made breakfast. They rode to a shallow creek and stopped.

"Across this creek, a half day's ride is Wyoming," Two Hawks said.

"How do you know that?" Jack said.

"I traveled this country for months last year to stay ahead of the army," Two Hawks said. "And I looked at Emmet's map."

"Speaking of Emmet, let's get back. Breakfast should be about ready," Jack said.

Jack and Two Hawks returned to camp, where a breakfast of fresh baked rolls, scrambled eggs, bacon, and coffee was waiting for them.

"Any chance we can make Rock Springs by sunset?" Emmet said.

"If we push hard, we can make it by eight o'clock," Two Hawks said.

"You make good rolls," Jack said as he bit into a warm roll.

"Ma taught me how to bake them and bread, and even a cake," Emmet said.

"I wouldn't go bragging about that in a saloon if I was you," Jack said.

"How are you with cookies? I love cookies," Two Hawks said.

"Ah, for Christ's sake," Jack said. "Let's get moving before you two start exchanging recipes."

★ ★ ★ ★ ★

After breakfast, Amy gathered the entire family on the porch, and she and Duff told them the news.

"That's wonderful. I'm happy for you both," Maria said.

"I don't understand, Grandma," Sarah said.

"Mr. Duff and I are to be married," Amy said. "We will be husband and wife."

Sarah looked at Duff. "Does that mean I call you Grandfather?"

Duff lifted Sarah onto his lap. "You can call me Grandfather, Grandpa, Mr. Duff, or whatever you like, young lady," he said.

Chao-xing looked at Amy. "Where will you live?"

"I have a fine big house in town," Duff said. "We will divide our time between town and here."

Amy looked at Maria. "Once Emmet has finished building your home, of course," she said.

"Where do we live?" Sarah asked.

"With Pa and Maria, silly," Mary said.

"When is the big day?" Maria asked.

"As soon as the boys return," Amy said.

Maria rubbed her belly. "He better not wait much longer," she said.

"Lunch is in the oven," Chao-xing said. "I'd better see to it."

Amy waited for a few minutes and then went inside the house to the kitchen where Chao-xing was stirring a large pot of stew.

Even with her back to her, Amy could tell that Chao-xing was softly crying. Amy went up behind her and placed her hands on Chao-xing's shoulders.

"Jack will be home soon enough," Amy said. "Don't worry about that."

"I know," Chao-xing sniffled. "It's . . ."

"It's what?" Amy asked.

"He's been gone so long," Chao-xing said. "Jack is a good

man, but he's still a man."

"Oh, honey, if Jack wanted to tomcat around, he could do that right here in Fort Smith," Amy said. "I know my son. He doesn't make promises he won't keep. Clear your head of any thoughts of that, and let's have lunch."

A mile from Rock Springs, gunfire echoed softly around them and Jack, Emmet, and Two Hawks stopped their horses.

"Sounds like someone is celebrating the Fourth of July a month early," Jack said.

"Let's go before it gets dark," Emmet said.

They rode to the edge of town and dismounted in front of a large livery stable. An old man was standing out front, holding a double-barrel shotgun.

The old man looked at Jack's badge. "Did the railroad send for you?"

"Send for me for what, and what's all the shooting?" Jack said.

"The railroad coal miners are shooting up the Chinese workers that took their jobs," the old man said. "The Chinese work for half what the Americans do, and it started a riot."

Jack looked down the street to where all the gunfire was coming from. He removed the Winchester rifle from the saddle and said to the liveryman, "Take care of our horses."

As Jack turned and walked down the street, Emmet sighed and reached for the Winchester on his saddle. Then he and Two Hawks followed Jack.

At the center of town, in front of a small hotel, three wagons were overturned. A dozen men knelt in front of them and fired their rifles at the Chinese store across the street.

Dozens of residents stood on the wood sidewalks and watched.

The shooting suddenly stopped and a man stood up. "Come

on out, you stinking chinks, or we'll burn your store down around you," he yelled.

From inside the store a man answered in Chinese.

"Can't understand you, chink," the man shouted. "Ya got ten seconds before we burn you out."

Jack approached the man. "He said they did nothing wrong," he said.

The man turned and looked at Jack. "Who are you?" he asked.

"United States Marshal John Youngblood," Jack said. "Why are you shooting at the Chinese store?"

"These stinking slant-eyes showed up and took our jobs mining coal for the railroad," the man said. "I got mouths to feed, and no stinking chink is gonna take food off my table. That's why."

Jack sighed, and then turned around and tossed his Winchester to Two Hawks.

Then he turned back and faced the man. Almost too quick to follow, Jack grabbed the rifle from the man's hands, turned it, and cracked the man in the jaw with the wood stock.

As the man fell onto a wagon, Jack walked forward.

"I'm United States Marshal Jack Youngblood, and you people are breaking the law," he said. "Turn these wagons over and go the hell home."

The armed men stared at Jack.

Behind Jack, Two Hawks cocked the Winchester and Emmet put a hand on Two Hawks's shoulder. Two Hawks looked at Emmet, and Emmet shook his head.

"If I have to say it twice, you won't like the outcome," Jack said.

Slowly the men stood and righted the wagons.

"Now go home and cool off," Jack said. He looked at the unconscious man he'd cracked in the jaw. "And take your friend with you."

Once the men had cleared out, Jack turned to the crowd on the sidewalk. "Who runs this town?" he said.

A short man with a full beard stepped forward. "I am Mayor Langford."

"Where's your sheriff?" Jack asked.

"We don't got one," Langford said. "This is a railroad town under the jurisdiction of the railroad police."

"Any about?" Jack said.

"I wired the railroad," Langford said. "Should be here about midnight."

"In the meantime, what were you going to do, stand around and watch as they murdered those people in the store?" Jack said.

"You saw," Langford said. "There wasn't much I could do about it."

"You come with me," Jack said.

Langford stepped down and stood next to Jack. Together they crossed the street and stood in front of the Chinese store.

"Do any of you speak English?" Jack said in Chinese.

"I do," a man answered.

"Come out. Let's talk," Jack said.

The door opened, and a Chinese man dressed in miner's clothing stepped out. His long pigtail hung down to the center of his back.

"You are a marshal?" he said in English.

"Yes. Who are you?"

"Moy, the foreman of the Chinese crew."

"Tell your people they are safe," Jack said. "Then come across the street and have a cup of coffee with me and the mayor."

Moy turned and shouted in Chinese, then faced Jack and nodded.

As Jack, Langford, and Moy entered the hotel, Emmet and Two Hawks followed.

"He's a hell of a lawman, isn't he?" Two Hawks said to Emmet.

"You just realized that?" Emmet said.

There were a dozen tables in the hotel café, but just one was occupied with Jack, Langford, Moy, Emmet, and Two Hawks.

Moy opted for Chinese tea, which the café served to accommodate all the town's Chinese workers.

"How is it you speak Chinese?" Moy asked Jack.

"My wife is Chinese," Jack said. "She teaches me. Now what's this all about?"

"If I may," Langford said. "The Chinese work for half what the Americans do, and the railroad is in business to make a profit. It's really that simple."

"Is it worth starting a blood feud over?" Emmet said.

"That is not in my control," Langford said. "That's railroad business."

"What do you say, Mr. Moy?" Emmet said.

"It is true we work for half what the Americans do, but we also work twice as hard and long," Moy said.

"They do toil long hours, for sure," Langford said. "And I don't know how to solve this to a peaceful conclusion."

"Let's see what the railroad people have to say," Emmet said.

Jack, Emmet, and Two Hawks sat in chairs on the hotel porch and drank coffee.

"Nice piece of work today, Jack," Emmet said.

"The day ain't over yet," Jack said.

"The days after your great war, when I was a young man, I would watch as men set down tracks all across the country," Two Hawks said. "White men, freed slaves, and Chinese. I thought at the time, how odd that your government would hire ex-slaves and import Chinese from halfway around the world and yet ignore the millions of us who came first."

Emmet looked at Two Hawks.

"I never quite thought of it that way," he said.

Rolling a cigarette, Jack looked at Two Hawks. "And if offered a job of back-breaking hard labor for very little pay in the hot sun for months at a time, you would have taken it?"

"Hell, no," Two Hawks said. "I said I thought it odd. I didn't say I was stupid."

Jack struck a match and lit the cigarette.

Emmet looked at his pocket watch. "It's a quarter to midnight, let's go meet the train."

Jack stood up. "I'll get that pipsqueak mayor."

Jack, Emmet, Two Hawks, and Langford stood on the end of the long platform and watched as a dozen men armed with pistols and rifles stepped off the train. They formed two columns of six and waited for railroad executive Alan Brooks to step off the train.

Brooks was a tall man wearing an expensive suit. A long cigar was unlit and clenched between his lips.

Next off the train was District Railroad Police Chief Bill Watts. He was a hard-looking man about the same age as Jack.

Brooks looked at Langford. "Again, Mr. Mayor?" he said.

"I best go arrest those men who started the trouble," Watts said.

"Arrest them for what? Trying to put food on their table?" Emmet said.

"Who are you?" Brooks said.

"United States Deputy Marshal Emmet Youngblood," Emmet said.

Watts looked at his men. "Let's go, boys," he said.

Jack stepped forward. "Let's not," he said.

Watts eyed Jack's badge. "This is a railroad matter," he said.

"This matter is whatever the hell I say it is," Jack said. "Now back off, or you'll be the first one I lock up."

"Watts, stand down," Brooks said. "The mayor and I will discuss the matter at the hotel."

After Brooks and Langford walked toward the edge of the platform, a stunning woman with blond hair came off the train, escorted by a man of about thirty.

"The railroad shall hear of this inconvenience," she said.

"Indeed," her escort said.

The woman stopped and looked at Jack. "Make sure my bags are delivered to the hotel," she said.

"What?" Jack said.

"My bags on the train. Go get them," the woman said.

"Your bags?" Jack said.

"And don't lose any of them."

"Your bags and you can go take a flying—" Jack said.

"Excuse me, miss," Two Hawks said. "I am Comanche scout Sergeant Major Two Hawks. I recognize you from your picture in the newspapers. You are Lillie Langtry, the famous actress of plays and shows."

"I am," Lillie said.

"I will consider it my honor to see that your bags are delivered to the hotel," Two Hawks said.

"Well, at last, a man with etiquette here in the wilderness," Lillie said. "Please join my companion Mr. Wilde and me for a drink at the hotel."

"I will, Miss Langtry," Two Hawks said.

"Come, Mr. Wilde, let's get to the hotel," Lillie said.

As Langtry and Wilde walked to the end of the platform, Jack looked at Two Hawks. "Who the hell is she?" Jack said.

"A famous play actress," Emmet said.

Jack looked at Two Hawks. "How come you know who she is?"

"How come you don't?" Two Hawks said.

While Brooks, Moy, and Langford sat at a table with Jack and Emmet, Two Hawks joined Lillie Langtry and Oscar Wilde at a private table in the room reserved for VIPs.

"I will leave six railroad police in town to keep the peace," Brooks said. "The offer to the men is the best I am authorized to make at this time. If there is any additional trouble, with or without gunplay, my men will arrest any man partaking, and they will be prosecuted. Am I understood?"

"So the men will get three-quarters of what they used to get, and the Chinese will get the same," Langford said. "The men won't like that, Mr. Brooks."

"They will like being unemployed even less," Brooks said. "At least they are back to work." He looked at Moy. "And the same goes for the Chinese, Mr. Moy. I will tolerate no further violence of any kind."

"There will be no violence on behalf of the Chinese," Moy said.

"Good," Brooks said. "I will return in September, and we will meet again."

Moy and Langford left the table.

"Mr. Brooks, you know as well as I that this won't sit well with the Americans," Emmet said. "I give it a month, maybe two, before you have a riot on your hands."

Brooks sighed openly. "I can't say I disagree with you, Marshal," he said.

"Goodnight, Mr. Brooks," Emmet said.

The room had four beds, as the railroad needed to maximize capacity for workers staying in town.

"Two Hawks must still be with Miss Langtry and Mr. Wilde," Emmet said.

As Jack removed his shirt, he said, "Who is she exactly?"

"Some say she is the greatest living actress here and in Europe," Emmet said. "I've read about her in the newspapers."

"And that other fellow?"

"Oscar Wilde," Emmet said. "He's a famous playwright from England."

"You mean he sits around writing stories all day, like dime-store novels?" Jack said.

"I think it's a little more than that, Jack," Emmet said.

As Jack turned down the sheets, the door opened and Two Hawks walked in. A wrapped parcel was under his right arm.

He gently placed the parcel on the dresser and said, "That Miss Langtry is a real lady, and that Mr. Wilde gave me this notebook that has what he called a first draft of a book he is writing."

"Oh, hell, a year ago you would have scalped the both of them," Jack said as he got into bed.

"A year ago, given the chance, I would have scalped you too," Two Hawks said with a sly grin.

Chapter Twenty-Five

Jack carried two sacks of extra supplies from the general store to the hotel, where the horses were saddled and ready to go.

Emmet was on the porch, smoking his pipe.

"Where's Two Hawks?" Jack asked as he packed the saddle-bags.

"Saying goodbye to Miss Langtry and Mr. Wilde," Emmet said.

"You're kidding," Jack said.

Emmet stood up and walked down to his horse.

"Did you send the telegrams?" Emmet asked.

"I did."

Two Hawks came out of the hotel and walked down to his horse. He held a white lace handkerchief in his left hand.

"Miss Langtry gave me her personal handkerchief," he said as he tucked it into a shirt pocket.

"That's great," Jack said. "Now if you're done holding hands with Miss Langtry, we'll be on our way."

Emmet stirred the fire with a stick and then tossed on some brush and twigs. They were camped along the shore of the Green River, northwest of Rock Springs.

Beans and bacon cooked in a pan over the fire.

Jack smoked a cigarette as he scanned the river.

"He's been gone an hour," Jack said.

"Yeah, but I see him coming," Emmet said.

Jack filled a cup with coffee, looked north, and watched Two Hawks ride into camp.

"They crossed the Green River about two miles north of here," Two Hawks said as he dismounted.

"How far ahead of us are they?" Emmet asked.

"Five days. No more than that," Two Hawks said.

"Grab a plate of food," Emmet said. "We have six hours of daylight left. Let's make the most of them."

They crossed the Green River and followed the northwest trail left behind by the herd until dark.

Around the campfire, Emmet studied his maps.

"I can't figure this out," he said. "Right now we're in the valley between the Wyoming Range and the Wind River Range. If they stay on this path, it leads directly to the mountains, and cattle won't climb mountains no matter how much you prod them."

Two Hawks grabbed a cup of coffee, sat next to Emmet, and looked at the maps. He traced a path with a finger.

"My guess is they will turn east into the Great Divide Basin, where there is good water and fertile grazing grounds," Two Hawks said.

Emmet studied the map. "And then to where?"

"The Rockies are to the west, the Bighorns to the east, and the Bighorn River sits between them," Two Hawks said. "They will go there."

Emmet looked at the map again. "God's country," he said.

"Depends on your god," Two Hawks said.

While Amy visited with Duff at the newspaper, Chao-xing took Mary and Sarah shopping at Greenly's General Store. Each girl had a quarter, and each was allowed to buy whatever she wanted with her money. They went directly to the candy counter.

Greenly had a list of seven orders for custom-made shirts. Chao-xing purchased the materials, buttons, and collar stays. At the register, the runner for the telegraph office entered the store with two telegrams.

One was addressed to Amy. The second was addressed to her.

"Girls," she said to Mary and Sarah. "You have five minutes to buy your candy. I'll be outside."

Chao-xing left the store and sat on the bench by the front window. She looked at the telegram addressed to her. It came from a place called Rock Springs. Her hands shook just a tiny bit as she opened the flap. The entire telegram consisted of just three words.

I love you.

It was signed JY.

Chao-zing folded the telegram, tucked it into a pocket, and felt a tear roll down her cheek.

The girls came out with bags of candy.

"There she goes, being happy again," Mary said.

"What did you get for candy?" Chao-xing asked.

"Everything," Sarah said.

"Good," Chao-xing said. "Let's eat some."

As Emmet floated on his back in a shallow section of the Bighorn River, he looked up at a bright blue sky overhead.

"This is mighty pretty country, Jack," he said. "A man could get lost out here."

Floating next to Emmet, Jack said, "We *are* lost out here and have been for two days now."

"I'm talking about a man's soul, Jack," Emmet said.

Swimming nearby, Two Hawks suddenly stood up and looked to shore.

"Say the wrong word, and forget losing your soul—you will

lose your scalp," he said.

Emmet and Jack stood up and looked at the two dozen mounted Shoshone Indians. The leader, an old man, sat atop a tall horse.

"Stay as you are," Two Hawks told Emmet and Jack. "Do nothing until I tell you to. My Shoshone is limited, but I'll try to find out what they want."

Two Hawks walked to the shoreline and stood naked before the mounted elder.

"I am Two Hawks, scalp for the army," Two Hawks said in broken Shoshone. "My two bends in the river are marshals for the . . ."

"Do you speak English?" the elder asked in English. "Because you are butchering my language."

"Yes," Two Hawks said.

"I am Chief Washakie of the Shoshone people," the elder said. "Tell the marshals to come out and get dressed. You look ridiculous with your dinks flapping in the wind."

Dressed, Emmet, Jack, and Two Hawks sat around a campfire and drank coffee with Washakie. The old chief had developed a taste for coffee with condensed milk while held captive by the army twenty years ago, and could never quite get his fill of the sweet mixture.

"We are after some very bad men," Emmet told Washakie. "Murderers and cattle thieves. Our path has led us from Arkansas to this valley. Have you seen men driving cattle through these grounds?"

Washakie looked at one of his men, and the Shoshone brave brought the old chief a long, well-worn pipe. The brave placed a stick into the fire and then lit the pipe. Washakie puffed until the tobacco burned evenly, and then he looked at Emmet.

"By the white man's time, I am eighty-five years old,"

Washakie said. "This is the hunting grounds for our reserved land. Many herds pass through, and the ranchers pay their respect by visiting the Shoshone tribe and bringing gifts. A week ago my scouts tell me a herd of about four hundred passed through. A dozen rode over the herd when half that number would do. One of the riders was a woman."

"A woman?" Emmet said.

"They traveled to the north?" Two Hawks said.

"Yes. My scouts followed them for twenty miles before turning back," Washakie said.

"This woman, did your scouts recognize her?" Emmet asked.

"No."

"Any of the men?"

Washakie looked at the brave who lit his pipe. The man stepped forward.

"One of the men I have seen before," the brave said. "Driving several other herds. I do not think the herds belonged to him. I can tell by the way a man treats his cattle if they are his or not."

"Chief Washakie, we must continue to ride to track these men," Emmet said. "If we come back this way, we will stop and pay our respects."

"We will ride with you for a while," Washakie said.

Although he was eighty-five years old, Washakie mounted his horse under his own power with little trouble. Washakie and Emmet rode point, followed by Jack and Two Hawks, and then the twenty braves.

They rode about ten miles before parting ways.

Emmet gave Washakie a gift of five pounds of coffee, two cans of condensed milk, and an unopened pouch of his tobacco.

Washakie and his men went east to their reservation.

Emmet, Jack, and Two Hawks continued north.

"I'll scout ahead," Two Hawks said.

Chapter Twenty-Six

"We been out here a week and haven't seen so much as a jackrabbit," Jack said as he scrubbed his chest with a bar of soap.

"Our supplies are running low," Emmet said as he washed his hair with a bar of soap. "The map shows the town of Sheridan is a day's ride north. We'll stop there."

They were in a water basin formed by a tributary of the Belle Fourche River. The basin was fairly shallow and warmed by the hot Wyoming sun.

Emmet rinsed his hair, stood up, and noticed Two Hawks riding in hard from scouting ahead. He dismounted at the edge of the basin, removed his holster and slung it over his horse's saddle, then removed his boots and jumped into the basin fully clothed.

When he surfaced, Two Hawks said, "I can't stand the stink of my own clothes. Hand me the soap."

Jack tossed Two Hawks the soap.

"A few miles north, two riders broke west," Two Hawks said. "The rest of the bunch continued north with the herd."

"West? Into the Bighorns?" Emmet asked.

"It would appear so," Two Hawks said.

"Why would they do that?" Emmet asked.

"Only one way to find out," Jack said as he emerged from the basin and walked to the fire where coffee was boiling in a pot.

Emmet looked at Two Hawks. "You know what he means, right?"

"We'll have to split up," Two Hawks said.

"The horses need rest and grain," Emmet said. "We could stay here the night and get a fresh start in the morning."

"I saw some wild turkeys not far off," Two Hawks said. "I'll go hunt one for supper."

Jack bit into a turkey leg, chewed, washed it down with a sip of coffee, and said, "How far ahead did you say they split up?"

"Two, maybe three miles at most," Two Hawks said.

"And just two riders broke away?" Jack said.

"To the west," Two Hawks said.

"What's on your mind, Jack?" Emmet said.

"One of us has to follow the two," Jack said.

"One of us, Jack?" Emmet said.

"I'm a better tracker than you, Emmet, and I'm better mounted," Jack said. "You and Two Hawks continue on and pick up supplies in town. I'll catch up with you afterward."

Emmet looked at Two Hawks, and Two Hawks nodded.

"Break me off a wing, would you?" Jack said.

"Here," Two Hawks said. "They turned west here."

Jack dismounted, as did Emmet and Two Hawks.

Jack loaded his saddlebags with extra supplies and ammunition for his Colt and Winchester.

"They went in for a reason," Jack said. "And that reason has to lead to somewhere. I'll catch up with you there."

"You watch yourself, big brother," Emmet said.

"Two Hawks, take care of my kid brother," Jack said as he mounted his horse. "Or I'll skin you alive."

Jack rode west toward the Bighorn Mountains. Emmet and Two Hawks continued north.

By midday, Jack was in the foothills. He stopped to rest his horse for an hour and to eat a cold lunch of biscuits, jerky, and water.

Then he continued on. By late afternoon, the trail left behind by the two riders slanted northwest and directly to the Bighorns. With four hours of daylight left, he could make camp or continue. He decided to continue.

The terrain was rocky and dry, dangerous for a horse. He dismounted and walked his horse over steep hills and continued to follow the trail.

The two riders, also on foot, took Jack to a steep plateau of grasslands.

Jack paused and rubbed his horse's neck.

"We got an hour of daylight left," he told his horse. "Let's see where they take us."

About a mile along the ridge, the trail took Jack directly to a parting in the mountains. Narrow, about six feet wide at most. The riders entered one behind the other as the opening was too narrow to ride side by side.

After a half mile or so, the pass widened a bit and was not so claustrophobic.

Night fell early as the surrounding cliffs blocked out the low sun.

Jack made camp and gathered up what wood and brush he could find for a fire. As beans, bacon, and coffee cooked, Jack gave his horse a good brushing and fed him a bag of grain.

After eating, Jack smoked a cigarette and drank coffee with his back against his saddle. The narrow opening in the cliffs blocked out the stars and moon overhead and, as the fire dwindled, darkness enveloped him like a stifling blanket.

He kept his mind clear. It would do no good to think of Chao-xing and home. A lawman on the trail had no right to think of home, as it shortened his odds of returning to it.

When the fire was extinguished, Jack settled in to sleep, feeling as if he were inside a closed casket.

"I'd like to help you, Marshal, but herds come through the grasslands near the Bighorns all the time," Sheriff Gaffney said. "It's a route into and from Montana. Sheridan is a small town with limited resources, and you're asking about one herd passing through in hundreds of square miles."

Emmet and Two Hawks were in Gaffney's office on the main street in Sheridan.

"Montana is major cattle country, isn't it?" Emmet said.

"As are Wyoming and Nebraska, but Montana is a place a man can really disappear in," Gaffney said. "You could drive a herd straight through Montana into Saskatchewan and not see another living soul along the way."

"Where's the nearest telegraph station?" Emmet said.

"Billings," Gaffney said. "Three days' ride from here."

"We'll be at the hotel overnight," Emmet said.

"Wish I could be more help," Gaffney said.

Emmet and Two Hawks left Gaffney and walked several blocks to the small hotel they'd registered in. The streets were muddy. Cowboys were everywhere, most of them drunk.

As they passed a group of celebrating cowboys, one of them grabbed Two Hawks.

"Hey, Cochise, how about a little drink?" he said and waved a bottle.

"Ah, you know they can't hold their liquor," another cowboy said.

The group of cowboys laughed, but only for a moment. Two Hawks spun quickly, brought his right knee up, and drove it into the cowboy's testicles. He dropped the bottle of whiskey and fell to his knees. Two Hawks pulled his knife, grabbed the man by the hair, and held the blade to his throat.

"Cochise was a great leader of his people," Two Hawks said. "A man admired and respected. You drunkards aren't worth the fleas on a mangy dog's back."

A drop of blood appeared on Two Hawks's knife.

Emmet saw the blood and stepped in.

"United States Marshal," Emmet said. "And it looks to me that you boys have done some celebrating, and now it's time to go home. Sergeant Major, lower the knife."

Two Hawks lowered his knife, and the cowboy grabbed his throat.

"Go home, or go to jail," Emmet said to the cowboys. "Which?"

Slowly, the cowboys left the street.

Two Hawks replaced his knife and looked at Emmet. "Let's get a steak," he said.

The only available hotel room had two beds and one window and it faced the back alleyway. Even with the window wide open the air was hot and heavy.

Emmet sat on his bed, smoked his pipe, and studied his maps.

"They'd stay clear of towns all the way to Canada," he said. "If we go to Billings to send a telegram, it will take us out of our way."

Prone on his bed, pipe in his mouth, Two Hawks said, "It would."

"By the time we reach Billings, they'll be in Canada anyway," Emmet said. "We can't leave Jack in those mountains alone."

"Don't worry about your brother," Two Hawks said. "Worry about whoever he runs into."

Emmet looked over at Two Hawks. "I'm more worried about what my mother would do to me if I came home without him," he said. "Ma is the only person alive to ever knock Jack on his behind. I'd hate to think what she'd do to me."

Two Hawks grinned and puffed on his pipe.

"Maybe next time, we should take your mother?" he said.

There was no reason not to, so in the morning Jack prepared a full breakfast before continuing on. While he ate, he treated his horse to a full bag of grain and topped it off with a large carrot.

The narrow pass went on for another quarter mile before it widened enough for Jack to mount his horse. He rode at a moderate pace as the still-rocky terrain was dangerous ground for a horse.

Suddenly the pass ended and opened up to a lush and very green pasture. Jack dismounted and looked around. He was in a valley inside the Bighorn Mountains. Was this the secret holy ground Two Hawks spoke of?

The grass had long since overgrown, and the trail of the two riders was difficult to pick up. He walked his horse north for a while until he was sure they traveled in that direction, then he mounted up and rode most of the morning.

With the mule loaded down with fresh supplies, Emmet and Two Hawks rode northwest out of Sheridan toward the Bighorn Mountains.

Two Hawks scouted ahead and picked up the trail of the stolen herd. He rode back to Emmet, and the two followed the trail until noon.

They ate a cold lunch and rested the horses for one hour.

"They turned the herd west directly into the mountains," Two Hawks said.

"Like you said, cattle won't climb mountains," Emmet said.

Two Hawks looked at the Bighorns in the distance.

"We will know by nightfall," he said.

Around noon, Jack decided to take a break and rest his horse, when he spotted something in the distance.

He dismounted and dug the binoculars out of his saddlebags and zoomed in. He was shocked to see three small cabins and a corral in the middle of a field. The corral was filled with horses.

The cabins appeared deserted. Jack scanned the immediate grounds and spotted not one person about.

He tucked the binoculars away, mounted up, and rode to within a hundred yards of the cabins.

From the saddle Jack watched the cabins and corral. The horses eyed him with mild curiosity but quickly lost interest in him.

No one came out or went in to the cabins.

Then Jack noticed the hammock strung between two birch trees. Someone was sleeping in it with one arm slung over the side.

Jack dismounted, quietly pulled his Colt, and walked his horse to the cabins. He tied the horse to a post near the corral and walked to the hammock. The person sleeping in it was just a kid still in his teens.

Jack holstered the Colt and then flipped the hammock over. The kid hit the ground face-first. Jack immediately placed his right boot on the kid's back.

"United States Marshal," Jack said.

"I didn't do nothing," the kid said. "I swear, I didn't do nothing."

"Are you armed?" Jack said.

"What? No. I don't even own a gun, Marshal."

"I'm going to let you up, kid," Jack said. "Give me any trouble, and you'll wish you hadn't."

"I won't."

Jack removed his boot. Slowly the kid stood and grinned at Jack. He was a handsome kid, thin as a reed and with a winning smile.

"What's your name, kid?" Jack asked.

"Parker. Robert Parker."

"They call you Bob?"

"Butch. My friends call me Butch," Parker said. "On account of I worked in a butcher shop over at the Great Salt Lake. My folks are Mormons."

"What the hell are you doing here, wherever here is?" Jack said.

"Working for Mr. Cassidy."

"Who is Mr. Cassidy?" Jack said.

"He's the rancher I work for," Parker said.

"Is there anybody here besides you?" Jack asked.

"Not now. They all left."

"Let's go on the porch and talk in the shade."

Jack led Parker to the porch where they sat on wood chairs. Jack rolled a cigarette and said, "Who is this Cassidy?"

"He has a small ranch, but I think he spends most of his time rustling," Parker said. "So do the others."

"What others?"

"A fellow calls himself Dutch Henry and claims to be a horse thief," Parker said. "A woman calls herself Cattle Kate, and this big Cherokee they call Blue Duck. He's a mean one, Marshal. I'd steer clear of him. This fellow called Kid Curry. The others I didn't get to know their names real well."

"Cattle thieves, the lot of them," Jack said. "What are you doing here with the likes of this bunch?"

"Mr. Cassidy said he'd pay me one hundred dollars to watch the extra horses in the corral until they get back," Parker said.

"Back from where?"

"A couple of days ago, they took the whole damn herd north," Parker said.

"North where?"

"I don't know. I only hear little bits at a time."

"How big is the herd?"

"Maybe six thousand head."

The number surprised Jack. He struck a match and lit the cigarette.

"Am I in trouble, Marshal?" Parker asked.

"Unless you do exactly as I say," Jack said.

"My only part was to watch the horses, that's all," Parker said. "I don't know nothing else."

"Are there supplies in the cabins?"

"Lots."

"Pack enough to last you to get home," Jack said. "Then you set those horses free. Did you come in the back door or the front?"

"The narrow pass," Parker said.

"You leave the same way," Jack said. "Go pack your gear."

Thirty minutes later, Parker sat atop his horse and looked down at Jack.

"Thank you, Marshal. I sure appreciate you not arresting me," Parker said.

"Keep your nose clean, Butch, and I'll never have to," Jack said.

"You bet," Parker said and rode east toward the pass.

Once Parker was out of sight, Jack entered the three cabins and inspected them. There was a healthy supply of food, blankets, firewood, and clothing, but nothing incriminating.

In the third cabin, on the table he found a detailed map of a trail that led directly to Canada. He folded the map and tucked it into his shirt pocket.

"I've never seen the like," Two Hawks said as he inspected the trail left behind by the large herd. "Must be six thousand, maybe more, and twenty riders."

Seated by the campfire, Emmet stirred the pan full of beans and bacon.

"Headed north as we figured," he said.

"Do we plan to camp here and wait for your brother?" Two Hawks said.

"I think that's a good idea," Emmet said.

"Perhaps I should backtrack the trail into the mountains?" Two Hawks said.

"No need," Emmet said.

Two Hawks turned west and spotted Jack riding his tall horse along a trail coming from the mountains.

"He found it," Two Hawks said.

Emmet waited for Jack to arrive. When he slid down from the saddle, Emmet handed Jack a plate of beans, bacon, and cornbread.

"Thanks, little brother," Jack said. "And this is for you."

Jack removed the folded map from his pocket and tossed it to Emmet.

"Compliments of Kid Curry, Cattle Kate, Dutch Henry, and Blue Duck," Jack said.

"Blue Duck?" Emmet said.

"I hate that son of a bitch," Two Hawks said. "He's a traitor to his own people. Takes up with the likes of Belle Starr and the Clantons, and kills his own kind for whiskey and money."

"It doesn't surprise me none he's riding with this bunch," Jack said.

Emmet looked at the map. "Clear run straight into Canada," he said. "Somebody knows the territory. They don't come within forty miles of a town the whole way."

"And they're halfway there by now," Jack said. "By the time we reach Miles City, they will be across the border into Canada."

"At twenty dollars a head, do you know how much money that is?" Emmet said. "A hundred and twenty thousand dollars, maybe more."

"It's a bunch of money for sure," Jack said.

Two Hawks looked at Jack. "What did you find in the mountains?"

"Most amazing thing," Jack said. "This narrow pass wide enough for just one horse opens up to a hundred square miles of green valley. On the northwest side, the outlaws built some cabins and a corral. This has to be the secret place you spoke about."

"When our business is finished, I will explore that valley," Two Hawks said. "It will be a fine place for my son to grow up."

"Jack and I can track the herd from here on," Emmet said. "I can tell Judge Parker you kept your end of the bargain."

"Yeah," Jack said. "No need for you to carry on when you're already here."

"No," Two Hawks said. "I will ride to the end, as I gave my word. I was still a young man when Blue Duck murdered Buffalo Hump, believing it would make him the leader of my people. Instead it made him an outcast and hated by my people as well as the whites. It is time he paid for his crimes."

Emmet and Jack exchanged glances.

"Did you know Blue Duck was involved in this when you sent for us to make the agreement?" Emmet asked.

"I had suspicions, but no evidence," Two Hawks said.

"And now you want to ride with us to kill him?" Jack said.

"If someone murdered your Judge Parker in cold blood, would you not want to kill the man responsible?" Two Hawks said.

"I expect I would," Jack said.

"Well, let's pack up and ride if we're going," Emmet said. "We can be in Montana by sunset."

Jack tossed his empty plate to the ground and looked at Two

Hawks. "Old Blue Duck won't be so easy to kill," he said. "Neither am I," Two Hawks said.

CHAPTER TWENTY-SEVEN

Sitting atop his tall horse, Jack surveyed the Montana landscape.

"I have to admit this Montana is some beautiful country," Jack said.

"We've been riding in it for four days, Jack, and you just noticed?" Emmet said.

In the distance Jack spotted Two Hawks riding toward them.

"Here he comes," Jack said. "Might as well make camp and have us some lunch."

By the time Two Hawks arrived, beans and bacon were cooking in the pan, and the coffee was ready.

"Miles City is a half day's ride from here," Two Hawks said. "It sits on the Yellowstone River."

Emmet handed Two Hawks a cup of coffee.

"They have the telegraph and railroad," Two Hawks said. "And the army fort sits just outside of town."

"Well, let's eat and rest the horses a bit, and then we'll go see the army," Emmet said.

Fort Keogh was home to the 5th Infantry and two hundred soldiers under the command of Colonel Garrison. He met with Emmet, Jack, and Two Hawks in his office, along with one of his senior officers, Captain Jones.

"Blue Duck?" Garrison said. "Is that son of a bitch loose in Montana?"

"More like passing through, Colonel," Jack said.

235

"By now they're in Canada or close to it," Emmet said. "With your aid, we can cut them off when they reenter Montana. It won't be difficult to track where six thousand head crossed the border. Blue Duck and the rest will probably take the same out-of-the-way route back to avoid detection."

Garrison looked at Jones. "Opinion, Captain?"

"It bothers me, sir, that so many outlaws are right under our noses," Jones said.

"As it does me," Garrison said. "Take twenty men and whatever arms necessary, and take the railroad north to Glasgow. I'll wire Colonel Henry at Fort Glasgow to supply the like. Your orders are to capture or kill as many of these outlaws as possible when they cross the border."

"Yes, sir," Jones said. "I'll see to the arrangements at once."

"Colonel, I'd like to send a wire to Judge Parker in Forth Smith and advise him of our whereabouts," Emmet said.

"Captain, take the marshal to our telegraph station," Garrison said. "And stop by the mess hall and ask the cook to prepare some dinner for our guests."

While Emmet, Jack, and Two Hawks feasted on steaks in the mess hall, Garrison and Jones just took coffee.

Garrison read the map Jack took from the Bighorn Mountains. "I can certainly see how such a well-thought-out route could hide even a herd twice as large," he said.

"Colonel, have you Gatling guns?" Jack asked.

"A half dozen," Garrison said. "Do you think Gatling guns will be necessary?"

"If we set up Gatlings a hundred yards apart and catch the bastards in a cross fire, they won't be able to advance, and the back door will be closed," Jack said. "They'll have no choice but to surrender."

Garrison nodded. "Captain Jones, plan on taking two Gatling guns."

"Yes sir," Jones said.

Garrison looked at Jack. "Good thinking, Marshal. Will you men stay the night at our guest quarters?"

"Thank you, Colonel," Emmet said.

"Colonel, would your cook have any chocolate ice cream?" Two Hawks asked.

"That was good thinking about the Gatling guns," Emmet said as he smoked his pipe in bed. "It would be good to take as many of those killers as possible back to stand trial in Judge Parker's court."

"Old Parker has been itching for ten years to get old Blue Duck into his court," Jack said. "What say you, Two Hawks?"

"Men such as Blue Duck should die as they live, in battle," Two Hawks said.

Rolling a cigarette, Jack paused and looked at Two Hawks. "Well, Sergeant Major Two Hawks, you just might get your wish."

Captain Jones arranged for a special run to Glasgow, and just one seating car was attached to the engine. Behind the riding car sat the boxcar for horses and a flatcar for weapons. Twenty cavalry soldiers lined the riding car. Their gear and weapons, including two Gatling guns, filled the flatcar.

What little Emmet, Jack, and Two Hawks saw of Miles City left them unimpressed, as the streets were muddy, and drunks appeared to be everywhere.

The train left at eight in the morning.

The engineer said they would reach speeds of nearly seventy miles an hour and would reach Glasgow in three hours.

Not ten minutes after the train left Miles City, Jack was asleep with his hat over his eyes and his legs stretched out.

Jones looked at Emmet. "How does he do that, just fall asleep?" Jones asked.

"Clear conscience," Emmet said.

Colonel Henry supplied twelve cavalry soldiers, one Gatling gun, and a junior officer named Lieutenant Books to supplement Captain Jones's twenty men.

They left Fort Glasgow after noon chow and, with Two Hawks riding scout, they headed toward the route taken by the herd into Canada.

By late afternoon, the group made camp while Two Hawks scouted well ahead.

Close to sundown, Two Hawks returned.

"They crossed northeast into Canada no more than two days ago," Two Hawks said. "There are no signs that they crossed back."

"Scout Two Hawks, tomorrow ride ahead and find a likely terrain where we can set up the Gatling gun to trap the outlaws," Jones said. "We'll need good cover for the guns, us, and the horses."

"I'll find such a place," Two Hawks said.

"Good. Grab some grub, and we'll make it an early night," Jones said. "We'll move out at dawn."

Emmet busied himself by reading his law book by the fire. He smoked his pipe as he read and turned pages.

Jack stripped, cleaned, and oiled his Colt revolver and Winchester rifle.

Two Hawks sat silently with a cup of coffee and stared into the fire, lost in thought.

Emmet closed his book and looked at Two Hawks. "Is something troubling you, Two Hawks?"

Two Hawks continued to stare into the fire as he said, "When the white man dreams of his future, what does he dream of?"

Stuffing his pipe with fresh tobacco, Emmet thought for a moment. "I suppose a good home, wife and children, food on the table, and some money in his pocket."

"When you are gone, do you wish to leave behind a name worthy of your children and grandchildren remembering?" Two Hawks said.

"Yes, of course," Emmet said. "All men do."

"My people dream of the same things," Two Hawks said. He turned to look at Emmet. "Except that we worry we won't leave any children behind to remember us."

Before the sun was up, Two Hawks had ridden ten miles. The trail left behind by the enormous herd was easy to follow, and he allowed his mind to drift a bit as he rode.

He wanted his son to remember him as a great leader, but there was no one left to lead. Soon there would be no one left behind to remember.

He wanted his son to remember him as a great Comanche warrior, but there were no more wars to fight, and the Comanche way of life was coming to an end all too quickly. In fifteen years, what was left of his people would live reservation life under the direction of the Washington government.

All that was left was for his son to remember him as a good man and a good father.

Maybe that would be enough?

Near noon, he began to search for a place for the army to set up camp where they could surprise the outlaws returning from Canada.

A few miles north, the herd passed through a valley surrounded by rocky, hilly terrain. The path narrowed to a hundred yards across and continued on for a mile before it widened again.

Two Hawks made camp and built a large fire the army could see for a mile or more, and then he sat beside the fire to wait.

He smoked his pipe and pondered his future.

The man who killed Blue Duck, that man would be remembered like Pat Garrett, who killed Billy the Kid and the coward who shot Wild Bill. Remembered for a very long time.

Two Hawks looked to the south and spotted a large cloud of dust.

"Excellent location, Scout Two Hawks," Jones said. He looked at Lieutenant Books. "Have the men set up the Gatling guns in the surrounding hills so when the outlaws ride past, we have them in a cross fire of about a hundred yards. We'll make camp in the hills. No fires after dark."

"Yes, sir," Brooks said.

By nightfall, Captain Jones and fifteen soldiers occupied the western hill, along with Jack, Emmet, and Two Hawks. Lieutenant Books and the remaining fifteen soldiers occupied the eastern hill.

Before eight o'clock, all fires were extinguished, and a two-man security detail was established. Captain Jones included himself in the watch detail.

Before turning in, Jones spoke to Two Hawks.

"Scout Two Hawks, in the morning take one man and ride north. See if you can pick them up coming our way," Jones said. "Then hightail it back here."

Two Hawks nodded.

"I'll go with him," Jack said.

Two Hawks looked at Jack.

"We'll leave at sunrise," Two Hawks said.

Chapter Twenty-Eight

Prone on the cliffside, Emmet watched the horizon through binoculars. Several of the soldiers were doing the same thing.

Drinking a cup of coffee, Jones stood next to Emmet.

"It's a good plan, Marshal," Jones said. "I wouldn't worry about your brother."

"The last thing I do is worry about my brother," Emmet said as he stood up.

"Then something else is weighing on your mind," Jones said.

"I could use a cup of coffee," Emmet said.

Emmet and Jones walked to the pit, where a large coffee pot was keeping warm in the fire. Emmet filled a cup, sipped, and said, "Ever have the feeling you missed something? Something important?"

"Only all the time, Marshal," Jones said.

"This bunch—not one of them is smart enough to devise a scheme like this," Emmet said. "Maybe Cattle Kate, but not alone. A plan like this took long-term planning and needed the right people."

"I don't disagree, but my job and yours is to capture them first," Jones said.

Emmet nodded. "I better get back to my binoculars."

Jack and Two Hawks rode north for twenty miles and then took up a position on a hill nearly a thousand feet above sea level.

While the horses ate their fill of grass, Jack and Two Hawks took up watch, Jack with his binoculars.

"You said the other day there were cabins in the pass at the Bighorns," Two Hawks said.

"Three, and a corral," Jack said. "The rest looks to be about a hundred square miles of valley."

Two Hawks stared north at the horizon.

"Are you still thinking of bringing your family there?" Jack asked.

"I have nowhere else to go where I can live as Comanche," Two Hawks said.

Jack rolled a cigarette and lit it with a wood match. "I understand your feelings," he said. "My mother is a quarter Sioux, so I am not without your blood."

"What are you trying to say?" Two Hawks said.

"It seems to me that if you go to the Bighorns and live in that valley, it is no different than living trapped on the reservation," Jack said. "Free, but trapped in a valley without walls."

Two Hawks slowly turned to look at Jack. "Sometimes you are not as dumb as you appear," he said.

"Thanks for the compliment," Jack said. "We'll discuss it later."

Jack held his binoculars to his eyes and turned them onto the speck of dust way off in the distance.

"Company," Jack said and handed the binoculars to Two Hawks.

After Two Hawks had a look, he said, "Ten miles off. We best ride back and tell that captain."

A soldier on watch lowered his binoculars and raced over to Jones.

"Captain, rider's coming in," the soldier said.

Jones, Emmet, and the others went to the cliff.

"Jack and Two Hawks," Emmet said. "Nobody kicks up dust

like Jack's horse."

Fifteen minutes later, Jack and Two Hawks raced their horses up the side of the hill and dismounted.

"Headed this way, the lot of them," Jack said. "They should reach us in the hour."

Jones turned to a soldier. "Run across to the other hill and inform Lieutenant Books. Tell him to make ready. Then we're on hand signals until they arrive."

Jack and Two Hawks helped themselves to cups of coffee and drank them at the edge of the cliff where they could watch north.

Emmet and Jones joined them.

"Well, Marshal, it looks like you're going to get your party," Jones said.

"Captain, we need as many alive as possible," Emmet said.

"How many of them die is entirely up to them," Jones said.

Two Hawks looked at Jones. "At the first shot, Blue Duck will turn and run."

"Then Blue Duck will get shot," Jones said.

Two Hawks turned and looked north. The dust cloud had grown larger.

Jones walked among his men. "Men, take your positions. Those on the Gatling guns, hold until I signal to fire."

Jones then went to the edge of the cliff and used hand signals to communicate with Lieutenant Books.

Emmet used his binoculars to follow the riders. When they were a thousand yards away, he lowered the binoculars and said, "Ten minutes, Captain. No more than that."

Jones went prone next to Emmet and used his binoculars to watch the riders. When they were within five hundred yards, Jones said, "I see a woman rider up front."

"That's Cattle Kate," Emmet said. "I recognize her from the newspapers."

Using his own binoculars, Jack said, "I see old Dutch Henry and Kid Curry."

"Blue Duck?" Two Hawks said.

"No," Jack said. "Wait. He's bringing up the rear."

"Hold steady, men," Jones commanded. "Wait for my command."

The outlaws rode closer until they finally entered the field of fire. Jones stood up and gave his men the command to fire.

The Gatling gun sprayed a hail of bullets several hundred feet in front of and behind the large group of outlaws. Some yanked hard on their reins and halted their horses. Some turned and saw the back door was closed. Others simply gave up on the spot.

Except one.

Blue Duck.

In the confusion of the moment, Blue Duck turned his horse to the west and raced him up the side of the cliff, turned sharply to the north, and disappeared over the embankment.

Jones gave the order to cease fire and then stood up.

"Thirty rifles and several Gatling guns are aimed at you, so if you value your lives, you'll surrender without bloodshed," Jones shouted.

"Don't shoot," Dutch Henry said. "We're bottled. We see that. We'll surrender peaceful like."

"Toss your guns," Jones yelled.

Emmet and Jack stood when the soldiers did and Jack said, "Now where is he going?"

"Who?" Emmet said.

Two Hawks raced his horse past the surrendering outlaws and followed the path Blue Duck took to make his escape.

"Son of a bitch," Jack said as he watched Two Hawks vanish over the hill.

Blue Duck had a lead of a thousand feet or more, but he was riding a large horse built for distance and not speed.

Two Hawks slowly closed the gap.

Blue Duck was unaware that he was being followed at the moment, but rode his horse as if the entire 5th Cavalry was on his tail.

And the large horse began to tire under Blue Duck's heavy weight.

Once the outlaws surrendered their firearms, Jones had twenty soldiers seat them in a circle.

Emmet, Jones, and Lieutenant Books approached the outlaws. It was then that Emmet realized Jack was gone.

"Son of a bitch," Emmet said.

Blue Duck turned his head to look back and was shocked to see Two Hawks gaining on him.

Blue Duck yanked the reins and cracked his boots against his horse, but the large animal had no more to give, and Two Hawks closed the gap quickly. Blue Duck decided to go for position and veered sharply to his left toward a hillside.

Five hundred feet behind him, Two Hawks followed.

The hill was steeper than Blue Duck anticipated and served only to slow his horse down even more. Exhausted, the horse nearly stumbled and fell twice before reaching the plateau.

As Blue Duck leveled his horse onto the plateau, Two Hawks burst over the hill, leapt from the saddle, and struck Blue Duck on the back.

Together they fell to the ground.

Both men got up slowly and stood six feet apart.

Blue Duck's right hand went to his holster, but in the fall his revolver came loose. He looked at Two Hawks.

"I know you, Two Hawks," Blue Duck said. "From the old days."

"I know you too, Sha-con-gah," Two Hawks said.

Blue Duck smiled. "No one has called me that in twenty years," he said.

"That is the name you had when you murdered Buffalo Hump," Two Hawks said.

"A useless, washed-up old man," Blue Duck said. "I put him out of his misery, as I will you."

"He was the leader of our people," Two Hawks said.

"What people?" Blue Duck shouted. "We have no people. Not anymore. All we have is what we take."

Two Hawks removed the Colt from the holster and aimed it at Blue Duck. "If we have no people, it's because men like you murdered them," he said.

Blue Duck looked at the Colt. "What do you want, old woman?" he snarled.

"This is your reckoning," Two Hawks said.

"My reckoning?" Blue Duck said. "Are you going to shoot me? Bring me back to hang at the end of the white man's noose?"

"No."

Two Hawks tossed the Colt to the ground and removed the telescopic tomahawk clipped to his holster. At the flick of his wrist, it extended from six inches to eighteen inches long.

Blue Duck smiled as he removed the Bowie knife from the sheath on his holster.

"What was that word?" he said. "Reckoning."

Two Hawks charged and screamed his war cry.

Blue Duck swung his Bowie knife, and both men came together. Blue Duck was larger and stronger, but Two Hawks was faster and more agile.

They slashed and thrust across the width of the plateau, each man cutting and wounding the other until they reached the edge.

Blue Duck's back was to the edge and he was just feet from falling over. He thrust with the Bowie knife. Two Hawks slashed down with the tomahawk, and the knife fell from Blue Duck's hand.

Two Hawks took a step back and waved the tomahawk at Blue Duck.

Blue Duck got to his knees as if to surrender.

Two Hawks stepped forward and held the tomahawk over-head.

Blue Duck grabbed the derringer hidden in his belt, cocked it, and shot Two Hawks in the side.

Two Hawks froze in place as he looked at Blue Duck. Slowly the tomahawk fell from his grasp.

Blue Duck stood up, grabbed Two Hawks by the arm, and spun him around and threw him over the edge of the cliff.

"Say hello to Buffalo Hump when you meet him in the spirit world," Blue Duck said.

Blue Duck turned and walked toward his horse just as Jack raced over the hill. The derringer had one shot left. Blue Duck fired and missed as Jack jumped from the saddle and tackled Blue Duck.

They hit the ground hard. Jack jumped to his feet, grabbed Blue Duck, and yanked him up.

"Where is Two Hawks?" Jack yelled.

"Gone," Blue Duck said.

Jack's rage was at a pinnacle, and his strength matched his fury. He beat and pounded Blue Duck until he was a bleeding pulp on the ground.

Jack went to the edge and looked over. Two Hawks was unconscious on a large rock fifteen feet below. After the rock was a sheer, one-hundred-foot drop.

He grabbed the thirty-foot-long rope from his saddle and tied one end around the saddle horn. Then he looped the rope around his waist and slowly descended the cliff to Two Hawks.

Two Hawks was alive, but bleeding heavily from the bullet hole in his left side.

Jack lifted Two Hawks over his left shoulder and, holding the rope in his right hand, he scaled the cliff. It was slow going, and by the time Jack lifted Two Hawks onto the plateau, he was exhausted.

Once Two Hawks was safe, Jack pulled himself up and over. The first thing he noticed was that Blue Duck was gone.

Jack sat and gasped for air. When his breathing returned to normal, he stood, lifted Two Hawks in his arms, and carried him to his horse.

While Captain Jones questioned the prisoners, Emmet watched and waited for Jack to return.

Finally he appeared with Two Hawks in tow. Two Hawks appeared unconscious. Jack had tied him to the saddle.

"Captain, do we have any medical people with us?" Emmet asked.

"Two, in fact. Why?" Jones said.

Jack wandered over to the campfire where Two Hawks slept. The two medical people were keeping watch.

"How is he?" Jack asked.

"Small bullet. It struck nothing vital," one of them said. "He'll have quite a bellyache for a few weeks, but he'll recover fully, I expect."

"Good," Jack said.

He walked over to Emmet and Captain Jones. The prisoners were tied together in a large circle with a fire in the middle of them.

"Any of them give you anything?" Jack asked.

"Most of them are as dumb as yesterday's fish," Jones said.

"All we have are tracks left behind by a herd," Emmet said. "That's not enough evidence to convict a one of them, and they know it. All they have to do is keep quiet, and they'll walk away from this in court."

"That's the lawyer in you talking, little brother," Jack said. "If I have to babysit this bunch all the way back to Fort Smith, it's going to be for a reason."

"What are you saying?" Emmet asked.

Jack stepped over the prisoners and stood in the center of the circle.

"Who wants to go home?" Jack said.

The prisoners looked at him but stayed silent.

"You made one bad mistake," Jack said. "You left a witness alive on one of your raids, and he can identify several, if not most of you. So, I'll ask again, who wants to go home?"

Cattle Kate said, "What do you mean, go home?"

"I know the lot of you aren't smart enough to organize a plan such as this," Jack said. "I'm a United States Marshal. In exchange for your cooperation, I can arrange for amnesty."

"Full pardon?" Cattle Kate said.

"That's the deal," Jack said.

Cattle Kate nodded. "I'll talk, but I want it in writing."

Jack helped Cattle Kate to her feet. "Emmet, get your writing paper," he said.

Cattle Kate talked for hours. While Emmet took detailed notes, Jack grew bored and went to check on Two Hawks.

He was awake, sitting up, and eating a bowl of beef stew.

Jack sat beside him and rolled a cigarette.

"Blue Duck?" Two Hawks said.

"I had him, but I had to let him go to save your life," Jack said.

"You should have let me die," Two Hawks said.

Jack struck a match and lit the cigarette. "And cheat your son out of a father?" he said.

"I still would have killed you a year ago," Two Hawks said.

Jack grinned. "I know," he said.

"But . . . I suppose it's better a boy grows up knowing his father," Two Hawks said.

Jack nodded. "I know," he said.

Emmet was studying his notes when Jack joined him at the fire.

"Well?" Jack said.

"When we get back to Fort Glasgow, we have some telegrams to send," Emmet said.

"You do," Jack said. "I got a steak with my name on it."

"Quite a stunt you pulled," Emmet said. "There were no living witnesses."

"That kid Robert Parker, he's a living witness," Jack said. "And that reminds me."

Jack walked over to the prisoners and stood in the center of the circle. "Which one of you bastards is Mike Cassidy?"

The group looked at him.

"I won't ask a third time," Jack said.

A man at the end of the circle answered.

"Me. I'm Mike Cassidy."

Jack walked to Cassidy and kicked him in the face with his right boot.

"Robert Parker says goodbye," Jack said.

CHAPTER TWENTY-NINE

Judge Parker was at his desk when an assistant delivered the telegrams to him. They were from Emmet, sent from Fort Glasgow in Montana. He told the assistant to wait in case he needed to reply.

Parker read the telegrams carefully and then he wrote several detailed notes.

"Send this one to the State Attorney General," Parker said as he handed the assistant a slip of paper. "And this one to the Attorney General in Washington. Wait for replies."

Jack and Emmet had breakfast with Colonel Garrison and Captain Jones in the officers' mess hall.

"We'll hold the prisoners in the stockade until arrangements can be made to transport them," Garrison said.

"We'll have a train with a team of marshals sent to pick them up," Emmet said.

"It's too bad Blue Duck got away," Garrison said.

"My fault, Colonel," Jack said.

"I read the reports, Marshal," Garrison said. "I would have done the same thing under the circumstances."

"That reminds me, Colonel," Emmet said. "We couldn't have done any of this without the help of Two Hawks."

"My doctor told me this morning he'll be fit to travel in about two weeks," Garrison said. "After that, he's free to do as he pleases."

"Thank you for that, Colonel," Emmet said. "And that reminds me, we have one last item to attend to."

As Jack and Emmet walked the hall of the infirmary, they heard Two Hawks yell from a room, "Sponge bath? I'd sooner scalp you than have you give me a sponge bath."

A nurse exited a room with a bedpan in her arms. She looked at Jack and Emmet. "He's a mite . . ."

"Testy," Jack said.

"He's all yours," the nurse said.

Jack end Emmet entered the room. Two Hawks was sitting up in bed with his pipe clenched between his teeth, billowing smoke.

"What's the problem there, Two Hawks?" Jack said. "Don't you want a pretty nurse bathing you? From the smell in here you can use it."

"That smell is the cheap tobacco in my pipe," Two Hawks said. "And it still smells better than you white-eyes."

"And here I thought we was starting to be friends," Jack said.

Emmet removed a folded document from his shirt pocket, unfolded it, and handed it to Two Hawks. "Do you read English?"

"Like Noah Webster," Two Hawks said.

"Well, when you get around to reading it, that's our agreement for the full pardon as promised," Emmet said. "You might want to hold on to that paper for future reference."

Two Hawks glanced at the paper and nodded.

"Well, we have a train to catch," Emmet said and extended his right hand to Two Hawks.

After they shook hands, Emmet looked at Jack.

Jack extended his right hand. Two Hawks extended his right hand. They shook and Two Hawks said, "This doesn't mean that if our paths cross again in the future, I won't kill you."

"I know," Jack said. "But that ain't likely."

CHAPTER THIRTY

"Dammit, Emmet, you've had your nose in that damn book for two days now," Jack said.

"Emmet closed the book and said, "When we get home, I don't have much time to take the bar exam. If I miss it, I'll have to wait an entire year."

"Good, then you'll have time to build your house," Jack said.

"Well, the train is stopping," Emmet said.

"About time," Jack said. "My ass is as sore as if I rode bareback on a mule cross-country."

"Well, nothing's changed," Jack said as he and Emmet walked their horses through the streets of Dallas to the Hotel Fort Worth.

"We were just here two months ago. What did you expect would change?" Emmet said.

At the hotel, they stopped by the livery to care for the horses before checking in at the lobby desk.

The desk clerk remembered them. "A message for you, Marshal," he said.

"Which one of us?" Jack asked.

"Both, I guess."

Emmet took the envelope, opened it, and read it quickly.

"Room four-eleven," Emmet said.

Judge Parker filled three glasses with whiskey and gave one each to Emmet and Jack.

"I don't mind telling you it took some doing to get the Attorney General to agree with this crazy scheme of yours," Parker said.

"But they did agree?" Emmet said.

"Yes, they agreed," Parker said. "They had no choice but to agree."

Jack tossed back his whiskey and said, "Then let's get to it. I want to go home."

"I suggest a shave, a bath, and clean clothes before we do anything else," Parker said. "Then we'll meet for lunch in ninety minutes."

Captain Armstrong of the Texas Rangers and Dallas Sheriff Lang were with Parker at his table when Emmet and Jack arrived for lunch.

"I believe we all know each other," Parker said.

"Nice to see you boys again," Armstrong said.

"I ordered steaks all around," Parker said.

"Is she here?" Emmet asked.

"She's here, and that also took some doing," Parker said.

"She's waiting on us in my office," Lang said.

"Captain Armstrong, are your Rangers in place?" Parker asked.

"I have six men on the street," Armstrong said.

"Then let's hope for a peaceful transaction," Parker said.

Larkin was at his desk when Judge Parker, Captain Armstrong, Emmet, and Jack walked in unannounced.

Larkin, stunned, nearly dropped the pen he was dipping into an inkwell.

"What is . . . ?" he said.

"Christopher Titus Larkin?" Parker said.

"Yes. What is . . . ?"

"I'm Judge Isaac Parker, and I have in my possession a duly noted warrant written by the Attorney General in Washington that places you under arrest," Parker said.

"What? This is outrageous!" Larkin said.

"The charges are organizing a large group of outlaws to rustle cattle from ranches across the west for the purpose of selling them to black-market ranchers in Canada," Parker said.

"You can't be serious!" Larkin said. "This is preposterous."

Parker looked at Emmet, and Emmet stepped forward.

"You divided the outlaws into three groups," Emmet said. "So at least one group would be ready to ride at a moment's notice. Then, when you received a telegram concerning cattle transactions, you simply sent the closest group to rustle the herd. Upon delivery in Canada, the buyers then wired the money to a special account. Your account. Simple, but genius."

"Genius except for one fact," Parker said. "Sheriff Lang, if you please."

The door opened, and Lang escorted Cattle Kate into the office.

"In exchange for her testimony, she will be granted full immunity," Parker said. "And by the way, accessory to murder is added to the charges."

"Murder? I've never left my desk," Larkin said.

"But the men you sent to steal the herds did," Parker said. "Captain Armstrong, will you take Mr. Larkin into custody."

"With pleasure, Judge," Armstrong said.

"I think we're done here," Parker said.

Parker, Emmet, and Jack stood at the bar of the Yellow Rose Saloon. Each had a shot glass of bourbon whiskey.

"Think the charges will stick?" Emmet asked.

"They'll stick," Parker said. "It's just a matter of who will hang and who will get life."

"When do you think there'll be a trial?" Emmet asked.

"That depends on the Attorney General," Parker said. "You're taking the bar exam in a few months, aren't you?"

"Early fall," Emmet said.

"I can ask to have you sit in on the trial as a consultant," Parker said. "Be good experience for your career."

"I appreciate that, Judge," Emmet said.

Across the saloon, three cowboys stood up at a table and surrounded a man passing by. The man was a Sioux Indian working as a cowhand.

"They let anybody drink with the men these days, even a stinking squaw," one of the three said.

"Is that right, squaw?" another of the three said. "Are you a drinking man or just a drunk like all them other little Indians?"

Jack, Emmet, and Parker turned to watch.

"I'm not looking for trouble," the Sioux said.

"Well, you found some," a cowboy said.

The three cowboys started shoving the Sioux until he fell to the floor, and one of them put his boot on the Sioux's back.

"See? Can't hold their firewater," a cowboy said.

Jack tossed back his shot, said, "Son of a bitch," and started walking to the three cowboys.

"Marshal Youngblood," Parker said.

"Let him go, Judge," Emmet said. "Jack's earned some fun."

CHAPTER THIRTY-ONE

Riding side by side, Jack and Emmet rode along the road on the reservation.

"When are you going to retire that nag and get a real horse?" Jack asked as he glanced at Emmet's pinto.

"When you quit acting like an overgrown child, I'll get a new horse," Emmet said.

"What are you . . . ?" Jack said.

"Two hundred and seventy-seven dollars and eighty-three cents in damages," Emmet said.

"Those fellows had it coming," Jack said.

"I know they did," Emmet said. "But three tables, eleven chairs, and a dozen bottles of whiskey. And how on earth did you break a chandelier?"

"Like I said, they had it coming," Jack said.

"Yeah, lucky for you Judge Parker allowed you to pay for the damages out of our expense money," Emmet said.

"Forget that," Jack said. "I'll race you home."

"Let's not," Emmet said.

"I suppose we can ride along like a pair of old women the rest of the day," Jack said.

"We could," Emmet said as he yanked hard on the reins and the pinto took off running.

"No fair!" Jack shouted.

After lunch, Amy, Chao-xing, and Maria took coffee on the

porch, while Mary and Sarah had glasses of lemonade.

"How is that new article for Mr. Duff coming along?" Maria asked.

"Nearly complete," Amy said. "I'll drop it off to him tomorrow. When I saw him yesterday, he said he had a big story that would surprise me."

"He didn't say what?" Maria asked.

"If he told her, it wouldn't be a surprise," Mary said.

"That is true," Maria said, and then a sudden wince made her hold her stomach. "The baby just kicked," she said.

"At five and a half months, they will do that," Amy said. "Jack kicked like he was trying to escape."

Mary looked at Chao-xing. "Why don't you have a baby?" she asked.

"Mary, what did I tell you about the bag of mind-your-own-business?" Amy said.

"That I should hold it like I should hold my tongue," Mary said.

"Correct, and I suggest you do so," Amy said.

"Come, girls. I'll play you a game of Chinese checkers," Chao-xing said.

After Chao-xing and the girls went inside, Amy said, "Tomorrow we'll take a ride over to see Doctor Jefferson."

"I'm fine, really," Maria said.

"And we want to keep you that way," Amy said. "The last thing we need is for you to get sick when Emmet comes home."

"Okay, I'll see the doctor," Maria said. "Would you like more coffee?"

"I would."

Maria stood. "I'll get the pot," she said and went inside.

While Maria was inside, Amy noticed something on the road. After a few seconds, she stood up and opened the screen door.

"Maria, Chao-xing, come quickly," Amy said. "Your men are home."

ABOUT THE AUTHOR

Ethan J. Wolfe is the author of the western novels *The Last Ride, The Regulator, The Range War of '82, Murphy's Law, Silver Moon Rising, All the Queen's Men* and *The Devil's Waltz.*

The employees of Five Star Publishing hope you have enjoyed this book.

Our Five Star novels explore little-known chapters from America's history, stories told from unique perspectives that will entertain a broad range of readers.

Other Five Star books are available at your local library, bookstore, all major book distributors, and directly from Five Star/Gale.

Connect with Five Star Publishing

Visit us on Facebook:
https://www.facebook.com/FiveStarCengage

Email:
FiveStar@cengage.com

For information about titles and placing orders:
(800) 223-1244
gale.orders@cengage.com

To share your comments, write to us:
Five Star Publishing
Attn: Publisher
10 Water St., Suite 310
Waterville, ME 04901